Love Letters
IN THE SAND

WHEN I FALL
IN LOVE

Love Letters
IN THE SAND

DIANN HUNT

summerside
PRESS™

Summerside Press™
Minneapolis 55438
www.summersidepress.com
Love Letters in the Sand
© 2011 by Diann Hunt

ISBN 978-1-60936-113-6

Scripture references are from the following source: The Holy
Bible, King James Version (KJV).

All characters are fictional. Any resemblances to actual
people are purely coincidental.

Cover design by Chris Gilbert | www.studiogearbox.com

Interior design by Müllerhaus Publishing Group |
www.mullerhaus.net

*Summerside Press™ is an inspirational publisher offering fresh,
irresistible books to uplift the heart and engage the mind.*

Printed in USA.

ACKNOWLEDGMENTS

To my husband Jim who truly is my hero. Thanks for walking the beaches and bouncing off ideas with me. I love you.

To my kids and grandkids for bringing joy into my life every single day and filling my world with stories.

To Amy Luetke—and the Sunday night Bible study group that meets at Mark and Cheryl Pollock's house—for the Ebenezer gift idea.

To brainstorming buddies Colleen Coble and Denise Hunter for pushing me to write conflict no matter how much I kick and scream.

To my amazing agent and friend, Karen Solem, who never gives up on me.

To my friend and editor, Susan Downs, who tossed me a lifeline when I was drowning. You'll never know how much that meant to me. Also my new friend and editor, Nancy Toback, for her sharp eyes and editing expertise.

To the creative Summerside Press team, the copy editors, and the sales reps, who breathe life into my stories. Thank you for allowing me to partner with you on this project.

To those of you who share your time to travel through these pages with me, I hope you find joy in the journey.

Can't wait till next time. Until then, God bless you all!

DEDICATION

With much gratitude and respect, I dedicate this story to
my nephew, Staff Sergeant Scott G. Meyer, for his sacrifice
and service to our country. I am proud to be your aunt.

PROLOGUE

Summer 1940

Julia Hilton took a deep breath, shoved her bedroom window upward, and slipped through the opening, taking care not to wake her parents. The very idea of her daughter sneaking around would send Julia's mother to bed for a month.

The aged oak tree peeked into her window and held out a gnarled branch. Landing on a safe ledge, Julia put her weight on the limb and edged her way down. The tip of her saddle oxford brushed against a twig that snapped and fell to the ground. A cautious breath stuck in her throat as she waited for any sound inside the dark house.

Nothing.

The air stirred, shaking loose the sweet scent of honeysuckle from a nearby vine. She continued downward until her feet finally settled on the safety of the ground. Brushing her hands on her skirt, she looked ahead of her. Soft moonlight lit the waves that rolled back and forth on Lake Michigan's shoreline.

The speed of her pulse matched her steps racing toward their meeting place. Once she reached the large rock, she stopped and leaned against it. Stefan wasn't there yet, but she knew he'd come soon.

The night breeze caused her shoulder-length hair to tickle her neck as she turned her face toward the moon. Farther down the beach, quiet laughter and conversation lifted with the wind, along with Judy Garland's voice singing "Over the Rainbow." Probably a love-struck couple had a car radio on behind them while they sat on the beach, talked of a future together, and no doubt stole a kiss or two beneath a starry sky. She smiled.

"There you are." Stefan raced up behind her, his strong arms locking around her waist in a playful manner, his leathery cologne tickling her nose.

She squealed. "You scared me."

He laughed and turned her around to face him. Specks of moonlight shone in his eyes of summer blue, with an intensity that took her breath away.

Pulling her into his strong embrace, he whispered, "I don't want to leave you."

The words sent shivers through her. "Don't go."

He pulled back and faced her. "My furlough is over. The army frowns upon no-shows."

Her lower lip set into the most genuine pout. "What if we join the war?"

"Don't worry. We'll get through this. Even Hitler can't live forever." He smiled, but she could tell it was forced, for her benefit.

Julia's eyes burned and she blinked rapidly, determined not to cry. She didn't want to make this any more painful for them.

Stefan's finger tipped her chin upward. "You remember the plan?"

She nodded, her heart so full she thought it would burst.

"Tell me," he said.

"Two years from today, August second, we meet back here at seven o'clock in the evening. If one of us needs to change our plan, we'll send word through my brother somehow."

The love in his eyes, the gentle touch of his arms...the moment burned in her heart, branding her to him forever. Why couldn't the world leave them alone, let them be happy?

"If something happens—"

"It won't," she said.

"If you change your mind—"

"I won't." No matter what her mother said, Julia would not let her mother's prejudice keep her from the man she loved. "I'll help Mother understand."

"And if she doesn't?"

"It doesn't matter. I'll be here," she said. "You'll write to me?"

"Every day."

He gave her a tender kiss then lifted her hands into his and pulled her close once again, her feet moving in rhythm with his to Gene Austin singing "Love Letters in the Sand."

Hot tears burned her eyes. She wanted to be grown up about this. They could get through it. Yet, everything in her ached to belong to Stefan Zimmer forever. "I wish we could get married now."

"Me too," he said. "But you'll be old enough when I get back."

She nodded, daring to imagine her life with him and wishing like everything she weren't seventeen.

"At least your brother likes me," Stefan said with a smile.

"Joe would never hold your German ancestry against you. He's not like that." She looked down and whispered, "I never knew Mother was that way."

"It's the war," he said. "It changes people."

No matter how her mother had treated him, Stefan still showed her respect. "I suppose," she said, not wanting to talk about that now. She wanted to linger in the feel of his muscular arms around her, the scent of his clean skin, to hear the sound of the water lapping to shore and the strains of the distant song.

Once the song finished, Stefan picked up a nearby twig, bent down, and drew a heart in the sand. Then he wrote their initials inside the heart. Above the heart, he wrote one word. *Forever.* Then he stood, intertwined his fingers with hers, and looked into her eyes.

"I love you, Julia Hilton."

"I love you too."

She would wait. No matter how long it took, Julia would wait for Stefan.

Nothing could separate them for long. Not her age. Not the war.

Definitely not her mother.

CHAPTER ONE

Summer 1957

Julia tucked her marker between the pages of her book, placed it on the stand, then walked toward the impatient knock at the front door. One peek through the peephole and she saw her mother on the other side. Her back stiffened. She took a deep breath and turned the knob.

"Hi, Mother, come on—"

Before Julia could finish the words, Margaret Hilton shoved past her daughter while clawing through her purse. She finally pulled out a handkerchief then, with great excitement, waved it like an American flag.

Julia rolled her eyes and closed the door. Her mother should have gone on Broadway. She loved theatrics. Determined to appear unaffected by her mother's drama, Julia settled into the chair across from her. "How are you today, Mother?"

"I'm hot," she snapped, as though Julia should have known. Mother blotted her face and neck with the handkerchief. She pulled the neckline of her dress away from her chest and blew down the hole.

This was serious.

"Would you like some iced tea?" Julia asked.

"Of course I would like some iced tea." More snapping. "But what I need is a fire hydrant." Frantic, irrational wiping.

Julia practically ran to the kitchen.

Pulling two glasses from the cupboard, she snatched the ice tray from the freezer and punched out the solid cubes, allowing them to drop into the glasses with a clink. Maybe her mother was coming down with a fever or something. She'd been acting so strange lately. Forgetting things, hot all the time. It was early summer, but 70-degree weather hardly merited a fire hydrant. Glasses filled and ready, she turned to go to the living room, but instead plopped two more ice cubes in her mother's glass for good measure.

"Here you are," Julia said, serving her the chilled drink.

Julia watched in disbelief as her mother, the epitome of Emily Post and unwavering etiquette, guzzled her tea like a boozer.

Neither said a word. Julia gaped. Her mother took a deep breath, patted her lipstick with the hankie, which now lay limp and wrinkled in her hand, then smiled as though nothing out of the ordinary had occurred.

When Julia finally found her voice she said, "So what brings you here this bright, sunny day?" Maybe she shouldn't have said the word sunny.

"Your father insists that we take a trip overseas." Another pat on her forehead with the handkerchief. "I complained about being a little tired after the fundraiser for the hospital and he says we need a vacation, a change of scenery."

Julia couldn't agree more. She might have a couple of peaceful weeks all to herself.

"We'll be gone a month."

"A month?" This was going to be a good summer, indeed.

"Yes. We'll be touring Greece, Italy, oh, who knows where all."

Julia was pretty sure if she were offered a trip like that, she'd remember where she was going.

"You know, Julia, you really should dust more," her mother said, running a finger along the stand where she placed her iced tea, leaving the trail of her fingerprint behind. "At any rate, we've hired a contractor to build an addition off our living room. We want a room with larger windows for a greater view of the lake. They're coming on Monday. I don't know how your father expects me to have a room worked on if I'm not here to oversee it."

"Why don't you postpone the remodel until you return?" Julia asked.

Her mother sputtered and coughed. "Oh my, no." Hand to her chest and a moment to catch her breath. Julia had no doubt her mother would have made a wonderful Scarlett O'Hara, given half the chance. "Contractors are busy this time of year. We have to take them while we can get them."

"Who did you hire?"

"Hammer Haven. I've heard they're quite good."

Julia nodded. She had no idea about the contractors in town.

"Besides, your father insists the contractor has the plans, knows what we want, and he mentioned that you could come and housesit to oversee the project. So I suppose it's settled."

Now it was Julia who sputtered and coughed. She considered asking her mother for the hankie. "Whoa, wait. You want me to come and stay at your house for a month?"

"What? School lets out this week, doesn't it?"

"Well, yes, but—"

"Honestly, Julia, it's not as though it would be a chore. After all, our home does overlook a breathtaking view of Lake Michigan. Your little house is fine, but admittedly doesn't offer the amenities that ours does."

No argument there. Expectations. Her mother seemed to think when she said, "Jump," Julia should obey. No matter that she was thirty-four years old and had a life of her own—well, okay, maybe not a life, per se, but she certainly didn't live with her parents.

"It's just that I enjoy staying in my own home."

"Of course you do. But a month isn't all that long. It's a way to give back to your parents for all they've done for you."

Did her mother just flutter her eyelashes? Julia was pretty sure she saw that.

Despite her efforts, Julia's chin hiked. "I would have to bring Beanie with me," she said, referring to her calico cat, a perfect blend of black, tan, and white fur. Also, an uncanny mix of Dr. Jekyll and Mr. Hyde. Heavy on the Mr. Hyde side.

Her mother harrumphed. "You have to bring that little beast with you? I swear she's half tiger."

As if on cue, Beanie sauntered into the room, plumed tail and white padded paws heading straight for Julia's mother. Beanie did a figure eight around her legs, purring with absolute innocence. It was a grand performance, Julia had to admit. Drama must run in the family.

"Oh, for goodness' sake. She'd better not scratch up my furniture."

Beanie could soften the hardest of hearts—when she wanted to be fed. But if she had a full belly, look out.

The elder Hilton walked to the front door. "Oh, we'll be leaving on Saturday. Shouldn't take you long to pack." Mrs. Hilton glanced around the room. "You won't need much."

Julia didn't miss the way her mother said it more as a directive than a comment.

Closing the door behind her mother, Julia scooped Beanie into her arms and let out a long sigh. She spotted the pad of paper on the stand beside her sofa. "Time to make a list of what to pack."

* * * * *

When the last student had left the room and her books were put away for the summer, Julia grabbed her handbag and left the smell of chalkboards and erasers behind. Almost three months' of freedom before she had to return in September to return to school.

A quiet walk along the shores of Lake Michigan was just what she needed today. Breathing deep of the lake air, her skin tingled to the warmth of the sun. The sound of the waves calmed her thoughts.

"Hey, friend, how was your official last day of school?" Becky Foster skidded to a halt, causing her auburn curls to bounce upon her shoulders. The wind kicked up a notch, and she flopped a hand on top of her straw hat.

Assigned to introducing Julia with the ways of Beach Village Junior High School when Julia joined the staff nine years ago as an English teacher, the home economics teacher and Julia had become the best of friends.

"Good. I see you got my message."

"Yeah. A walk on the beach sounded good to me too."

"I was going to ask you in person, but I didn't see your car, so I figured you weren't home yet." Not only were they best friends; they were also neighbors.

"I stopped by the store after school."

They took a few steps. "You mentioned something about your mom. What's going on there?" Becky asked.

Julia explained about the house-sitting adventure.

Becky whistled. "Why do you have to stay there? Couldn't you just check on the house every day?"

"You know Mother. She says a home unattended is just inviting trouble."

"Oh."

"She worries about tramps settling in."

"Oh my."

"I know. But then that's Mother." Gloom fogged the edges of Julia's mind.

"Still, I can't imagine staying there for a month. A balcony off your bedroom overlooking Lake Michigan. That has to be so awesome."

"Yeah, that will be nice." Julia knew she shouldn't complain, but she just didn't have it out of her system yet. Still, Becky had a way of putting things into perspective. Becky grew up in a family with nine kids and she was smack dab in the middle. Four older brothers and four younger sisters. Since Becky was the oldest of the sisters, her siblings all came to her to solve their problems. Though the family never had much materially, there was plenty of love to go around. Julia had always envied Becky's family get-togethers during the holidays. Julia's family gatherings, consisting of her parents and only Julia, now that her brother was gone, were stark in comparison.

"You'll still have your privacy, since they'll be gone, and an amazing view in the meantime."

"Yeah, I'll just be breathing sawdust into my lungs, listening to the scream of an electric saw, and the incessant pounding of a hammer." Julia sighed. "If it's not done to perfection, you know who Mother will blame, don't you?"

"That stinks."

"No kidding."

"Well, you didn't ask for the job. You'll just have to tell them what they get is what they get."

"That would go over well. She's not been in the best of moods lately."

"Oh? Is she feeling all right?"

"I don't know. Maybe she's just preoccupied with the trip."

"That would do it for me," Becky said. "Oh, no. Don't look now, but here comes Eleanor—I-think-I'm-Elizabeth-Taylor Cooley."

Julia looked up to see their former classmate, dressed in a black one-piece swimsuit with white shoulder straps. Her short stylish black hair was curled to perfection—obviously she hadn't been in the water. Her shapely legs took long strides toward them, causing men on the beach to gape and stare.

If there was one thing Julia didn't need today, it was an encounter with Eleanor Cooley.

"Hello, girls. Fancy meeting you here." Her voice dripped with insincere charm.

They followed with small talk. Then, "Hey, Becky, I needed to talk to you. You promised to bake those cookies for the kids' camp next Monday. How about I come pick them up, say, around four o'clock?"

"A couple dozen, right?"

Eleanor let out a long, breathy sigh. "Here's the problem. Three of the other cookie bakers dropped out on us, so I had hoped you would be able to make up the difference."

"Meaning?"

"I'll need about twelve dozen from you."

Becky's eyes popped.

Eleanor put her hand to her chest. Julia couldn't help noticing the similarities between Eleanor and Julia's mother.

"Oh, dear, is that too many?" Eleanor asked with a slight pout.

It frustrated Julia to no end how Eleanor put pressure on people while she herself came out smelling like a rose. "Are you making any cookies?" Julia asked.

"Oh my, no," Eleanor said. "No one could eat anything I make. That's why we employ cooks in our home. So we don't have to cook." She smiled sweetly and Julia resisted the impulse to trip her.

Julia turned to Becky. "I'll help you, Becky," she said. "Just come over to my parents' Monday morning, and we'll spend the day baking." She lifted an encouraging smile and Becky's shoulders relaxed.

"Wonderful. It's settled then," Eleanor said. "I'll come by around four to your parents' house and pick up the cookies." She studied Julia a moment. "So why will you be at your parents'?"

Julia knew that one was coming. Eleanor had to be in-the-know about all the goings-on around Beach Village. Begrudgingly, Julia explained the construction situation.

"Sounds lovely. Well, I'd better go. I need to go to the beauty parlor this afternoon. Tah-tah."

Julia and Becky watched, speechless, as Eleanor strutted off down the beach, amid wolf calls from immature boys with nothing better to do.

Becky sighed. "Some girls have all the luck." They continued walking.

"What are you talking about? She's not prettier than you are. She just thinks she is."

"Yeah, and every guy in the country agrees with her."

Julia sneered. Eleanor had been Julia's thorn in the flesh since high school. No one had a chance with a guy if Eleanor was interested in him. Julia remembered how she had tried to keep Stefan away from Eleanor so she wouldn't "steal" him.

Stefan Zimmer.

She hadn't thought of him in years. Well, in months, at least. Weeks? All right, days. She pushed all thoughts of him aside. For now.

Besides, barely in her thirties, Eleanor had already been married once, divorced, and was once again scouring the area for an available man. She collected men on the beach like some people collected lake rocks.

"Hey, you still with me here?" Becky said.

Julia blinked. "What?"

"I said, I'm going into the record store this afternoon. Do you want to go along?"

"You have so many records now, you could start your own radio station," Julia said. "What are you getting this time?"

"The new Pat Boone release, *Love Letters in the Sand*. It's a remake. Have you heard it?"

A pang shot through Julia's heart. Heard it? She could have written it.

"Oh, it's so dreamy. But then again, so is he."

Julia had a word for the song, all right, but dreamy wasn't it. The song was painful. A love gone bad. She knew all about that.

"I hope I can find a guy like that."

Becky would be a wonderful wife to some lucky man one day. She had a zest for life like no one else Julia had ever met. And she made the best cookies in the state.

"You will. All you have to do is offer him a chocolate mint cookie, and he'll propose right on the spot."

"Those mint cookies are why I never get a date. If I could lose twenty pounds, it might help."

Julia noticed how the last golden rays of sunlight played on Becky's auburn curls. "Becky, you're beautiful just the way you are. Anyway, a guy who looks only on the outside of a woman is shallow, and you don't want him."

"Spoken like a true friend."

"You know it's true."

"Well, how come you make cookies and they never show up on your body?"

"It's my mother's metabolism. The only good thing she ever gave me."

They laughed the kind of laugh that best friends share when they're having a relaxed time together.

They continued walking and discussed Julia moving in to her parents' home and when they could start on the cookies. Twilight had settled over the lake by the time they returned to where they started.

"Well, I'd better get home. I promised my brothers I'd bake them a batch of caramel cookies," Becky said, climbing into her cherry-red Rambler.

"Have fun."

"I will as long as this gets me home in one piece." She patted the dashboard of her car and waved.

Julia waved and watched as Becky's Rambler sputtered and jerked along the parking lot. Julia shook her head and smiled. She'd better get home. She had some packing to do.

* * * * *

Lukas Gable glanced out the massive window overlooking the city of Chicago while the attorney shuffled through papers on his desk. Mr. Schultheis took several puffs on his pipe, filling the room with the scent of expensive tobacco.

Finally he handed Lukas a copy of his uncle's will. Lukas stared in disbelief at the paper that offered him legal ownership of his aunt and uncle's estate.

Mr. Schultheis grunted. "Snuffed out before they had a chance to get old," the old man said. He shook his head. "Too bad. Your uncle was so excited about that new plane of his."

"Yeah."

Mr. Schultheis shook his head. "For a long time, Catherine refused to go up in it with him...until that day."

"Guess it was their time to go."

"Yes, I suppose it was. Your family has had a time of it. Your dad, as I understand, died of, what, a heart attack awhile back?"

Lukas nodded. "I didn't know you knew my family."

The old man let out a deep, raspy cough. "Only through your aunt and uncle. Your uncle thought a lot of his brother and told me so. By the way, how's your mom?"

"She died about six months ago. Pneumonia."

The lawyer scratched his head. "Is that right? I'm sorry to hear that."

"Thanks." The truth was, this inheritance couldn't have come at a better time. Lukas had so many bills to pay in connection with his mother's healthcare, he didn't know how he was going to manage it. If there was one thing his parents were proud of, it was keeping their bills paid. He had to do the same—in their honor, even if he had to dig ditches to pay off every last bill.

"Well, with no children of their own, it had always been Mr. and Mrs. Zimmer's desire to bequeath their entire estate to you." Mr. Schultheis took another puff from his pipe. "Mind you, there aren't a lot of assets there, but it's a pretty good start."

A knot lodged in Lukas's chest. It was just like Uncle Clay to do something like this. Lukas loved the summers he'd spent at their home when he was growing up, but after Julia, well, he was glad to leave there. Now to go back and face the memories, wondering where it all went wrong...

Mr. Schultheis shuffled through the paperwork on his desk. "Your name change caused a bit of confusion in finding you."

"Sorry about that."

"Stefan Zimmer is a good, strong German name. Don't know why you would change it." Mr. Schultheis paused as though waiting for more of an explanation.

Lukas said nothing. He owed no one an explanation of his past.

Mr. Schultheis picked up a paper and read from it. "So, Lukas Gable." The curious attorney let the words hover between them, baiting Lukas for more.

"Yes sir" was all Lukas said.

Mr. Schultheis took another puff of his pipe, held it in his hand, then shrugged. "To each his own, I guess."

Silence.

"Well, young man, it's official," Mr. Schultheis said, handing Lukas a copy of the will. "It will take some time for everything to shake out in court, but you can take immediate possession of the property. No one has contested the will."

Their handshake signaled a fresh start. With his mother gone, there was no reason to stick around Chicago. Plus the fact he couldn't afford to live there any longer, not with her medical bills following him. She'd lived in an apartment, and there was no estate—only bills left. He was in a dead-end factory job. This would give him an excuse to start over. He'd sell his uncle's house, pay off his mother's debts, look for a job, and buy a small place to call home—wherever that might lead him. He had no ties. Maybe he'd use his teaching degree—the one he'd never put into practice, much to his mother's dismay—and find a job in a classroom so he could have time off in the summers to work on building boats. Maybe even start his own business one day. There was enough money in his uncle's estate to give him a little time to get things in order before the house had to be sold, but just a little time. Hopefully there wouldn't be much to do to prepare the home for sale.

There was no denying that he wished the house were located somewhere other than Beach Village, Wisconsin. Anywhere else would have been preferable. But those days were in the past and it was time for him to move on. Julia would have moved on by now. It had been, what, seventeen years? She'd probably relocated to another town, maybe another state. She hadn't seemed all that close to her parents. Nothing to hold her there.

Yes, this was a good move. In fact, maybe this was his second chance to put his past behind him so that he could move on.

One thing for certain, he was about to find out.

CHAPTER TWO

After a meal of salmon, broccoli, and salad, Julia and her parents settled in the living room for tea. Julia eased into the Queen Anne chair and tried to get comfortable. The furniture was beautiful to look at, but she'd always wanted a fluffy cushion to sink into—this wasn't it.

"That was a delicious meal, Mother," she said.

"It was good, but we could have used a little chocolate for dessert." Margaret Hilton lifted her teacup to her lips and took a dainty sip.

Chocolate? Did her mother say chocolate? She never ate candy, that Julia could remember. Was she going through a second childhood or what?

Julia looked over at her father, who gave her a wink. Maybe he knew something she didn't. She'd have to talk to him later when they were alone.

"You know, you could cook like that if you set your mind to it, Julia."

Though Julia loved her mother, she didn't always appreciate her opinions. Her dad didn't seem to mind. Granted, her mother was beautiful. Stately, tall, slender, hair dark as midnight normally wrapped in a French twist at the back of her head, elegant jewels adorning her neck and ears from her neck and ears. But the woman could be as prickly as a wire brush.

A slight nip in the late spring air made their stone fireplace a welcome presence. The warmth from the dancing flames in the hearth filled Julia with nostalgia. She couldn't say all of her childhood was bad.

Even what happened with Stefan wasn't her mother's fault. In the end, it turned out her mother had been right. Yes, her mother had control issues, but the truth was their relationship struggled most after Joseph's death. Maybe most mothers who had lost a child reacted this way. It took time to heal. Who knew that better than her?

Julia's glance shot to the familiar picture on the stand of her mother and brother. Joseph wore his army uniform and a bright smile. He looked so much like their mother, tall, slim, dark hair and eyes. Julia, on the other hand, had many of her father's lighter features. Some people told her she favored Debbie Reynolds. She couldn't see it, of course, but appreciated the compliment just the same.

Another nearby picture flashed a smiling Julia with her dad. Seemed there were more pictures of their family divided than together. Mother took Joseph and Dad got Julia. Just like his and her towels.

"Sure is sweet of you to take care of the house for us while we're gone, Julia," her dad said with a smile.

"Well, it is a daughter's duty to take care of her parents," her mother said.

Dad tossed Julia an apologetic glance.

"I'm happy to do it for you, Dad." Julia hoped her mother caught her drift, but she doubted it. Suddenly her mother's face turned rosy-cheeked. Maybe she was working up a temper. Wouldn't be the first time.

"I think we've covered everything. If you think of any questions, I'm afraid you'll have trouble reaching us for a while," her mother said, scooting away from the fireplace. "Once I have a better handle on our itinerary, I'll call you." She wiped her brow with a handkerchief.

"She won't need us," Dad said. "Julia is quite capable of handling things on her own."

Her mother leaned back against the sofa. It was then Julia noticed the dark circles beneath her eyes. It was a big job to get ready for an extended vacation. No doubt the time away would do her good.

The grandfather clock in the den struck nine. Julia noticed her dad's glance locked on the heirloom. How he loved that clock, a wedding gift from his parents. Not long ago Mother had wanted to get rid of it because it didn't fit the décor in the room, but Dad had refused. She threw a fit. He held his ground. One of the few arguments Julia had heard him win, and she was quite proud of him for it.

Julia took a drink of her mint tea and listened as the moments ticked by. She would stay long enough to be social and then be on her way.

"So what are your plans this summer, Julia?" her mother asked, yawning.

Julia shrugged. "Get some things done around the house. Watch over your house and the construction. Read some books I've put off for a while, enjoy the beach, that sort of thing."

"Well, I hope we're not keeping you from enjoying your summer," Dad said. "We could try to find someone else to come over."

She had a choice? Funny, her mother never mentioned that.

Mother's eyebrows furrowed. "Of course we're not keeping her from anything. She still has plenty of time to go somewhere once we get back." Her voice had a snarl in it.

"I'm doing what I want to do this summer, Dad. I'm going to relax, spend lots of time on the beach, just enjoy myself."

"Nothing wrong with that, I guess," he said, scratching the evening whiskers on his face.

"I've started making these gifts called Ebenezers. I collect smooth rocks from the lake shore, put them in a large glass container with a candle, wrap a bow around it, and stick on a marking pen and a card with the scripture from 1 Samuel 7:12."

Her father looked interested. "What does that say?"

"'Then Samuel took a stone, and set it up between Mizpeh and Shen and called the name of it Ebenezer, saying, "Hitherto hath the LORD helped us."'"

"Whatever is it for?" her mother asked.

"To write on the stones of remembrance special moments that God brings into our lives, using the Israelites as our example."

"What a unique idea," her dad said. "Very creative."

"I can't take credit for it. Our pastor came up with the idea." And indeed she couldn't take credit. The truth was Julia needed such a gift to remember…God. They hadn't had a good talk in forever.

"You would do well to remember that rocks don't exactly go with every décor." Her mother yawned again.

Julia got her mother's not-so-subtle hint that she wanted to go to bed.

"I'd better get home and take care of Beanie. She'll wonder where I've been all evening." Standing to her feet, Julia collected her cup, saucer, and purse.

"Oh, for goodness' sake, the way you coddle that cat," Mother said.

Julia walked over and planted a kiss on her dad's cheek. "Good night."

"Good night, sweet girl." He gave her hand a squeeze.

"Good night, Mother." Her mother squinted her cheek as though bracing herself for Julia's kiss.

"Have a wonderful vacation," Julia said before she slipped through the massive front door. Once outside, she pulled her jacket tighter around her. She wasn't sure which was colder, the night air or her mother's attitude.

* * * * *

"So is that everything you need?" Becky put the box down in the hallway with a dozen or so other boxes and brushed her hands together.

"That's all I need for now," Julia said.

"How many boxes is that? Where are you going to put everything?"

"Now, Becky, don't start. You know I need my books, my makeup, my clothes, hats, shoes, Beanie's kitty litter, food and water bowls, all that."

Becky laughed. "Your little hoarding secret is safe with me. It's the plague of teachers, I'm afraid."

Julia looked at her and chuckled. "I guess."

"Just remember, you won't be here forever." Becky pointed to the recipe books, the records, and the yarn.

"I need to keep myself occupied," Julia said with a more defensive tone than she'd intended. Good thing Becky didn't know Julia planned another trip home to bring in more shoes, some books to get ideas for the next school year, and the quilt her grandma had made her. She couldn't sleep without it. She and her grandmother had been very close.

"Yeah, that's the excuse I always use too." Becky glanced around the room with a whistle. "Would you look at this place? What a beautiful home."

"It's too stark for my tastes."

"Oh, but what fun we could have filling it up." Becky laughed.

"That's true." Julia dropped the box she was holding.

Becky's attention turned to one of the boxes. "You must spend a fortune in books. You ever heard of the library?"

True enough that her friend was thrifty. She had learned to be, growing up in a house with nine kids. Julia, on the other hand, was able to buy what she needed—and wanted. "Sometimes I like to refer back to quotes, Becky. An English teacher must have her resources."

Becky shrugged. "If you say so."

They rifled through more boxes, putting things where Julia wanted them. "Hey, why don't we listen to some records?" Becky thumbed through Julia's parents' records on the stereo cabinet in the living room. "Never mind." Her nose scrunched in distaste. "These aren't our style."

Julia smiled. "Not to worry." She shoved a box toward Becky. "I brought records, remember?"

Her friend bent over and looked inside. She giggled and lifted the 45s from the box. "You've brought everything but the kitchen sink."

"I may go back and get it."

"Oh my goodness, I love Elvis Presley!" Becky squealed like a high school girl. "He's so dreamy." She hugged the record close and sighed with sheer pleasure. "'Hound Dog' is my favorite." After stacking a few records on the player, she placed the mechanical arm over the vinyl and turned the knob, causing one to drop. The record needle rode the grooved disk while Elvis belted out, "You ain't nothin' but a hound dog."

Becky and Julia immediately launched into a jitterbug around the room. With every thump of the beat, they kicked, swung, and twirled enough to lose a good fifty calories before the song's end. In the grand finale of the tune, Julia gave a leg kick that could have won her a spot with the Goldwyn Girls. Her foot swooped down and walloped something hard, causing her toes to protest in pain. Breaking glass crackled in the silence between the changing records.

Fortunately, no toes were broken. If only she could say the same for the framed picture of her mother and brother—the-last-gift-Joseph-had-given-to-his-mother-before-he-died framed picture.

* * * * *

"Hi. I'm George Hammer of Hammer Haven Construction." George extended his hand and Lukas grabbed it in a hearty shake.

"Thanks for coming out so soon," Lukas said, stepping aside so George could enter the house, a whiff of fresh-cut grass following him inside.

"No problem. Things don't start getting busy till next week."

They walked over the stained carpet, frayed at the door's edges, and began their tour of the house. Lukas was painfully aware of the repairs they'd have to make, the musty smell of a basement that flooded, and the water spots on the ceiling. His aunt and uncle had let the place run down. There was much to do here before he could make it sellable. Which presented another problem. How could he pay off the medical bills if he had to sink a lot of money into repairs?

"So you're new in town?" George asked.

"Yeah." Lukas had no intention of revealing his history in this town to anyone.

"What did you say your name was again?"

Lukas paused a moment. Though he had changed his name almost two years ago, it still took getting used to when he introduced himself. "Lukas. Lukas Gable."

George nodded. He looked around the house and the two of them discussed what changes they could make to the old homestead.

"I won't sugarcoat things," George said. "This will take a bit of work to make it marketable, in my opinion. New flooring in the kitchen." He glanced up at the ceiling and pointed toward the water spots. "New roof. Some of your pipes look rusted. I doubt that your insulation is up to code."

"Yeah, that's what I figured too," Lukas said. "I don't have a lot of money, so I may have to do it in stages."

"Do you plan to live here or just improve it for an investment?" George asked, as they settled into friendly conversation.

"I'll stay here until it's sellable. Then I'll get something smaller. With no family of my own, I don't need a place this big. Plus, I need the money the sale will bring." Oops. Lukas wished he hadn't said that. No need to give more information than necessary.

"I'll be honest with you. Not much real estate moving these days. Can't really say why, other than people around here are just conservative when it comes to spending money. Seems to me they haven't gotten over the Depression and the war days yet."

The news made his stomach plunge. Maybe he'd have to come up with another plan for making money. He didn't want to stay in this town any longer than necessary.

"What kind of work do you do?" George asked as they walked on the wooden floors from one room to another.

"I have a teaching degree. But what I enjoy is building wooden boats."

"Really?" George scratched his jaw. "I don't think we have anything like that around here. Might be a good place to start a business."

Lukas released a guarded grin. "Maybe. I'd have to do it part-time, though, till I could make some money."

"Where did you learn to build boats?" George asked.

"My uncle taught me."

George looked at the pipes in the bathroom. "Got anything going for the summer?"

"Not yet."

"Ever worked construction?" George asked.

"Yep. When I came back from—uh, yeah, for a few years I worked with a home remodeling business, before I went to work in a factory." He noticed the question on George's face. "The teaching degree was my mom's idea, not mine."

George smiled. "You could probably do the work on your house here by yourself."

"Take me too long." Lukas was sure the hospital wouldn't be willing to wait that long for payment. "But if you'd give me a discount, I could definitely help you."

"Sure, I could do that." George stroked his chin. "As a matter of fact, I'm a small business. My partner just left town and I'm on my own. I have a room addition scheduled to start on Monday and no one to help me. 'Course, I have the usual subcontractors, but I could sure use some help. Don't suppose you would be interested?" Hope lit George's eyes.

Lukas stood there a minute, considering the idea. He'd get a discount on his home repairs and make some money in the process. Sounded like a win-win to him.

"You don't know my work. That's a pretty big gamble."

George shrugged. "You can swing a hammer, that's a big plus right there. Besides, I'm desperate. You're a risk I'm willing to take at this point. I have to get someone to help me. It would take me too long to finish by myself. These people aren't that patient." He glanced at the kitchen cupboards. "You could paint these."

Lukas nodded.

George turned to Lukas. "I've already had the concrete guys out there. The slab has been poured for the room and the footers put in. I've obtained the permits, so we'll be ready to get started on Monday."

"Sounds good to me." Lukas grinned and reached toward George's hand. "You've got yourself a deal."

They shook hands and settled in the kitchen for coffee to talk out the details of income and work expectations.

"You said you're by yourself. You ever been married?" George asked.

"Nope."

"That makes two of us. I figured you to be a smart man."

They laughed.

"Never found a woman who could tame me—though plenty have tried." George grinned and leaned back in his chair, clasping his hands behind his head.

Lukas smiled and sipped his coffee.

"Well, I'd best be going." George dropped his chair with a thump and swallowed the last of his coffee. "Guess I'll see you bright and early on Monday." He grabbed a pen and pad of paper from his pocket. "Here's the address." He handed it to Lukas. "Can't tell you how much I appreciate it."

Lukas said good-bye and once George drove off, he sat back down at the table to finish his coffee. He picked up the paper George had given him, thinking he'd better go try to find the place before Monday. He remembered some of the streets from when he had lived here in the summers as a teen, but he needed to refresh his memory.

When he glanced at the paper, the words hit him like a punch in the gut. He wouldn't have to look up the address. He knew it all too well.

* * * * *

Beckoned by the cool night breeze, Julia stepped from her parents' bedroom onto the balcony, allowing the moonlit sky, scattered with twinkling stars, the whisper of the night waves rolling to shore, and the sweet scent of summer to envelop her. She drank in the scene, the sounds, the scent, everything.

Her mind's eye envisioned a young man and woman pledging their love to one another at the water's edge. He bent over and wrote something in the sand then caressed her in a long embrace.

Julia closed her eyes and allowed herself, just one more time, to bask in the luxury of that memory. To feel his breath next to her ear and her heart pounding so hard she could barely breathe.

A bird cawed overhead and her vision shattered like the broken frame on her mother's living room floor.

What had started this flood of memories of Stefan? Maybe her mother was right. She should date more often. It might make her forget.

"Where are you tonight, Stefan Zimmer?" The words crowded her throat and caused her eyes to fill. If only she could forget him, let him go. Why was she struggling to control something she obviously never had? Control? A thought surfaced that nearly cut off her air supply.

She was becoming her mother.

* * * * *

The night air offered a perfect evening for a walk on the beach. Lukas passed couples, hand in hand, strolling along the water's edge, no doubt dreaming of a future together. The same way he and Julia had done so many years ago.

He looked across the great expanse of the lake, mesmerized by the shimmering moonlight in the rippling waters. Where had everything gone so wrong? He truly had thought their love was so much more than teenagers' puppy love.

Bending over, he picked up a large rock, carved his name in the sand, then watched as the water carried traces of it back to the depths of the lake. He moved on. The truth was he hadn't thought of Julia in quite some time. He had dated plenty of women since those days. Yet not one of them could make him forget...her.

He supposed his aunt and uncle's gift and coming back here to Beach Village stirred up all the old memories that now haunted him like the Ghost of Christmas Past.

A seagull cawed overhead, its wings silhouetted against the moonlight. Lukas took a deep breath. Maybe if he knew where Julia was, how she had moved on with her own life, it might give him some closure. If he could talk with her, just once, to clear things up, to know where it all went wrong, he could move on. He was almost sure he could.

The creak of wooden doors opening caused him to look up toward the house on the hill. He hadn't realized he'd walked this far. He now stood near Julia's parents' home—at least, it used to be. He doubted they still owned it. Her mother had talked of moving the summer he and Julia parted.

A woman stood on the balcony overlooking the lake. Dressed in a long white robe, her face was lifted toward the night sky, shrouded in the gentle shadows of moonlight. The rhythm of his heart ran wild in his chest as he looked on her beauty. It didn't matter that her face was a blur. His eyes refused to see anyone but Julia Hilton. In breathless wonder he took in her silhouette wrapped in the perfect blend of a velvet sky and soft moonlight, and his heart seemed to pause.

The woman stood there a few moments then turned and stepped back inside the house, closing the French doors behind her.

The image of Julia popped like a balloon at a celebration party. Only this wasn't a celebration, there were no balloons, and definitely, no Julia.

CHAPTER THREE

"What are you going to do about the frame?" Becky said over the phone the next morning. Julia poured herself a cup of coffee and sat at the kitchen table.

"I don't know. I'll think of something." Julia prayed the answer would come to her. She didn't want to think about how her mother would react to the news. Nerves twisted her stomach. Here she was, a grown woman, and still afraid of upsetting her mother.

"Too bad you can't just replace the glass in it," Becky said.

"Yeah, I'm going to check into that too." Julia heard Becky chewing something. "What are you eating?"

"Oh, sorry." Becky hesitated.

"Come on. Tell me." Julia fingered the coiled telephone cord.

She sighed. "Brownies."

"Tell me you didn't get up and bake them this morning," Julia said.

Silence.

"Becky?"

"You told me not to tell you, so I won't."

Now Julia sighed. "You don't have to be nervous for me, Becky. It will all turn out all right. Besides, chocolate will not solve life's problems."

"No, but it sure helps."

"Okay, then bring the rest of them over and share them with me."

They laughed together.

"Do you want to start on those cookies after church or wait till tomorrow?" Becky asked.

Julia thought a moment. "I need to go and pick up yesterday's mail, then I was planning to read awhile. Would it be all right if you came over and we made them tomorrow instead?"

"Isn't that when the construction guys are coming?"

"Yes, but that's no problem."

"All right, then, if you say so. I'll be there in the morning."

"Sounds perfect," Julia said, taking another sip of coffee.

"Have you heard from your parents yet?"

"Not yet." Julia's stomach twisted some more.

"I thought sure they'd call you by now."

"Mother will probably call every day that they're on land once the construction starts."

Becky agreed. "Hey, it's getting late and I'm not dressed yet. I'll see you at church in a few."

"See ya."

Julia finished her coffee and looked off the living room where her parents were planning the room addition. She could only hope the contractors knew exactly what they were doing and she wouldn't have to answer any hard questions.

Before she walked away, she had pretty much convinced herself she could do this. In fact, she doubted she would have much interaction with the workers at all. Why, she would hardly even know they were there.

* * * * *

Lukas tossed and turned most of the night. By the time the alarm went off, he wondered if he'd slept at all. He quickly took a shower, dressed, and stumbled into his first day on the new job.

He didn't know why his stomach churned like a summer storm. So he was going to Julia's parents' home. He doubted they still owned it after all this time. He could have asked George but didn't want him to know he knew Julia's family. That might prompt too many questions.

George knocked on the door with Lukas right behind him. The door opened. "Hi, I'm George Hammer. This is Lukas Gable. We're here to work on your room addition."

Lukas looked up. It seemed as if the whole world took a collective breath. Julia. Same beautiful sandy-colored hair, pulled back into a ponytail. She hadn't aged at all. Same sweet smile with a tiny dimple on one side. Same green eyes, shining with the innocence and vulnerability that had one time peered into the depths of his soul.

Same familiar ache in his heart.

She wouldn't—couldn't—recognize him. Since the reconstructive surgery, he hardly recognized his own face. Yet, when she looked at him, her gaze lingered a moment, causing the breath swirling in his chest to stop.

"Nice to meet you both," she said, moving to the side. "Please, come in."

Same soothing sweet voice. She walked toward the living room and they followed her.

Lukas's heart hammered against his chest. His palms grew sweaty. "Come on, after all this time?"

George turned to him. "What? Did you say something?"

Lukas shook his head. That's what he got for talking to himself.

"I'm afraid my parents will be gone over the next four weeks, but if you have any questions, I'll be happy to help as best I can. They assured me you had worked out all the details before they left?" she said.

"Yes. Your father called me and told me they were leaving. We went over the latest instructions, and I think we'll be just fine. I don't believe I caught your name," George said.

"Julia." She glanced at Lukas. "Julia Hilton."

Another skip of his heart. Her last name was still Hilton. A shot of hope soared through him, then his thoughts skidded to a screeching halt. What was he thinking? This woman dumped him, pure and simple. He wasn't about to go there again.

"I'll be in the kitchen this afternoon if you need me." She turned to Lukas. "Can I get you guys anything to drink?"

His tongue seemed to stick to the roof of his mouth. He just stood there, gaping at her, feeling like a stupid teenager.

George smiled. "I think we're fine. Thanks." He turned to Lukas. "Ready to get to work?"

"Huh? Oh, yeah. Yeah."

George grinned. Julia didn't seem to notice Lukas's discomfort. She turned and headed for the kitchen—at least that was the direction Lukas thought the kitchen was. After all these years, he couldn't be sure.

His hand reached up to his longest scar. Things were different now. Way different. She didn't know him. Some days, he didn't even know himself.

"Are you okay?" George asked when they got to the truck.

"I'm fine, why?"

George's eyebrows lifted. "You just seemed a little, well, over the moon when you saw that woman."

Lukas shrugged. "She just reminded me of someone. That's all."

"I see." He picked up one end of a two-by-four and Lukas grabbed the other. They hoisted it from the back of the truck. "Take my advice, don't think twice about that one."

"Oh? Why is that?"

"She's known as the Ice Queen around here. Has turned down just about every guy in town, from what I hear."

Lukas stifled a grin. "Did she turn you down?"

"No sirree. I never got up the nerve to ask her."

Lukas laughed. "Sounds like a challenge to me."

"You'd better be careful. You could get your heart broken with a girl like that."

"I doubt it," Lukas said, knowing good and well George was right. Julia had already broken his heart once. A second time would be plain stupid on his part.

"You seem pretty sure of yourself," George taunted. "How about we make a wager on it."

"I don't bet," Lukas said.

"I'll give you an additional 15 percent off the work I do at your house and let you pay my cost for any supplies—in addition to the 10-percent discount I already quoted for the work you do."

Lukas's eyebrows raised. "And what do you want from me?"

"You have to keep working with me through August. These are my busiest months."

"Okay, so what's the bet?"

A slow grin played across George's face. "You have to be able to get Julia on at least three dates."

Lukas thought a moment. He didn't want to put himself in a position to get hurt again. But that was years ago. His jaw twitched as he thought of their past.

George dangled the carrot. "Fifteen percent off."

Lukas could sure use the discount, but did he really want to be alone on a date with Julia again? He thought about it a moment. Julia would never recognize him. And this could give him a chance to get to know her again, find out what she'd been up to all these years.

"Three dates?"

"Three dates."

So he might get a bruised ego out of the deal; 15 percent was worth it, wasn't it? He needed the money. And maybe he could get to the truth of why she'd dropped him.

"All right." Lukas shoved out his hand to shake on it. "You're on."

With the agreement made, the two men spent their morning sawing lumber and putting up the framing for the walls.

Julia walked into the room about ten o'clock with chilled glasses of iced tea.

"I thought you might enjoy a bit of a break." She walked over to George and handed him a glass then walked over to Lukas. Their eyes met and Lukas thought he might drop the glass, but he held on tight—as a life support, if nothing else. "Hope this helps with the heat," she said to him, smiling.

He took one glance at her and all intelligible speech scattered from his mind. He wanted to say something, anything, but his mind was a blank slate, like a foundational block with nothing on it. He simply looked at her. Drank in her beauty, remembered their shared kisses, their words of love written in the sand. Their promises.

She blinked and immediately turned away, taking no further notice of him. He could have been a fly on a board for all she cared. His gaze collided with George's. A grin split wide across his face before he took a drink. Lukas wanted to slug him.

Putting aside his glass, Lukas picked up nails and a hammer. He pounded one nail after another into the wood, working off steam. He didn't think he had a hefty ego, but he'd continued working out at the gym since his army days, and his build was fairly decent for a thirty-six-year-old, if he did say so himself. He'd been a skinny kid when she knew him. Maybe he needed to show off his muscles a little more. Women liked that.

He'd get her to come around. What did it hurt? Three dates, nothing serious. No one would get hurt.

Not this time.

* * * * *

"I hope I've brought everything I need," Becky said, bringing in the last bag of groceries.

She and Julia pulled food items from the bags. Milk, butter, chocolate chips, peppermint flavoring, nuts, sugar, eggs...

"My goodness, you have enough here to make hundreds of cookies," Julia said.

"You heard Eleanor. At least twelve dozen."

"Yeah, you're right. Guess we'd better go to work."

"I even brought my own mixer, so we could get done quicker." Becky lifted her hand mixer from a bag.

"Swell."

Becky measured ingredients into a large mixing bowl. "So when do I get to peek at the construction guys? Are they single?"

Julia giggled. "You're awful. A woman is supposed to play hard to get." No need to mention how the blue in Lukas's eyes made her skin tingle—just the way Stefan's had done—and how his arms looked strong enough to protect her through the fiercest of life's storms. His smile...

Becky put her hands on her hips. "I found a wrinkle on my face this morning, Julia. Right here." She poked her forehead with her finger and left a smudge of flour behind. "I don't have time to play hard to get." The electric beaters started to whir.

Julia shook her head and started her own mixer. A sugary scent stirred in the air.

They spent the afternoon whipping up batches of peanut butter, chocolate chip, chocolate mint, and oatmeal cookies. Finally, Becky took the last of the cookies from the oven and placed the pan on a rack on the counter.

"Time for some iced tea," Julia said, brushing the hair from her forehead with her arm.

"Sounds great."

Once the glasses were filled, Julia sat down at the table and lifted her feet onto an empty chair.

"A little reward from the fruit of our labor," Becky said with a grin. She carried a plate of cookies to the table.

"Something sure smells good," George said when he walked into the kitchen with his empty glass.

Lukas walked right behind him.

Julia dropped her feet to the floor.

"Why don't you two take a break and join us," Becky said.

Julia gave her a discreet kick beneath the table.

"Ow."

The guys looked at them.

"Just let me get you some more iced tea." Julia jumped from her chair before anyone could comment. A knock at the front door caused her heels to practically spark fire as she came to a sudden halt. Julia and Becky locked eyes.

Eleanor.

One deep breath then Julia left the room to let her in. "Hi, Eleanor. Come on in."

Eleanor stood there in her pedal pushers and matching top, hair swept into soft curls. For some reason the whole look irritated Julia.

"How are the cookies coming along?" Eleanor asked as she followed Julia to the kitchen.

"We're all finished. In fact, we were just sitting down to try some."

Once in the kitchen, Eleanor's eyes grew wide when she spotted the guys.

"Oh."

"Eleanor, this is George Hammer and Lukas Gable. They're working on Mother and Dad's room addition."

A raised eyebrow and smirk replaced the surprise on Eleanor's face. "Nice to meet you," she said sweetly.

The guys stared at her—a little too long to Julia's way of thinking. She knew she and Becky were about to fade into the wallpaper.

"Can I get you some iced tea, Eleanor?"

"That would be swell." She looked for a chair and George jumped up and brought one toward her.

"Why, thank you. I so admire men who can make things. Tell me, how did you two get into this business?"

Julia and Becky sat open-mouthed as Eleanor seemed to hang on the guys' every word. By the time they were through the cookies, Julia and Becky had been completely forgotten, and the guys walked away with looks of confidence, as though they had won Eleanor over. But Julia knew the truth. Eleanor was no more interested in them than the man in the moon. She merely pulled them into her web, like every other guy in town, to be visited later, if she so desired.

After Lukas and George went back to work, Julia and Becky put the cookies in containers for Eleanor.

"You didn't tell me the guys working for you were so dreamy," Eleanor said.

Julia shrugged. "I hadn't noticed."

"Oh, come now, Julia. You may be cold but you're not blind."

Julia whirled around to say something but stopped herself. Becky shot her a warning glance. The last thing they needed was for the guys to hear them fighting like schoolgirls over boys.

"I'm going to the bathroom. I'll be right back."

Julia closed the door in the bathroom and stared at herself in the mirror. Her face was red. One of these days she'd learn not to let her emotions control her. She wet a washcloth, soothed the back of her neck, and took a deep breath before going back out to face Eleanor.

Just as Julia was about to turn the corner to go into the kitchen, Eleanor's conversation with Becky stopped her.

"Come on, Becky," Eleanor said above a whisper, "you have to admit those guys are good looking. I saw the way Julia looked at Lukas. If he shows her the least bit of interest, she'll cave, I know she will."

"I don't think so," Becky said. "Julia's not won over by good looks and muscles alone."

Eleanor gave a forced laugh. "You have to admit, it's a good place to start."

Silence.

Julia started to move forward then stopped when Eleanor spoke up again.

"Here's the deal. I think Julia will fall for Lukas, and before the room extension is finished, they'll be an item. You say she won't fall for him and nothing will come of their knowing one another. If I'm wrong, I'll pay you twenty-five dollars. If you're wrong, you pay me twenty-five dollars. Oh, and you can't tell Julia about this. Deal?"

Julia knew Becky had the good sense to turn down this deal. Becky's car was barely making it, and she had used some of her savings to buy her sister a dress for a school dance. If she lost more money, there was no telling when she'd get another car and she had to have a car to work.

"Deal," Becky said.

Julia couldn't believe her ears. Why would Becky make such a deal with Eleanor? Was it pride? Was she so certain that Julia wouldn't be interested in Lukas?

Trying to hide her disappointment and act as though she heard nothing, Julia smiled when she came into the room. The more she thought about it, the more she realized their little "deal" shouldn't cause her worry. After all, she had no intention of dating Lukas Gable.

Lukas walked into the room, all broad-shouldered, bulging muscles, and heart-stopping grin. "We're going to head out for the day. Be back tomorrow." His eyes locked with Julia's. "Thanks for the cookies," he said. "They were delicious."

She tried to swallow but couldn't. Words bunched in her throat but her mouth refused to open. Instead, she merely nodded and watched his back as he walked away. His broad, strong, rippling-with-muscles back. When she turned toward Eleanor and Becky, she didn't miss the look of triumph on Eleanor's face. She was planning her victory party, no doubt about it.

Julia would show her.

Becky would win this bet. Julia had no intention of dating Lukas Gable. She looked toward the window and watched his long legs climb into the truck.

No intention whatsoever.

CHAPTER FOUR

"Want to go out for Chinese?" Julia asked Becky when everyone finally left the house.

"I'd better not. I'm trying to save my money for another car."

Julia's heart squeezed. Why did Becky make that bet with Eleanor? She needed to be more careful with her money.

If only Julia could talk to her about it. But she knew Becky would be embarrassed for having let Eleanor back her into a corner that way. Plus, Eleanor said she couldn't tell Julia.

"Hey, I've got a better idea," Julia said. "I have some fruit in the fridge. We can eat that, then take a walk on the beach."

"Good idea," Becky said. "Then we can come back and have another cookie. Sure glad you saved a few more for us."

After they ate a mixture of strawberries, pineapples, bananas, and melon, she and Becky walked along the lake's shoreline. The night air was sweet with the scent of toasted marshmallows from a distant campfire in someone's backyard. The rhythmic lull of the incoming and outgoing tide relaxed Julia.

"So what did you think of the guys?" Becky asked.

"What guys?"

"The workers who came to your house."

"What's to think? They seemed to do an okay job. Though I don't know much about construction."

"I don't mean that," Becky said. "I mean, didn't you think they were cute?"

"Oh, that. I don't know. Haven't thought about it." Okay, maybe she had thought about it, but she didn't feel like talking about it.

Becky shook her head. "What's with you? Good-looking men like that, unattached, and you don't notice? Have you given up on love forever because of that one crush long ago?"

A pain shot through Julia. "It wasn't a crush, Becky. I was in love with Stefan. Why can't people believe that? Just because I was seventeen at the time didn't mean I couldn't love someone. It was love—pure, innocent, but very grown-up love."

Becky grimaced. "Sorry. Didn't mean to upset you."

Remorse settled over Julia. If only she could learn to hold her tongue. "I'm sorry too. It's just that I truly loved him."

They took a few steps in silence.

"Does that mean you'll never give anyone else a chance?" Becky asked softly.

Julia shrugged. "I don't know. I've just never found anyone else who came close to Stefan."

"Maybe you're looking for another Stefan rather than looking for someone else, period. You know what I mean? Don't try to make everyone be like him."

"I'm not trying to do that. Can we change the subject?"

"Sure. But for the record, just let me say, I think George is pretty cute." She giggled. "But you're right. Lukas doesn't seem your type."

That intrigued Julia. "How so?"

"Oh, I don't know. You never seem impressed by the body-builder types. And Lukas is definitely the body-builder type. Probably has women falling at his feet, and most likely the ego to prove it."

"Yeah. You know how I feel about men and their egos."

"I sure do. We'll just have to keep looking for you. There has to be someone out there I can fix you up with."

Julia laughed. "Ever the Cupid. Trust me, if I find someone I'm interested in, you'll be the first to know."

And one thing Julia knew, bet or no bet, her interest wasn't in Lukas Gable.

* * * * *

With the smell of fried beef still in the air, Lukas finished his hamburger and chips when the phone rang. "Hello?"

"Hey, I forgot to tell you earlier today that I belong to a gym in town. Figured a big husky guy like you might want to check it out. I'm headed over there now. Want to go?"

Lukas thought a minute. "Sure. Where is it?"

George filled Lukas in on the directions and they made plans to meet in fifteen minutes. Filling up Sauerkraut's food and water bowl, Lukas gave his dachshund a vigorous scratch behind the ears. Sauerkraut grabbed his hot dog chew toy and ran to his doggie pillow near Lukas's easy chair in the living room while Lukas looked on with a laugh. "See you later, Sauerkraut."

In no time Lukas and George were pumping iron in the gym.

"So what did you think of Julia?" George wanted to know.

Lukas climbed off the bench press then picked up some hand weights. "One, two, three." Lukas sucked in air on the downward thrust and blew out short breaths with every lift. "She was all right."

"Just all right?" George eyed him with a mischievous grin.

"What are you getting at?"

George lifted twenty-pound dumbbell weights. "Come on, you know she's better than all right. I saw the way you looked at her."

"She's all right." Lukas put the hand weights back and headed for the walking track.

George followed him.

"Well, the bet's still on, remember. Interested or not, you have to get her on a date. And to be honest, I didn't see her hanging on your every word."

Lukas could tell George was teasing, but the man was starting to get on his nerves.

"I'll get her attention, don't you worry about that," Lukas said. He picked up the pace and walked the track with purpose, discouraging further conversation.

Lukas wondered how he'd get Julia's attention. He agreed she didn't seem all that interested. She was nice and civil, but nothing in her body language, eyes, talk, none of it gave any indication she was interested in him. Still, he'd never been one to give up easily. Maybe, just maybe, he could come up with a plan.

* * * * *

The next day sawdust littered the cement floor as George and Lukas worked on the room addition. Lukas pounded another nail then wiped his forehead with the back of his arm.

"Hey, George, I'm going to get a glass of water," he said.

George grinned at him. "I wondered when you'd get around to business." He winked.

Lukas ignored him and walked to the kitchen where he spotted Julia knitting at the table. A sweet smell came from the oven. "That's nice," he said, pointing at the yarn in her hands. "What are you making?"

Her fingers stopped working and she looked up. "Oh, it's just a scarf for one of Becky's sisters. She has a birthday coming up."

He went over and lifted the soft yarn in his hands, intentionally brushing Julia's fingers as he did so. "Nice. Really nice." His eyes met hers and his heart was an instant mixture of pain and—and…he was afraid to analyze what else. "Very nice, indeed," he said again, eyes still focused on her.

She blushed. Something she did so long ago that he had always thought made her look more beautiful than ever. He mentally shook himself. No good could come from thinking that way.

"So your parents are on a trip?" His words were abrupt and, the way Julia blinked, told him unsettling as well.

"Um, yeah."

"They were lucky you were able to help them out. Do you live in the area?" He wanted to pace himself, not ask too many questions and scare her off.

"Yes, I do. I've lived here all my life."

Her comment sent goose bumps up his arm. *And what about the summer of 1942, where were you then?*

"How about you?" She rose from her chair. "Here, let me help you with that." She took his glass and went to the freezer for ice cubes.

"I'm not from around here. I recently moved into a place here in town."

"Oh? What brought you here?"

His mind scrambled for an answer. "My parents visited here a couple of times when I was a kid. I always liked the area."

She smiled the kind of smile that made his gut do a flip-flop. He wished she'd stop that.

"I've always loved it here. It's not for everybody, though. Some people prefer the big city." She filled his glass with water from the faucet and handed it to him.

Why didn't you write back to me, Julia? I've waited all this time. Why? Why? Why?

An odd smell filled the air. "What's that sme—"

Just then a cloud of smoke seeped through the oven door.

"Oh, my cake!" Julia grabbed the mitts from the counter and sprang to the oven. Lukas spotted a fire extinguisher, grabbed it, and sprayed inside the oven then opened a window to bring in fresh air. She tossed the charred cake, pans and all, into the sink.

Her cheeks were rosy again, from embarrassment or the heat of the oven, he wasn't sure.

In the midst of the chaos the phone screeched.

* * * * *

Julia dashed to the phone and attempted to catch her breath. She mouthed a silent "Thank you" to Lukas then said, "Hello," into the phone. The voice on the other end of the line forced her stomach to bottom out with a thud. "Mother. How are you?"

"Why on earth are you out of breath, Julia? Is everything all right?"

"Everything is fine, Mother," she said, assuring herself that indeed, everything was fine. The stove was intact, the house was fine. She could always make another cake. "Are you having a good time?"

"There's hardly been time to enjoy it yet," she said. "It makes me nervous when your father plans things. I never know what to expect. We're on a cruise right now."

"A cruise?"

"Yes. It's a Mediterranean cruise. We met up with it in Germany. We're actually on land right this moment, as you've probably guessed, since I'm calling. Some town I've never heard of."

It sounded so wonderful to Julia, yet her mother didn't sound all that thrilled. "How positively romantic, Mother."

"Oh, you and your romance. The beds are lumpy and the room

is so small—though they have many smaller rooms. I don't know how people do it. I've hardly slept a wink. I know your father was trying to do a good thing. I just wish he would have asked me first."

Julia's heart squeezed for her dad. These days he couldn't win no matter what he did. She didn't know what was going on with her mother, but she hoped she'd get over it soon. "Once you get settled and catch up on your rest, you'll have a good time."

"Maybe." Her mother didn't sound convinced. "Did the workers get started on our room?"

"Yes, they did," Julia informed her. "They're working on the framing."

"Wonderful. I sure hope they do a nice job."

"From what I can see, it looks great."

"Good. They come highly recommended. Your cat hasn't ruined my furniture yet, has she?"

"No, Mother. Beanie is behaving herself quite nicely."

"Well, you see that she does. Your father is motioning to me, so I guess I'd better go. He sends his love. I'll check back in with you later." She clicked off.

But what about your love, Mother? Do you send your love too?

* * * * *

"Did you make any headway?" George asked when Lukas rejoined him in the room addition.

"I don't know what you're talking about. I went in for a glass of water."

"No luck, huh?" George laughed.

If Lukas didn't need money from the sale of the house, he wouldn't have to worry about discounts and George's stupid challenge. Even so, he wondered if it was worth getting his heart trampled on again.

"I wasn't trying anything. Like I said, I went for water."

"If you insist. You might want to get started on that, though. I mean, if you want the discount to kick in for your house remodel. I'm guessing it could take you awhile. Ice queen and all that."

Lukas looked around. "Be quiet. She'll hear you."

George laughed and went back to sawing. Just as Lukas raised his hammer then lowered it to hit the nail, Julia stepped into the room, distracting him. The hammer came down hard on his thumbnail. Not the nail he was going for.

Jerking his hand away, he grimaced, held his thumb in a tight fist, and clenched his teeth so tight his head pounded along with his thumb.

The saw continued its high-pitched whine. George didn't seem to notice Lukas's pain until Julia ran over to him.

"Are you all right?" she asked.

The worried look in her eyes made the pain feel better. Much better. He didn't want to let her know, but that stupid bet was out there taunting him, forcing him to be civil to the woman who had altered his world.

"I'll be fine."

"Let me see it. It's all my fault." She opened his hand to look at his thumb and his jaw tightened. Not only was he in pain, but her fingers on his hands sent a wave of pleasure that he didn't want. Once she saw his thumb, she looked up at him, "Please, let me see to it. You're going to have a purple thumb. I'm so sorry."

The look in her warm green eyes fringed with thick lashes, her soft skin, silky hair, the touch of her hand on his...

"It wasn't your fault. I shouldn't have looked up." Why was he excusing her? This woman crushed not only his thumb but also his heart.

"Anyone would have. It's a natural response. Follow me," she said.

Lukas followed her a few steps then tossed a glance back at George and gave a shrug. George just shook his head and held up three fingers.

* * * * *

Lukas punched his pillow into place, shoved his arm behind his head, and stared at the ceiling. He never dreamed he'd find Julia still in town and unmarried. How was he supposed to forget her when she was here and available?

What was he thinking? She wasn't available to him. Her intentions were clear the moment she stopped writing to him, what, after one letter? How could they have a love that would last a lifetime, when she couldn't even stay with him a month after he left the States?

He had thought they were both mature enough, that their love would see them through. Obviously, he had been wrong. She was too young. Another punch to the pillow, more punch than he'd intended.

The effort made his thumb throb again.

The cuckoo clock struck one. The same clock he brought home from Germany and gave to his aunt and uncle after the war.

If he didn't get to sleep soon, he'd be of little use to George on the job tomorrow. He blew out a sigh. He'd just have to let Julia go and forget that she was "available." But how could he? His stomach flipped at the mere thought of her. Eyes the color of Lake Tahoe's Emerald Bay, hair the color of sun-warmed sandy beaches, that same sweet smile that had seen him through the worst days of the war.

He'd seen her looking at his scar today. Most women told him it made him look ruggedly handsome. Something told him Julia didn't feel that way. Beauty and the Beast. That's what they were. Only he didn't foresee a happy ending for them.

If only he hadn't let George talk him into that challenge of getting her on three dates. So what that he was giving him a discount on his home repairs. He should have said no. On the other hand, he did need the money. And he did want to talk to her. Another sigh. He'd get her on three dates, get closure on their prior relationship, get the discount, pay off his mother's medical bills, then move back to Chicago or somewhere, anywhere but here. He was not about to put himself through the torture of seeing her in town over and over again.

He'd been through enough.

CHAPTER FIVE

Bullets split through the night air, slicing through live targets, missing others. Grenades whined and exploded in all directions, leaving a smoky fog in their wake. Stefan turned to three wounded comrades. One waved him away and inched his body to a place of safety. Stefan turned his attention to the other two. He crawled on his belly to get to them. Both were lying in the open, tattered clothes covered in blood and dirt.

Stefan heard others crying out around him, telling him to get back, but he paid them no heed. He had to help these two men—at least get them hidden in the nearby ditch.

"I'm here," Stefan said. "I know you're both hurt bad, but I need to get you out of here before they come back." Stefan's gaze lifted toward the skies while he tugged on the first man's clothes. No sign of the enemy... yet. "Can I lift you—"

"No, Stefan. No time." The first man coughed up blood.

"Stefan, take this. Hurry," the second man called. A bloody hand lifted a picture.

Stefan reached out and took the photo of Doug Spencer and his girlfriend.

"Tell her I loved her," Doug said.

"You can tell her, but I'll hold on to this for you," Stefan said, stuffing the picture into his pocket.

"They're coming back. Take cover!" the first man said before another wild cough raged through him followed by his last breath.

Stefan turned to help Doug but he was gone too. Tears filled Stefan's eyes, but before he had time to mourn his friends' passing, the angry growl of airplane engines drew dangerously close. Stefan had to crawl to the gully and fast. The enemy planes gained on him with each second. The rough terrain, thick with dirt and debris, tore his clothes and clawed at his skin. Just as rapid fire kicked up dirt around him, he jumped into the gully face-first, unaware of the sharp rocks and twisted metal awaiting him.

Bright lights overhead. White coats worked around him. Mumblings. Medical instruments. A mirror. "Mr. Zimmer, what do you think?" Smiling faces. He looked into the mirror...and saw the face of a stranger.

His own scream woke Lukas up. He broke out in a cold sweat and wiped his arm across his forehead. Sauerkraut lifted his head to look at Lukas then walked over to check on him. Lukas swung his legs over the side of the bed. "It's all right, buddy," he said, scratching Sauerkraut behind his ears. "Just another nightmare."

The dresser mirror reflected his scars. Lukas absently touched them. That night, that photograph, changed everything.

With the cold hardwood beneath his feet, Lukas walked down the hall to the kitchen. Sauerkraut lagged behind him as if to say, *What are you doing up at this hour?* Lukas grabbed a glass of water from the refrigerator. Over a decade and he still had that same nightmare. Would it ever leave him?

He sat down at the kitchen table. It wasn't like he could have prevented those deaths. He'd tried his best to help Doug and Joe. But it wasn't enough. His friends were gone.

And Lukas would never be the same.

* * * * *

"Thanks for coming with me, Julia," Becky said. "You know how much Etta thinks of you."

"Of course I would come. I'm just so sorry Etta is going through this. Poor thing."

Julia and Becky walked up the steps to Cindy's Soda Shop and Becky opened the door. They looked around the room filled with black tables and pink and black upholstered booths, a wooden floor, and a pink jukebox standing on a far wall.

"Over there," Becky said, pointing toward the woman who sat at a booth on the other side of the room. School pennants dressed the walls.

Etta's large brown eyes, swollen and puffy, turned to them. Tears stained her rosy cheeks. Wadded tissues littered the table. She sat sipping a very large chocolate malt with whipped cream, minus the red cherry, which she'd most likely already eaten.

This was serious.

"Oh, Etta, I'm so sorry," Julia said, extending a hug.

"Thank you." Etta pulled a long, deep sip of malt through her straw.

"You poor thing." Becky offered a hug as well. She exchanged a sorrowful glance with Julia. "Now, tell us what happened."

Etta sniffed a time or two then patted the end of her nose with a tissue. "Well, you know Jimmie and I have been seeing each other for almost a year." Another pat of the tissue against her nose and the corners of her eyes. She looked at them. "He dumped me for another woman." Fresh tears fell down her face and dripped on the table.

For an anguished moment, no one said anything.

"I know you don't want to hear this, but there will be other guys," Becky said.

Shock registered on Etta's face, as though she'd swallowed a goldfish whole. Then she glared at her sister. "You're right. I don't want to hear that." Softness settled into her expression and voice. "I love Jimmie,

Becky. You know that." Etta slurped the last of the malt from her straw then waved her hand at the waitress. "I'll take another, please."

Becky and Julia gasped.

"This is no way to handle your problems, Etta," Becky said. "You have to get a handle on things."

Etta stared down her sister and said through clenched teeth, "I want my chocolate malt."

Becky raised her hands. "Okay, okay." She ordered a hamburger, fries, and cherry Coke. Julia made a duplicate order.

"So, my parents are remodeling," Julia said.

Becky and Etta stared at her.

"Well, I thought it might help Etta to talk about something else."

Etta gave a half smile. "Thanks, Julia. Is that why you're staying at their house while they're away?"

Julia nodded.

"In fact, got a couple of cute guys on the job," Becky said. "I've got dibs on one, but the other one is available."

For some reason that comment irritated Julia. She reasoned, of course, that Becky was trying to keep Julia's interest off Lukas.

"I told you, I love Jimmie."

Becky grabbed her sister's hand. "Listen to me, Etta. I know you don't want to hear this, but Jimmie is no good for you."

Etta jerked her hand away.

"It's true and you know it. He calls it quits, goes out with someone, and then comes back to you. He puts his nights out with the guys ahead of you. It's as though if nothing else works out, he'll come and get you."

Etta winced.

"I'm sorry, sweetie, but that's how I see it. You're better off without him."

Coins dropped into the jukebox and Julia glanced over at the girl dressed in a flirty skirt, complete with a crinoline slip, matching top, bobby sox, and saddle oxfords.

Elvis Presley began singing "Heartbreak Hotel" and the tears gushed from Etta's eyes once more. Julia wanted to bop the girl in the flirty skirt.

Once Etta regained her composure, she stirred the ice cream in her glass and watched it swirl. "I guess you're right about Jimmie." A few more tears trickled down her cheeks. "What am I gonna do?" She fell against her sister, who held her tight.

"You're gonna make it. Julia and I will see to it."

Julia locked eyes with Becky and smiled, all the while hoping a wonderful man would come into Etta's life so she would stay away from Jimmie. And for some strange reason, hoping too that the man wasn't Lukas Gable.

* * * * *

Lukas was bone tired after working all day. The framing wasn't going as quickly as he would have hoped. Julia was gone most of the afternoon, which suited him just fine. The less he saw of her, the better.

He liked that his aunt and uncle's home was in the country. He loved the isolation of it. A woman he had dated told him he'd become a recluse if he wasn't careful. Maybe she was right.

Cows grazed in the meadows. Wildflowers popped up in clusters along the roadside. Cobwebs laced through wire fences. A balmy breeze with the smell of earth and freshly mown grass blew through his car window. Elvis Presley crooned "Love Me Tender" on the radio. He reached over to turn it off. He wasn't in the mood for a love song.

Just as he looked up, a dog hobbled into the street and he had to slam on the car brakes, barely missing the old hound. Carefully he pulled to the side of the road and got out of the car to check on the mutt, which had barely moved out of the way.

Fear lurked in the golden retriever's dark, melting eyes. He growled and edged away from Lukas as he approached.

"I'm not going to hurt you, boy." Lukas slowed his pace and eased gently forward. "Just want to see if you belong to anyone."

The dog took another step backward, cautiously growling but not baring his teeth. It was as though he wanted to protect himself but wanted to trust Lukas at the same time.

The poor little fella only had three legs. As Lukas spoke soft words and leaned in, the dog stood in place, this time seeming to let down his guard a tad.

With caution, Lukas pulled a packet of crackers from his pocket, opened it, and squatted in front of the hound. He hoped to spot a collar with information to return the dog home. There was no collar. Bones protruded through his thin skin. Patches of hair were missing, exposing pink skin. Dirt covered his paws and legs. Matted hair dangled in clumps under his belly.

"Where you from, buddy?"

Lukas held out the crackers and the dog sniffed and nosed into his outstretched hand. The hound stuck out his tongue and quickly snatched the treat. Seeing that Lukas didn't move, he finished it off, sniffed a couple of times at Lukas's bare hand, then looked at him with friendly eyes. Lukas dared to scratch him behind the ears. The dog whined and leaned into him.

"Okay, you're coming home with me. Come on, buddy."

The hound immediately followed him, jumped in the car, and soon they were on the road.

"Scooter. That's what I'll call you."

Scooter's right ear cocked and he seemed to understand. Lukas laughed at his new friend. He'd get him a collar, take him to the vet for shots, and get him on the road to health. With all of his current bills, what were a few more? Unfortunately, he might have to stick around for a while to get rid of some debt, but he could do it. The town was big enough to avoid Julia. Once he finished this job with George, he'd be fine.

Turning his attention to Scooter, Lukas wondered how the dog had lost his leg. Obviously, the hound had been abused. But no more. Lukas would take care of him. Animals he could handle. Women, not so much.

* * * * *

Julia sat down in her chair and Beanie hopped up on her, circled a couple of times, then curled into a ball on her lap and began to lick her paws. Smiling, Julia stroked Beanie and purring whispered at the back of the feline's throat. After a bit of bonding with her pet, Julia picked up the phone receiver on the stand next to her and dialed Becky's number.

"Hi, Becky. Just thought I'd check in and see how Etta is getting along."

"Oh, she's doing all right. So far she hasn't talked to Jimmie."

"That's great. I'm sure it's hard, especially when she thinks she's in love."

"Yeah, that's the problem. I think they've been together so long that she's just afraid to venture away from the familiar, you know?"

"Yeah." Boy, did she know. Julia could write a book on that one.

"Sure wish we could find her someone."

Julia's stomach clenched. She hoped Becky wasn't going to play Cupid between Etta and Lukas. People should stop trying to play matchmaker.

"Speaking of finding someone," Becky said, "I sure think George is cute."

Julia smiled. George reminded her of Jerry Lewis, only a tad larger. "Oh?"

"Do you think I would have a chance with him? And don't tell me how beautiful I am. That's a best friend talking. I want concrete evidence."

Julia laughed. "Okay, okay. I saw him watching you in the kitchen on Monday."

"You did?"

Julia didn't miss the thrill in Becky's voice. "Yes. And I saw the way he smiled at you. He's definitely interested."

"Really?" She was practically giddy now. "I was afraid I was reading too much into it. I saw it too!"

"Just go in cautiously. Find out more about him. I don't want you to get hurt."

"Thanks, Jules. I should have asked you if you were interested in him. I don't want to mess things up for you."

Julia chuckled again. "No problem. I'm having too much fun on my own right now. After my last dating fiasco, I'd just as soon forget men for now."

Becky laughed. "What, you don't like a guy who stares at himself in the restaurant window the whole time he's with you?"

"Don't forget how he kept combing his hair."

"He was something else," Becky said.

"I'm pretty sure when he looked into my eyes, he was just checking out his own reflection."

At that Becky let out a guffaw that surely rattled her windows.

They discussed Etta and what they planned to do for the day. Then Becky promised to come over to Julia's the next day so Julia could have company and Becky could get to know George a little more.

Julia had no sooner hung up the phone than it started ringing.

"Hello?"

"Have they done a good job so far? They're not tramping mud and sawdust through the house, are they? Please tell me they're not doing a shoddy job, I just couldn't handle that."

"Hi, Mother."

"Well, you haven't answered my questions."

"They're doing a fine job, and no, they aren't ruining your carpets." Julia sighed and settled back into her chair. Something told her this would be a lengthy conversation.

"Well, that's a relief. Why I ever let your father talk me into going on this trip when our house is being worked on, I'll never know."

"Mother, forget what's going on here and try to enjoy yourself. It's a once-in-a-lifetime trip." For goodness' sake, she'd happily switch places with her mother.

"I don't want to be here," she snapped.

"Well, it won't be much longer now." Julia tried her best to appease her mother, but she would have nothing of it.

"I'm hot. I'm tired. And I want to come home."

"Does Dad know how you feel?" Julia twirled her fingers in the coiled cord of the telephone.

"Of course he knows. Why would I keep something like that to myself?"

Why, indeed?

"I demand to come home, Julia!" Her mother's voice hit desperation to the point that it scared Julia.

"Mother, it's going to be all right. Do you want me to talk to Dad?"

She hesitated and then said, "No, that's not necessary. I can handle him. But we'll be home sooner than expected, just so you know.

Then you'll be able to get back to your own home and I can oversee the remodeling."

Julia felt certain her mother needed a vacation, but the stress she was under now wasn't helping her in the least. She feared her dad would have to break down and come home. What a shame. He had such a lovely trip planned for the two of them.

"I don't mind being here if it helps, Mother," Julia lied. She didn't want to be here, but she didn't really have a choice. And at this point, she could see how desperately her mother needed that vacation. No one would get rest if she came home like this. Julia needed to pray more for her dad.

Her mother seemed to calm a little. "It's just so hot here. I hate being hot." Her anger seemed to dissipate like the slow release of air in a balloon.

"Where are you now?"

"Oh, how should I know? Somewhere in Italy. Tuscany or someplace like that."

Julia's heart sank. The money, the plans her dad had made, and her mother didn't appreciate any of it. "Aren't you enjoying yourself at all?"

"Well, I suppose I am some. If it just weren't so hot."

Julia couldn't imagine Italy was all that hot, but what did she know? "Well, I'll be praying for you both. Try to have a good time. I'll keep things under control here until you get back."

"All right," her mother finally said with more calm than she'd voiced in the entire conversation.

They soon clicked off and Julia stared at the phone. There was more going on with her mother than just worrying about the room addition. Julia wondered if her mother had crossed over to that delicate, older phase of womanhood. If that were true, from the stories Julia had heard about women in menopause, she decided she'd better pray for her dad's survival.

CHAPTER SIX

Becky wiped her feet on the mat then stepped into Julia's house.

"I'm so sorry. I'm making a mess of your floor." Her full red skirt dripped with water, and her hair hung limp upon her shoulders in auburn ringlets, weighed down by the rain.

"You could do a scene in *Singin' in the Rain*," Julia teased.

"Ha, ha."

"Don't worry about the floor. The house is so dusty from the construction, a little rain can't hurt it."

"I doubt your mother would say that," Becky said.

Julia handed her a towel, and Becky attempted to dry herself off. She wrapped the towel around her head just as George walked into the room.

Their gazes collided and no one said anything for the span of a heartbeat.

With a keen sense of observation, George said, "I see you were caught in the rainstorm."

"Yeah," Becky said, clearly swooning over his attentions.

"There's definitely a growing storm out there," he said, looking past her toward the window. He swiveled to Julia. "Not sure we'll stick around if this keeps up. Won't be able to get much done outside."

"I understand," Julia said.

Lukas stepped from the hallway into their living room but said nothing. Everyone looked around a moment.

"How about I make us some coffee," Julia said. "You can take a break and give the rain a chance to let up."

They followed her into the kitchen. Julia's stomach clenched. It seemed too much like a couples thing—boy, girl, boy, girl. Becky had definitely staked her claim on George, so that would leave Julia with Lukas, and of course she had no interest in him. None at all.

Thunder groaned. Lightning zigzagged through thick, ominous clouds.

"Ooo, I love days like this," Becky said, rubbing her hands together.

"You like storms?" George asked with a grin, clearly intrigued by her comment.

"Yes. I come from a big family. Dad's a farmer by trade, but last year he had to find a job at the factory to put enough food on the table. When we were kids, Mom tried to keep his mind off the weather and what it might be doing to our crops, by making popcorn and pulling out board games for the family to play. It was such fun. So each time a storm hits, I get excited about the possibilities of what I can do."

"That's swell. When I was a kid and a storm hit, Mom made us hide out in the basement in case of a tornado," George said.

"So you were scared?" Becky asked.

George thrust out his chest and hiked his chin a bit. "Maybe when I was a peanut, but nothing bothers me now."

Julia smiled. George was struttin' like a rooster. And by the dreamy-eyed look on Becky's face, she was enjoying the show.

George bumped Lukas's arm. "So how about you? Any childhood memories of storms?"

"Not that I can think of. Storms came and went. Didn't think much of them, I guess," Lukas said, reaching for the coffee Julia put down in front of him. "Thanks."

While Becky and George spoke of childhood memories, Lukas

sipped his coffee and Julia walked over to get her own cup, glancing at him as she returned to the table.

"So are you enjoying your new home, Lukas?" Julia asked, making an attempt at hospitality.

"It's all right."

"The town is friendly enough. At least, I hope everyone has made you feel welcome." She smiled.

He didn't. He merely shrugged.

"Have you tried out Cindy's Soda Shop yet? She makes the best fountain drinks and chocolate malts," Becky said.

"Yeah, I've been there. They are good," Lukas said with a grin.

Well, of all the nerve. He could be civil to George and Becky, but he practically ignored her. Why would he do that? Was it because he felt she was his employer? She considered that. Maybe that was it. He didn't know her, after all. There would be no reason for him to ignore her—unless he thought she was after him and he had no interest in her whatsoever! The very idea bored into her ego.

Not that she had a big ego, but Julia didn't exactly relish the idea of someone finding her unattractive. What woman would? Besides, she was probably imagining it all.

"So, Lukas, do you plan on going to the county fair?"

His grin disappeared and he put his mug on the table. After an uncomfortable silence, he said, "No."

Just then lightning split the sky and thunder cracked so loud, it caused everyone to look toward the window. Just the thing Julia needed to keep her tongue locked behind her teeth.

George stood and started to pace.

"Is everything all right?" Becky asked.

He craned his neck to look out the window toward their framework. "I'm worried about the framing. This is no ordinary storm."

"You don't think it'll just blow over?" Becky asked.

"I don't know." The worried expression on his face reiterated his comment. He paced some more.

"Doesn't do any good to fret. It is what it is. We'll just have to wait it out," Lukas said.

"I guess." George reluctantly took his seat at the table.

Intense rain pelted against the windows and rattled the house. Lightning continued to throw spears across the sky. Thunder, deep and menacing, growled and rumbled through a sky dark with nature's fury. An involuntary shiver ran through Julia.

"Since we don't have a basement, I think we should go into the hallway away from the windows," she said, at the risk of sounding like a worrier.

To her surprise, everyone scooted out from the table and followed her into the hallway. No sooner had they made their exit than they heard a loud thunderous roar like a train.

Becky gasped.

"Get down," George yelled.

Everyone hunkered down, covered their heads with their arms, and waited for the awful sound to go away. Julia's heart beat hard against her chest like the incessant pound of a native drum at wartime.

With relentless fury, the storm belted its wrath against the earth below. Strong winds whined through the trees. Lightning cast ghostly shadows upon the walls. Broken debris knocked forcefully against the siding as though to push its way into the house. The very foundations groaned in misery.

Julia prayed for their safety.

As the living room clock ticked off the minutes, the angry storm had its way, then, with anger spent, faded to a distant place, leaving a soft rain in its trail.

Lukas was the first to stand. "We'd better check out the damages." He walked toward the door. George followed him.

Once they were outside, Julia and Becky went to the window to see how the room held up in the storm.

"Oh, Julia, I'm so sorry," Becky said.

Two-by-fours lay scattered about the yard, along with heavy tree limbs and neighborhood debris. Patio furniture was gone, who knew where.

A sick thread of misery coiled around Julia's lungs and threatened her breath.

Becky gave Julia a worried stare. "Remember that movie we watched a while ago, *Abbott & Costello Meet the Mummy*?"

Julia nodded impatiently, wondering what in the world that had to do with what was going on.

"You sort of look like that."

Just as Julia was about to ask if she looked like Abbott, Costello, or the Mummy, the phone rang. They both knew there was only one person who would call at a time like this.

* * * * *

Lukas and George stared at the damage.

"Only a few boards lost. Won't take much to fix that," George said. "Could have been worse."

"Well, looks like we'd better get busy," Lukas said. He looked around. "I left my hammer inside. I'll be back in a second."

Lukas slipped back into the front door of the house. He didn't want to bother Julia and Becky. Julia was talking on the phone.

"I already told you yesterday that everything was fine, Mother. Stop worrying and enjoy your trip. Okay. Yes. I'll talk to you later. Bye."

Lukas stepped into view. "Well, that wasn't exactly the truth, was it?" He heard the irritation in his voice but couldn't help it.

"You have to understand my mother—"

"I understand a lot of things. The patio furniture is gone, did you notice?"

"Yes, but—"

"Honesty is always the best policy."

"Uh, would anyone like some tea?" Becky interjected.

"What is your problem?" Julia asked.

"I don't have a problem. You're the one who lied to your mother."

"I didn't lie. It would ruin her vacation to know the storm caused some problems. What could she do about it other than worry? You'll fix it before she comes home, so why put her through that?"

He gave her a cold, hard stare. Try as he might, he just couldn't help it. Her deceit drummed up old memories and the pain that went with them. He knew he was being a hypocrite. He hadn't exactly told her who he was. Yes, he'd given her his legal name, but he hadn't given her the full truth. Still, he couldn't stop his irritation.

Julia glared back at him. "Besides, I don't owe you an explanation."

Becky gasped.

Julia flipped her hair behind her shoulders the way she did when she was mad all those years ago.

"Hey, Lukas, I need your help with something." George looked completely dumbfounded when he entered the room and heard the two of them arguing.

"Coming." Lukas spotted his hammer and picked it up off the counter. His boots thumped hard on the floor as he made his way out.

He didn't care in the least that he'd offended Julia. Served her right. You don't just stop writing to someone to whom you've pledged your love and your life. Maybe she was just making excuses then too.

Making herself feel less guilty by telling herself she didn't want to "worry" him.

He kicked a clump of dirt out of his way, causing it to scatter and spray ahead of him.

"What was that all about?" George asked.

"The dirt was in my way."

"I'm not talking about that and you know it."

"I merely told her it was wrong to lie."

"Look, Lukas, I know we're just getting to know each other, and I really like the work you're doing for me here, but don't you think that was crossing the line? I mean, she's our employer, and you could mess it up for us here."

"Sorry," Lukas said, grabbing boards and stacking them close for easier access.

George joined him in moving the boards. "Why do you care anyway?"

Lukas dropped a board in place and shrugged. "It's the principle of the thing."

"A good worker and a man of principle? Guess I got lucky— or not."

They grabbed more scattered boards.

"Doesn't look like you'll be getting that 15-percent discount," George said.

Lukas looked at him and dropped another board. "Why not?"

"You're kidding, right? Do you really think she'll go out with you after that little confrontation?"

Lukas headed back into the yard. "Yes."

George looked interested. "And how do you plan to do that?"

Lukas looked him square in the face. "I'll think of something. But first, we'd better clean up this debris."

* * * * *

"What was that about?" Becky asked once George and Lukas went outside.

"I have no idea." Julia collected the glasses from the table and took them to the sink. Tightening the stopper, she poured dishwashing liquid into the sink and turned on the water faucet. She clanked the glasses together a little too hard and told herself to calm down.

"Are you all right?" Becky asked, stepping up to the sink with a dry towel in hand.

"I'm fine." She turned off the water and plunged the soapy dishcloth into a glass. "Who does he think he is, coming in here, telling me what to do? He's working for me, mind you."

"That took a lot of nerve, I have to admit."

Julia wondered if Becky was secretly delighted. There certainly was no chance of Julia and Lukas getting together now—not that there ever was a chance, but still.

Julia turned and faced her friend. "Why would he do that, Becky? Why?"

"I don't know." Becky picked up the glass, dried it, then put it in the cupboard.

"I'll tell you why. Because he's a judgmental jerk, that's why."

The pressure from Julia's firm hand and her rough handling of the glass caused her hand to break through. The glass sliced her pinkie finger right on the knuckle and it began to bleed in a steady stream.

"Ouch."

Becky grabbed a dishtowel and wrapped it around Julia's hand.

"Thanks."

"We need to get you to the doctor," Becky insisted.

"Oh, for goodness' sake. I won't bleed to death from my pinkie."

"No, but you need it stitched. I'm calling your doctor now."

Stitched? This was all Lukas's fault.

Becky looked up the number in the phone book and made an immediate appointment. She got another dishtowel and handed it to Julia. "Here, keep it wrapped in this fresh one till we get there. Press hard. Let's go."

Disgusted with herself—and Lukas—Julia reluctantly grabbed her light jacket and umbrella. As they headed to the driveway, Julia remembered Becky's car troubles.

"Here, drive my car." She dug in her purse and threw Becky her car keys.

"Okay. You get in the car and I'll let the guys know we'll be gone a bit."

Julia started to protest but Becky was already headed their way and George was standing within earshot, so Julia kept silent.

Once they pulled out of the driveway, Julia took a glance back at the house. Lukas stood in the yard, watching them. The remorse on his face made her feel a teensy bit justified...or sorry. She wasn't sure which, and right now, she just didn't want to analyze it.

CHAPTER SEVEN

He was an idiot. No doubt about it. Lukas pummeled his pillow then flopped his head into it.

"What was I thinking?" he said out loud.

Sauerkraut jumped onto his bed and nuzzled up to him with a whine.

"Thanks, buddy. I can always count on you to understand." Lukas scratched behind the brown dachshund's floppy ears. The happy hound's leg tapped a steady rhythm of pure pleasure.

Lukas smiled, then frowned. "I should have called and checked on her." He stopped scratching Sauerkraut and the dog shoved his snout under Lukas's hand. Carefully guarding his sore thumb, Lukas resumed scratching. "I should have kept my mouth shut, that's what I should have done."

Maybe he wasn't being fair. They had both been very young. Experience had taught him that women changed their minds. Often. So why couldn't he forgive her?

A dress purchase, different shoes, that type of change, he could understand. But to make a vow of love and turn on it—when he was fighting a war he didn't want to fight?

Maybe he should thank her. After all, if he hadn't been in the war, they might have married, and then they would have shared a lifetime of misery.

Yes, he should be thankful.

Sauerkraut kept nudging. Lukas lifted the hound's snout and looked him in the eye.

"Stay away from women, Sauerkraut. They'll break your heart and leave you wondering. Always wondering."

Sauerkraut's tail wagged furiously and he nudged again with gusto.

"All right, all right, I'll let you out."

Lukas got up and the dog jumped off the bed and chased happily after his owner. Sauerkraut slipped into the night, no doubt to get better acquainted with Scooter, while Lukas dialed Becky to get an update.

When he hung up, he was glad he'd called and checked on Julia. Knowing women, Becky most likely called Julia the moment they hung up to let her know he called. He liked that idea. Then maybe she wouldn't think he was such a bad guy.

On the other hand, he meant what he had said about lying. Though who was he to talk? He'd been doing his own share of it these days.

* * * * *

Julia's hand throbbed when she went to bed. She adjusted her pillow with her good hand and tried to get comfortable. The stitches hurt like the dickens, but at least her finger wasn't bleeding anymore.

"This was all his fault."

As soon as she said that, she remembered how she had caused Lukas to crush his thumb with a hammer. She figured now they were even.

She reached over and stroked Beanie, who was curled beside her in the bed. Something about animals calmed her—almost as much as her knitting. But she had been too upset to knit tonight—not that she could, with her finger wrapped up to the size of a hot dog.

That reminded her. The doily pattern she had at home would look very nice on her mother's living room stand. Maybe she would crochet her one. When it came to her mother's decorating tastes, though, Julia wasn't sure her knitting or crocheting was appreciated. Still, a gift now and then is always good for a relationship.

Funny that the word relationship made her think of Lukas. Why she let him get under her skin like that this afternoon, she couldn't say. He had chastised her, no question. The very idea sent hot adrenaline straight through her. She fisted her pillow and shoved it into a pile behind her head. She needed to get to sleep.

They still had plenty of time to get the room cleaned up before her parents came home. At least they'd found the patio furniture down the road. She was thankful she didn't have to worry about that.

A sliver of moonlight glowed on the ceiling. Her mind drifted to a night long ago when she slipped out of her room and ran to meet Stefan, pledging their love for one another and vowing to wait till he returned to her.

But he never came.

She thought Stefan had most surely been killed in action, but when she had visited his aunt one day, his aunt told her he was fine. Maybe Julia should have gone back and checked again.

Selfish to say, but death would have almost been easier to take. At least then she would have known—or thought that he still loved her. But the truth...hurt.

Still.

Why had she agreed to stay at her parents' house? It stirred up a past she had buried long ago. In her own home, she rarely thought of Stefan with his liquid-blue eyes, blond hair, and wide grin that could turn her heart to mush.

Well, almost rarely.

Thoughts tangled like a wild vine, wrapping this way and that as she considered the woman he might have married. Was she brunette? Tall? Short? Happy-go-lucky? Sensible? The thoughts tortured her.

"Is there no one else out there for me?" Her whispered words echoed through the room. Suddenly the image of Lukas came to mind and she gave an insincere laugh. "That'll be the day."

Beanie stirred, rolled onto her back, and kicked her paws up.

Julia frowned. "I'm glad someone is able to sleep."

With irritation she glanced at her pinkie. She'd had no idea a little finger like that could cause such pain. Switching off the light, she closed her eyes. Though she doubted the sleep would come....

* * * * *

Lukas pulled up to the beach parking lot. He'd overheard Julia telling Becky today that she planned to walk the beach tonight. He had no idea when but decided to take the chance of running into her. She'd been gone most of the day, so he didn't get a chance to see how she was feeling. At least that's what he told himself.

The damp scent of evening followed him. The moisture gave a crisp touch to the air. It felt good after working in the heat all day. They had almost finished the framing. Hopefully no more storms would come around until they had it under roof. He spotted a jagged piece of driftwood and picked it up, turning it over in his hands as he examined it. He finally threw it down and continued walking.

Farther down the beach, he thought he spotted Julia. Long, slender legs. Same graceful walk. Coming toward him. His breath grew shallow, his heart pounded in his ears, as their steps lapped up the distance between them. Seventeen years seemed to wash away in an instant. He wanted to run to her, scoop her into his arms, and pretend those years had never happened.

"Mommy, please, can I go play with Timmy?" A child nearby pointed toward another little boy who played on the sand near his mother.

"I told you, he's a nice little boy, honey, but his parents are poor. They have to stay with their own kind." She pulled her pouting son next to her and gave him a hug. "Here, let's have a cupcake." The little boy brightened. His chubby fingers reached for the cupcake, and the conversation appeared forgotten.

Lukas's jaw clenched. He'd heard that conversation many times before from many different people. The faces had changed, but the message was still the same. His family was different. Not only poor but also German. Those two facts just didn't sit well with most folks around here—especially during the war.

Obviously, things hadn't changed much.

Julia waved when she spotted him. He waved back then whipped around and headed to his car. He had been foolish to come here. He'd tell George the bet was off. He didn't want history to repeat itself.

He rubbed the scar on his face. He'd been through enough.

* * * * *

Julia watched Lukas walk toward the parking lot. Of all the nerve! One glance at her and he turned away. What was the matter with that guy? What had she done to him?

And to think that Eleanor thought Julia wouldn't be able to resist his charms. She grunted. What charms? The man had no manners whatsoever. Looked like Becky would have no problem winning their bet. Julia wasn't attracted to Lukas in the least.

By the time she got home, she was hot and tired and decided to take a shower. Once she got into her pajamas and slipped into bed, her phone rang.

"George asked me out." Becky's voice escalated three notches with every word. She could give Frankie Valli a run for his money.

"He did? That's great, Becky. How did it happen?" Julia propped her pillow behind her and leaned back against it, the smell of her bath powder scenting the air.

"He called me and asked if I wanted to go to dinner and a movie tomorrow night."

"Hmm, he's moving pretty fast." Julia picked up a nail file and set to work.

"Now, cut that out. At my age, I can't wait on a man to take his own sweet time." Becky's voice was so serious it made Julia laugh.

"Yes, you're so old. I'm happy for you, really, Beck." Julia was happy for her friend and annoyed that a shadow passed over her own heart.

"Thanks. I'm glad you like to see me happy," Becky said.

Julia sawed too hard on her nail and grimaced. "Well, of course I'd like to see you happy. Why wouldn't I?"

"You wouldn't get in the way of my happiness, would you?"

Julia didn't like where this was going. "What are you talking about?"

"I mean, you've been the greatest friend, ever since I took you in, helping you at school when you came, remember?"

"I remember."

"I've been there for you and you've been there for me, right?"

Julia stopped filing. "Uh-oh."

"Through thick and thin, we stand together."

Julia put the file back on her stand and sighed. "All right, spill it. What do you need from me?"

"Well, it's like this. George asked me out on the condition that we go on a double date...with you and Lukas."

Julia shot straight up. "What?"

"It's only one night, and—"

Obviously, having a date with George trumped her bet with Eleanor.

"Absolutely not. That's a ridiculous suggestion. I'm not interested in that self-absorbed, rude man at all. The fact that I've kept him on to work on the house is compassion enough on my part," Julia said. "Why would he want that, anyway? George doesn't need us there. I thought they were just coworkers. Lukas hasn't been here long enough for them to have become strong friends."

"Well, see, that's just it. George feels sorry for Lukas. He's new in town, doesn't really know anyone, and he could use a little social polishing. George is convinced that Lukas struggles with social situations because he's a loner. He means nothing by it."

"He's rude."

"Julia, that's not like you," Becky said, her tone chiding.

A slight twinge of guilt crossed Julia's heart. She ignored it. "No."

"Julia, please, please, please?"

"Becky, I saw him on the beach. He was coming straight toward me. I waved and he waved. Then he turned around and left." Julia's ego still smarted from it.

"Well, maybe he thought of a reason he had to hurry home."

"Nice try."

"I mean it. Maybe seeing you reminded him of something he had to do."

"Gee, thanks."

"You know what I mean."

"I'm not so sure I agree."

"Julia, if you do it just this once, I'll never ask you for anything again. I figure if I have the chance just once for George to get to know me, he'll ask me out again. But if I don't get this chance, we might miss something. My whole future rests in your hands. Can you live with that?"

"It's a risk I'm willing to take," Julia said.

"What?" Becky shrieked.

"All right, I'm kidding. But just for the record, I think it's wrong for you to take advantage of our friendship this way."

"You're right. It is." Before Julia could respond to that Becky continued. "So will you do it?"

Julia figured Becky must like George a lot to put her car—and maybe even their friendship—on the line this way.

"Julia, what about that 'not getting in the way of my happiness' speech?"

"Come on, Becky, you know that's not fair."

"Okay, you're right. I'll call George back and tell him I can't go out with him. The date is off."

"Please. He's an adult. He can still take you out."

"Maybe he's a little shy too. I don't know. All I know is that those were the conditions."

The disappointment in Becky's voice was palpable. Julia had hoped that Becky would feel guilty for putting that burden on her, but obviously her guilt was in check, and she was quite comfortable putting the ball in Julia's court.

"I doubt if he will want to go, anyway."

"I've seen the way he looks at you. Trust me. He'll want to go," Becky said.

Julia hesitated, not wanting to go, but not wanting to disappoint her friend.

"Please, Jules. Just this once, I promise."

"Oh, all right. But only this once. I can barely stand to be in the same room with that man, let alone on a date. I'm doing this for you, and you owe me big time, do you hear me?"

"Yes—yes, I do." Becky's excitement made Julia smile. "You are the best friend, ever. I mean that."

"Yeah, yeah."

"Hey, maybe we can go shopping tomorrow to pick out something for me to wear. Would you be able to do that in the afternoon?"

"Maybe I could swing it." Despite Julia's discomfort with it all, she couldn't help getting excited for her friend. She truly wished the best for her.

"Great. How about after lunch?"

"Sounds good."

"By the way, keep praying for Etta. Jimmie is still trying to get her back. No doubt his other girlfriend dumped him. I just wish he'd get out of her life for good."

"Oh, I'll pray for her." Julia didn't want to mention that her prayers probably wouldn't reach heaven.

"I'm just so worried about her. She's eating Mom and Dad out of house and home."

"I thought she'd moved out."

"She did. But she goes home to pour out her frustrations to Mom, and the next thing they know, she's eating...a lot."

"Doesn't she have a best friend she can talk to?"

"Yeah, but what I didn't mention was that her best friend is who Jimmie left her for."

"Oh, no. Poor thing."

"Exactly."

"How about we invite her on our shopping outing tomorrow?" Julia suggested.

"That's a great idea. Let's do it. Thanks, Julia."

"Sure. Etta's always welcome. She's a sweet friend. I hate to see her hurt like this. We'll help her through it."

"Yeah. Maybe we can get her a man—just not George," Becky said. "My sisterly affection only goes so far."

After Julia hung up, she went to her closet to see if she had anything decent to wear tomorrow night. She might need to buy something as well. Not that she cared about impressing Lukas in the least. But a woman had to look her best when she went out on a date, no matter who accompanied her.

CHAPTER EIGHT

The hair on Lukas's arms stood up. Sweat moistened his hands. Palpitations made his heart stutter. He stumbled in the sand, running from the memories, the cruelty of prejudice. The pain of it thundered across his heart. All those nights of fear, of his mother's tears, his father's wrath. Nights when his belly rumbled in rebellion and ached for relief. The storm of remembrance pummeled against his chest, leaving no room for breath. He shouldn't have come back. The wounds were rooted too deep in the soil of his inner man, twisting, turning, coiling deeper, deeper, deeper.

He thought he'd moved on, but he hadn't. He'd only moved away.

"Whoa, are you all right?"

"Oh, I'm sorry."

A dark-haired woman with worry in her soft brown eyes looked up at him, then at his hands that were on her arms as he attempted to steady them both.

She smiled—a smile that made him uncomfortable. He quickly dropped his hands.

"I should watch where I'm going."

She shrugged, clearly amused. "You had something on your mind. I could tell by the look on your face," she said. "You going to be okay?"

"Yeah. I'm fine. Thanks."

She thrust out her hand. "My name's Etta."

"Oh, uh, nice to meet you. I'd better go." He turned to leave.

"Don't you have a name?"

He swiveled back to face her and said quickly, "Stefan." With that, he took off running toward his car. It wasn't until he had settled into the seat, turned on the ignition, and backed out of the parking lot that he realized what he had done.

* * * * *

Lukas filled Scooter's food and water bowls and threw down fresh hay for the dog to sleep on. "Looks like you don't mind it much out here, ole boy." Scooter eyed him warily. Though Scooter was warming up to his new master, his reserve was still very much in place. He waited for Lukas to stand up and inch away from the bowls.

"Okay, you're safe. Go ahead and eat." Lukas stepped back a bit more and waited. Scooter watched him, looked at the bowls, looked back to Lukas, then slowly made his way over to eat.

Lukas just couldn't understand how anyone could hurt an animal.

Sauerkraut waited—not so patiently—as Lukas stepped inside the house. He jumped, barked, circled—did everything but flip when Lukas came into view. Lukas laughed. "All right, buddy, it's your turn." He pulled the dachshund next to him and gave him a playful rub on the top of his head. "Nice to see you held down the fort while I was gone." Sauerkraut whined and his tail wagged furiously.

The doorbell rang.

Lukas frowned and stood up, stretching his back in the process. "Who could that be at this hour?" He walked over and opened the door.

"George. What are you doing here?"

"Gee, thanks. Good to see you too." George stepped inside. "I needed to talk to you about something. You got a minute?"

"Sure. I just got home myself. Want a glass of lemonade?"

"That would be great." George followed Lukas into the kitchen.

"I came by earlier a couple of times, but you weren't home. I figured I'd give it one more try."

Lukas pulled a pitcher from the fridge, plunked a couple of ice cubes into glasses, and poured the lemonade. "Here." Lukas nodded toward the doorway. "Let's go back in the living room and sit down."

"Okay."

"Must've been important for you to come by a couple of times." Lukas took a drink then looked up with a start. "There's nothing wrong at the jobsite, is there? Vandalized or anything like that?"

"No, no, it's not that."

Lukas studied George. They hadn't known one another long, but they already had a good camaraderie between them.

"Well, you're new to town, and I figured you could use some friendship."

"I'm listening." Something told him to bolt.

"I figured you already know me and Becky and Julia. I thought it might be fun if the four of us—"

Lukas set down his lemonade and held up his hand. "Now, hold it right there. The fact that you've lumped all our names together makes me a bit edgy. I have no intention whatsoever of going on a double date, if that's what you have in mind."

"You're willing to give up that 15 percent, are you?"

"You didn't tell me that you would be setting up the dates."

"No, but I had to help you along," George said. "Seeing as how you almost blew it with her already."

"I thought the dates had to be solo, as in, me and Julia, alone."

"They do. But I thought this might get you started."

"Are you actually wanting me to win this bet?"

"No. But the truth is, I'm a little nervous to take Becky out alone. It's been, um, awhile since I've gone out."

Lukas sighed. "Look, Julia's a nice woman and all that, but—"

"Oh, come on. Name one good reason why we can't all go out as friends."

He could name about fifty, but he couldn't tell George about that.

"See, you don't have a reason. Is there someone else you're trying to be faithful to?"

"No." Lukas knew about being faithful. Julia was the one George should talk to about that.

"Great. Then it's a date."

"We don't have to set it anytime soon, you know."

"Sure we do. We're young. We need to go out, have fun, get to know people."

Lukas eyed him with suspicion. "You've already set it up, haven't you?"

"Tomorrow night, seven o'clock. We'll take the girls to Fred's Steak House then over to the theater to see *Tammy and the Bachelor*."

Lukas nearly choked on his lemonade. "Are you kidding me? Why would we go see a girl's movie?" He leaned his head back on the sofa and groaned.

"It won't be that bad. Besides, we'll be in good company." George wiggled his eyebrows.

Lukas stared at him. Then he looked heavenward. "Why are you doing this to me?"

George laughed. "It could be worse. You could stay at home and keep company with that three-legged dog of yours out in the yard."

As if on cue, Sauerkraut sauntered into the room. "And don't forget Sauerkraut."

This time, George stared. "You named a wiener dog Sauerkraut?"

"It seemed fitting at the time."

"Are you German or something?" George had no idea how his question shot through Lukas.

"Okay, I'll go on the date," Lukas said, avoiding the question. George was so happy with Lukas's consent to go, he didn't seem to notice Lukas hadn't answered his question.

"Great. It's all set then."

"Don't you have to ask Julia?"

"Becky's working on her as we speak," George said with a grin.

"You dog. I should have known."

The guys talked a little further about the details for their evening out with Becky and Julia, then George left.

Lukas closed the door behind George and looked down at Sauerkraut. "What have I gotten myself into?"

* * * * *

"I'm not sure what kind of mood Etta will be in. I haven't talked to her today," Becky said, as she pulled her Rambler into the driveway of her parents' home the following afternoon. Before she could get out, Etta came running out the door.

Her long black hair was pulled up in a ponytail with a chiffon scarf tied around it. The yellow skirt and blouse she wore amplified her bright dark eyes. She didn't look moody in the least.

"Hi, girls," she said, quite breathless as she climbed into the backseat of the car.

"Well, somebody's chipper today," Becky said, glancing at her sister through the rearview mirror.

"I've had a good day."

"Well, good for you," Julia said with a smile.

"Maybe Jimmie is finally leaving you alone?"

Julia knew Becky was fishing. Maybe she was thinking what Julia was thinking, that Etta had gone back to him.

"Yeah, I think he's finally got the message. Besides, I met someone else last night."

Becky had just started to pull out of the driveway but instead hit the brakes. "What? Who? Where? When? What's his name?"

Etta laughed as though she were keeping back the most enticing of secrets. "I bumped into him, literally—or should I say he bumped into me?" She giggled. "Yes, yes, that was it. He bumped into me. I could tell he was preoccupied, and I had a feeling he was going to run right into me. He did."

"Well, what happened, for goodness' sake?" Becky put the car into gear and backed out of the driveway and onto the street.

"Well, nothing happened. But I got a good look at him, and there was something so dreamy about his eyes." She sighed with sheer plea-sure, like a dog getting scratched in just the right place.

"Did you get his name?" Becky asked.

"Well, just his first name. Stefan." Her eyes got that faraway look again. "Isn't that a heavenly name?"

The name hit hard against Julia's chest. Silly, she knew. There were plenty of men named Stefan. She just didn't know any...except for one. It couldn't be him. He would never come back here. Would he?

"Listen, sis, you need more than just a first name. How do you plan to see him again?" Becky asked.

Becky most likely was thinking that Etta would just get her hopes up and it would all fizzle out again. Julia knew how the game of love could pan out—and sometimes, it just didn't.

"Well, you know what Mom says. 'If it's God's will, it will happen.'"

Julia and Becky exchanged a glance. Let Etta keep her dreams. Though Jimmie had broken up with her, Etta obviously didn't love him, or she couldn't have gotten over him so soon. It had taken Julia, what, seventeen years to forget Stefan? What was she thinking? She still hadn't forgotten him.

Yes, Etta was still at the stars-in-her-eyes stage of life, where everything turns up bright and happy—a place with cozy cottages and white picket fences. Though Julia envied the hope in Etta's eyes, she knew what was coming for her sweet, naïve friend.

Etta would have to deal with real heartbreak one day, the kind that burned in your stomach and tied you in knots. Heartbreak that seared images into your mind and broke your heart, day after day after day. Until one day, you just didn't care anymore. About anything.

Poor Etta. She'd learn. Just like Julia.

* * * * *

"I can't believe I let you talk me into this. I think you're abusing your employer/employee privilege," Lukas said.

George grinned and pulled the car to a halt at the stoplight. His fingers drummed on the steering wheel to the Everly Brothers' version of "Bye Bye Love" on the car radio.

When the light changed, he drove a half block then turned down another road. Lukas looked around, familiarity hitting him like a two-by-four.

"Does Becky live on this road?"

"Yeah. Right over there." George pointed. "Luckily, Julia said she'd go to Becky's house, so we don't have to drive to her house too."

"Does she live across town?"

George frowned. "I don't know, really. Since she said she'd be at Becky's, I just assume so."

When they drove past, Lukas barely recognized the house that was to be "their" home—his and Julia's—once they had gotten married. It didn't look so great back then, but someone had put a lot of work into it. He wondered if Julia ever thought about that house when she came to visit her friend.

George pulled the car up to Becky's house and cut the engine. "Well, buddy, ready to greet the girls?"

"Yeah," Lukas said.

When they stepped inside the house, one look at Julia nearly took Lukas's breath away. She wore a crisp white button-down blouse, a blue tapered skirt, and matching scarf. Her silky hair draped across her shoulders like a delicate shawl. Oh, how he wished he hadn't agreed to this.

"Hope you all are hungry," George said, rubbing his hands together. "I'm starving."

They laughed while Becky and Julia grabbed their purses and followed the guys out the door.

"Sorry you got roped into this," Julia said to Lukas as they walked to the car.

"Who said I did?" he asked.

"Well, didn't you?"

"Did you?"

"I asked you first," she said.

"Maybe. How about you?"

She grinned.

"George didn't have the guts to ask Becky out on his own."

Julia looked up with a start.

"Not that I mind."

A light smile touched her lips and he was drawn to it like bugs to a lightbulb. He coughed and looked away.

"So how's your finger?"

"It's fine," she said, raising it for inspection. "And your thumb?"

He held it up in all its blue and purple glory. "I won't be hitch-hiking anytime soon."

She grimaced.

"Listen, about what I said the other day—"

"Don't worry about it. You had your reasons," Julia said.

He didn't know what to say after that. He did have his reasons, but she wouldn't know about them.

"Didn't I see you at the beach—"

"Yeah, I'm sorry I had to take off in such a hurry." He couldn't add any more explanation without making something up, so he stopped there.

When they reached the restaurant and placed their orders, Julia was the first to speak.

"You guys are doing a great job on the room. I think even my mother will approve." She gave a slight laugh.

Lukas remembered her mother well. She was no laughing matter. "When are your parents coming back?" he asked.

"Not exactly sure, but probably another three weeks or so."

George cocked an eyebrow.

"They're in Europe on a cruise."

"But I thought—" George looked confused.

"My dad is full of surprises." Julia shifted uneasily on the booth's upholstery.

"Well, I know Becky has plenty of siblings, she's told me about her big family," George said. "How about you, Julia, do you have any brothers or sisters?"

Lukas didn't so much as twitch as they waited for her response.

She bowed her head a moment, as though to think of how to respond. For an uncomfortable moment, they all waited.

"I'm sorry. I still get choked up about it. I had one brother. Joe was killed in the war."

Becky reached her hand across the table and took Julia's hand. She smiled for reassurance.

"I'm so sorry," George said.

"Me too," Lukas said. If she only knew how sorry he truly was.

"The only thing we know is that many of the men in his battalion fell that day. One of Joe's comrades, wounded alongside Joe, wrote us that a German approached them, looked at their wounds, then turned away. He just left them there. To die." She stared at her fingers.

Lukas wanted to punch something. That wasn't how it happened at all.

"Hey, you were in the war, weren't you, Lukas? Maybe you could find out something for her."

"I was in the war, George, and I don't want to relive it. Don't even like to talk about it, if you must know."

"Sorry. Just thought a guy like you could pull some strings," George continued.

"No, George. I can't." Lukas's voice was firm and final. "There were a lot of guys who fought in that war."

The silence seemed to make a hollow ring around the table.

"I'm sorry, Julia. I'd rather forget the war," Lukas said.

She blinked. "Oh, sure. I understand. No problem."

Another silence.

"So, Julia and I went shopping today and had such fun," Becky said, obviously trying to steer the conversation away from their current topic, which was fine with Lukas.

Before anyone could answer, a woman stepped up to the table.

CHAPTER NINE

"Well, well, we meet again," Eleanor Cooley said, her voice dripping with charm, once again mesmerizing the guys.

"How are you?" Lukas asked with a grin. "Eleanor, isn't it?"

"Why, that's right. I'm flattered that you remembered."

"Who wouldn't?" George asked.

Beneath the table, Becky kicked Julia.

"Ow."

Everyone looked at Julia.

"Oh, sorry, I just hurt my foot."

They went back to their conversation. Julia gave Becky a frown and leaned in to whisper, "George said it, not me. Kick him."

"Oh, look, we're being rude, leaving Becky and Julia completely out of the conversation," Eleanor said. Her gaze flitted to Becky. "I found the loveliest gown at a boutique in Chicago. You should see it. Stunning. It cost exactly twenty-five dollars." Her gaze bore into Becky.

Becky squirmed in her seat and Julia felt sorry for her.

"Twenty-five dollars?" George's face was so red Julia thought he might break out in hives. "Women pay that kind of money for a dress?"

"Well, not everyone can afford to do that," she said.

Most likely meaning Julia and Becky could never do that.

"I don't know why they would want to," Lukas said.

Had he come to their defense? Or was he just being a man? Julia couldn't be sure.

"I think she understands me," Eleanor said, looking once again at Becky.

"Yeah, uh, sure," Becky said.

"Oh, good, here comes our food. I'm starved," Julia said when she saw the waitress approaching.

"Guess that's my cue to leave. Good to see you all again." Eleanor gave a wave of her gloved hand and headed toward the ladies' room.

Julia glanced over at Becky, who just stared at her plate. If she knew Becky, and she did, her friend's stomach was in knots right about now. That doggone Eleanor Cooley. Julia needed to reassure Becky that she was in no way interested in the likes of Lukas, but she had to do it in such a way that Becky didn't know Julia knew about the bet.

"Everything all right with your order?" George asked when he spotted Becky staring at her food.

"Oh, yes. Yes, it's fine. Thanks," she said brightly, fooling everyone but Julia about what was in her heart.

"You know, I don't know why you don't want to talk about the war," Julia said to Lukas. "It's not as though it happened yesterday. It's been well over a decade." Julia couldn't believe she was being so rude, so insensitive. But she had to help Becky, reassure her that she had no interest in Lukas. Whatever it took.

Becky gasped. "Julia!"

Though shame covered her, she held her chin up and plowed forward.

"I'm sorry, I'm not trying to be rude, but I just wondered." She picked up a chunk of cut steak with her fork and ate it.

"I understand," Lukas said. "It's just something I choose not to talk about." He stopped his fork midair and turned to Julia. "Period."

The irritating tone of his voice chased away her shame. Yes, she picked the fight, but he didn't have to happily go along with it.

"Fine."

"So, Becky, how do you like teaching?" George asked in a nervous voice.

He and Becky drifted into conversation about their jobs while Lukas and Julia ate their meals, saying not a word. Remorse set in. Much to her chagrin, she had ruined everything. In her effort to help Becky, she'd made everyone uncomfortable.

"Excuse me, I'll be right back," Julia said.

Lukas stepped away from the booth, allowing Julia to exit. She heard Becky excuse herself as well, and frustration filled her. If only she could have a few minutes to herself, to think things through and figure out how to get through this night, help her friend, and still keep a bit of her integrity before the night was over—if that was possible.

"Julia, wait up."

Julia turned around as Becky moved toward her.

"Are you all right?"

The concern in Becky's eyes made her feel worse. "I'm fine."

"I've never heard you talk like that. I know something is wrong."

"I'm fine, Becky. I just don't like him." Julia pushed through the bathroom door.

"You hardly know him. What made you turn on him that way? Was it talking about your brother or what?"

"No, it wasn't that."

"What then?"

Julia pulled a hairbrush from her purse and worked it through her hair. "Okay, maybe it was all that talk about my brother." She knew she wasn't being totally honest but had no idea how to fix it.

Becky edged toward her and put her hand on Julia's shoulder. "I'm sorry, Julia. I know it's still hard for you."

Not only was she rude, she was dishonest. Just like Lukas had said. Oh, why couldn't she just go home?

"I know Lukas is a nice man for someone, but honestly, Becky, I did this thing tonight only for you. Please don't ask me to do it again." Julia didn't miss the relief in Becky's eyes.

"I won't. Thank you for coming tonight so I could be with George. I think he'll have the nerve to go out with me alone the next time." She winked. "And to be honest, I'm glad you don't like Lukas."

Julia was relieved that Becky got the message that she wasn't interested in Lukas, and she hoped Becky wouldn't worry anymore. "Oh? Why is that?" Julia thought maybe Becky would tell her about the bet she had made with Eleanor.

"Can I borrow your brush?" Becky asked.

Julia handed it to her.

"He just doesn't seem your type. I can see why you're not attracted to him."

Julia wouldn't go so far as to say that. In fact, she had to admit she found him quite attractive.

"Oh?"

Becky shrugged, gave her curls one last touch-up, and turned to her. "I don't know. You always say you don't go for the muscle-bound types. They're usually trouble."

"Yes, I've said that." Now that she thought about it, she wondered why she said that. Just another way to protect her heart, she supposed.

Becky looked at her with an ornery grin. "You have to admit, he's muscle-bound."

She did not have to admit it. And she wouldn't. There was certainly more to building a relationship than physical attraction.

No matter how strong the pull.

* * * * *

Lukas was glad the movie was over and the evening had almost come to an end. This Julia wasn't the girl he had fallen in love with years ago, that was for sure. This one was opinionated, stubborn, and proud. She reminded him of someone—oh yeah, her mother.

George pulled onto Becky's street and Lukas could feel his shoulders start to relax for the first time all evening. They'd walk the girls up to the door, say good night, and that would be that. From here on out, he would relate to Julia Hilton strictly on a professional level. Maybe it was good they had gone out tonight. It snuffed out any idea he had of thinking he still carried a torch for her. In fact, he was sure he could take her on a couple of solo dates—three, to be exact. Long enough to get that discount George offered him and then get on with his life, without a single hitch.

George was right about one thing, though. It might not be easy to get her to go along with it. She didn't seem to care any more for him than he did for her. He'd have to get creative. Think of a way to get her to go out without considering it a date. It would take some doing, but he thought he could handle it.

Not only did his shoulders relax, his heart slowed to a steady trot and he decided the evening had possibilities after all. He could go home, get in a little TV. Too bad Ed Sullivan didn't come on until Sunday nights. He really liked that show.

"Oh, would you mind stopping here? That's my house," Julia said, pointing.

"This is where you live? Hey, since you live so close to Becky, how about I go and drop her off while Lukas walks you to the door?" George said.

"I guess that would be—"

George cut Julia off. "Great. You kids go ahead and I'll be right back."

Well, this didn't work out the way Lukas had hoped at all. He'd have to walk her up to the door without Becky and George. It would be awkward. What should he say? Should he shake her hand and treat her like the employer that she was? The very thought made his hands itch. This was like high school all over again.

Lukas ran a hand through his windblown hair. He got out of the car with her and one look at the house stopped him in his tracks. She obviously noticed and turned around.

"Are you all right?" she asked.

He couldn't believe what his eyes told him.

"Is something wrong?" Julia stepped closer to him.

Her nearness, the light scent of her perfume, mentally jarred him. "Oh, sorry. It's just that your house reminded me of a house—uh—a house—of someone I once knew."

"Oh." She smiled with obvious relief. "I love this house. When I was a teenager, I told myself I would live here one day." They walked up to the porch together.

"Really? Why is that?"

"Well, someone—" She blinked, her back stiffened, and she looked up at him. "It doesn't matter. That was years ago. Silly kid stuff."

He couldn't agree more.

A glance at the empty driveway made his stomach churn. Night shadows danced across the lawn. Where was George? Good grief. Would this night never end?

He turned back to Julia. "You can go on inside if you want. I'll just wait out here."

She fumbled with her key. "Well, you're welcome to step inside if you want, until George gets here."

He was about to say no but decided he wouldn't mind a sweeping view of her house, to see what she'd done with the place.

With one last glance toward the empty driveway, he accepted the invitation and stepped into her home. It smelled sweet, like watermelon. If memory served him, the house had three bedrooms, a kitchen, living room with a brick fireplace, one bath, and a basement.

A smile almost escaped him. They had been out in the rain that day and had run into this empty house to escape the storm. Soon they had found themselves wandering through the run-down property with dreams of one day fixing it up and calling it their own.

Julia had followed through with it. She'd made it her own. Without him.

"Nice place," he said, taking in the scrubbed hardwood floors, clean brick fireplace, painted walls with scenic pictures, davenport, coffee table, and chairs.

"Thanks," she said. "I like it."

Did she ever think about him while she was here? She had to remember, didn't she? Their past dreams couldn't vanish without a thought, could they? Or maybe she had just gone along with him on those dreams. Obviously, at some point, she had stopped dreaming— at least about him.

George's sedan pulled into the drive.

"Oh, here he is. Thanks for the quick tour. I'll see you tomorrow."

Before she could answer, Lukas was out the door. Something seemed to weigh his steps, as though cement were attached to his shoes. So much to think about tonight. But he didn't want to think. He wanted to forget everything. The date. The way a spark seemed to light Julia's eyes when she challenged him. The way her face glowed in the softness of candlelight.

With a quick grasp on the door handle of the car, he yanked it open and slammed it shut once he climbed inside.

"What's the matter, wouldn't she kiss you?" George teased.

Lukas turned to him. "Look, George, I appreciate that you've given me a job. I'm glad we've become good friends in a short time. But, please, don't ever ask me to do this again."

"Okay," George said.

Neither one said another word the rest of the way home.

* * * * *

Dressed in her pajamas, Julia was snuggling with Beanie on the davenport when the phone rang.

"Are you comfy and dressed for bed?" Becky asked.

"Yes. You?"

"Yep."

"So what do you think of George?" Julia asked, with a smile at the enthusiasm she could hear in her friend's voice.

"One word. Dreamy."

"You really like him, don't you?"

"Well, I don't know him very well yet, but I sure want to get to know him better."

"That's a good start," Julia said.

"He was just so sweet. And you should have seen him when he walked me to the porch. I know he wanted to kiss me, but he didn't dare. He kept shoving his hands in and out of his pockets. So nervous." She chuckled. "It was kind of cute."

"That's sweet."

"Listen, Julia, I'm sorry you had a rotten night. Really, I am. I won't ask you to do it again. And I'll never forget that you put yourself through a night of torment for me. I owe you."

"I'll say you do," Julia said with a laugh. "But it's all right. Lukas is okay, just not for me." She paused. "But he's a good builder, I'll give him that."

"Why did he stop on the sidewalk on the way up to your house?"

"You noticed?"

"George and I both noticed. Was he all right?"

"Yeah. He said my house reminded him of the house of someone he knew once," Julia said. "Might have been an old girlfriend or something. Who knows? Anyway, I let him come inside. He seemed impressed with my decorating abilities." She laughed.

"I can see why. You've done a beautiful job with your house."

Beanie stretched across Julia's lap and nipped at her hand.

"Well, I guess I'd better get going. Beanie's telling me it's time to fill her food bowl."

Becky laughed. "Nothing comes between Beanie and mealtime."

"Exactly."

"Sweet dreams, friend."

"You too," Julia said.

When Julia made her way to the kitchen, she wondered just what kind of dream she would dream tonight....

CHAPTER TEN

A week later, just as Julia turned out the kitchen light to head for bed, she heard a rattling at her front door. Beanie waited in the hallway for her to go to the bedroom. It was times like these that Julia wished Beanie were a dog. A very big dog.

Julia inched toward the coat closet, her eyes glued to the turning knob of the front door, the hair on her arms standing straight up. She quickly reached inside the closet and pulled out the baseball bat she kept there for just such an occasion as this.

Right when the door swung open, Julia lifted the bat high over her head, and just as she prepared to whop the intruder within an inch of his life, he yelled.

"Don't hit me! It's Dad!"

She stopped cold, arms frozen mid-air. "Dad. What are you doing here?"

He looked at the bat hovering dangerously over him. "Would you put that thing down? You're making me nervous."

With mouth gaping, she looked at him and said finally, "It's eleven o'clock, Dad. You're supposed to be in Europe. What are you doing here?"

He dropped his luggage, walked over to the davenport, sat down, and ran his fingers through his thinning salt-and-pepper hair.

Alarms went off in her brain. Julia was certain it had to do with the luggage perched in her living room.

"Dad, what's going on? You weren't due to come back yet."

"Your mother is driving me loco."

The alarms increased in volume. Her mother drove her loco almost every day, but she'd never seen it get to her dad. This was serious.

"I just can't talk about it right now, Jules. But I need you to go stay with her. Make sure she's all right."

"If you're worried about her, why are you here?"

"For peace of mind. I don't know what's going on with her. She won't go to the doctor. Maybe you can talk some sense into her. I told her I'd give her a couple of days to herself—since our trip seemed to bring all this on. She's probably had too much time with me."

Julia reached over and hugged her dad. "That's not it. In fact, I was wondering if maybe she's entered menopause." Julia felt a little embarrassed saying that to her dad. It wasn't proper to talk about such things in mixed company.

He scratched his jaw. "I hadn't thought of that. I don't know. I just know she needs to see a doctor."

Julia nodded. "I'll talk to her."

"You're the best daughter in the world. Thanks for staying with her, Jules. Just till this room addition gets done. I can't handle remodeling on a good day, let alone when your mother is going through whatever it is she's going through."

He wanted Julia to stay with her mother till the room addition was completed? Julia wondered if she could put herself up for adoption.

"By the way, I thought you'd be at our house. What are you doing here?" he asked.

"I come home on the weekends. I miss my house." She hoped he would take the hint.

"Sorry, honey. I know this hasn't been easy for you. The room addition is coming along. Appreciate you watching over it."

"No problem." She yawned. "Well, I'll grab a suitcase and head over to your house. The guest room is all ready, so go ahead and put your suitcase in there, Dad."

"You're the best." He reached over and pressed a kiss on the top of her head.

By the time Julia got her things put together and drove over to her parents', the house was dark. Good thing she had a key.

The lake swished softly in the darkness as she trekked up to the house. Moonlight gave her just enough light to see where she was walking. It might seem a bit eerie out here to others, but Julia loved this place at night. She'd spent so many evenings, just like this one, strolling the beach, listening to the sounds of the lake, breathing in its sweet scent, while she sorted through memories and tried to make sense of her life.

The very idea made her open her luggage and pull out a beach towel. She walked around to the back of the house and inched down the slope toward the beach. Once there, she spread out her towel and sat down, facing the lake.

Moonlight shimmered on the inky water. Darkness cloaked the far horizon. The air, cool and filled with night sounds, relaxed her. For a moment she sat there, still and content, wrapped in her surroundings, drinking it all in.

The grinding gears of a truck on a nearby road pulled her out of her reverie. What was with her parents? Was her mother truly in menopause or was there something else going on? Her mother had been difficult for as long as she could remember, so why was her dad just now seeing it? Was her dad changing or was her mother getting worse? She sighed. It seemed she would soon find out.

Just when the hope of her returning home for the summer was within reach, everything turned upside down. Her dad got her house, and she was stuck back at her parents' home—with her mother.

Though she and her mother had never actually gotten along, especially after Joe's death, Julia felt a little bit sorry for her. Margaret Hilton was a controlling, stubborn, arrogant woman. Her friends were surface and her family broken.

If only Julia knew how to fix it.

* * * * *

Julia awoke in the guest room to the noise of hammering. It had been a week since her date with Lukas and neither had spoken of it, nor had he asked her on another. Not that she expected he would.

She took in her surroundings, and the memory of last night with her dad rushed over her. Heaving a sigh, she threw off the covers. With a quick glance upward, she tossed a prayer for guidance.

Odd that she did that. When was the last time she had prayed, truly prayed? Church attendance was routine. It had never occurred to her not to go to church. It was just something she did. Like brushing her teeth. But prayer? Reading her Bible? She had stopped doing those things long ago...when life got harder.

It wasn't that she didn't believe in God. But He was busy running the world, and she was quite sure He didn't have time for her daily incidentals. Sometimes, when she thought of being a little blip on the planet, she even found herself doubting that He knew she was there. But then she always reminded herself that of course He knew. He was God, after all. And He was busy. So she tried not to bother Him much. Probably shouldn't even toss up this whole thing with her parents, but right now she was willing to try anything.

Dressed in her pajamas, robe, and slippers, Julia stepped into the kitchen to join her mother, who had just edged away from the coffee percolator heating on the stove.

Mother turned around. "Julia, what on earth?" She put her hand to her chest and took a minute to catch her breath.

"I'm sorry. I didn't mean to frighten you."

"Well, of course you frightened me. I checked on you last night and you weren't here, so I assumed you'd gone home."

The dark circles and puffiness beneath her mother's eyes told of her sleepless night. For a moment, compassion filled Julia, making her determined to help her parents get this matter straightened out. Besides, her dad couldn't stay at her house forever.

"I did go home."

Mother sat at the table and glanced at the coffee pot to see if it was percolating. It continued to hiss in response to the flames beneath it. With her finger, she doodled an invisible design on the table. "Your father left. I have no idea where he is."

"I know," Julia said, suddenly feeling as though she and her mother had switched roles. "He's at my house."

Her finger stopped moving and she looked up. "Oh."

"That's why I came here last night. He told me"— she searched for the right words—"that you and he—that he—well, that I should come here."

Her mother's chin lifted. "I don't know why he would tell you that."

The coffeepot began to percolate and fill the room with its rich aroma. The sound and smell swished Julia back to happier days when her parents sat at the kitchen table, sipping from their cups and talking together.

Mother rose to pour herself a cup of coffee. "Would you like some?"

"Sure." Julia had bought into those TV commercials and started her day with a cup of the brew. Though not a big fan of coffee, she drank it, she surmised, for the comfort of it.

Mother gave her a cup and sat down with her own drink. Julia couldn't remember the last time she'd sat down and had a peaceful moment with her mother.

"Is everything all right?" Julia asked.

"Obviously not."

"Dad says you're not feeling well."

Mother put her coffee cup down with a thump, causing it to slosh onto the table. She ignored the mess, which shocked Julia to the core.

"I feel absolutely fine. I don't know why he keeps saying that. Just because I don't go along with every little thing he wants to do, he says there's something wrong with me. I wanted to come home. Is that a crime, Julia? Well, is it?"

Julia was speechless. Did her mother really want an answer, or was this a rhetorical question?

"No, it isn't a crime. I have just as much right to my likes and dislikes as he does." Mother stood to her feet, walked over to the sink, and grabbed a dishcloth. Then she walked back to the table and cleaned the spilled coffee. "This trip was for him, not me." She walked the dishcloth back to the sink, washed it out, and draped it over the hump separating the two sinks.

"It was a nice trip, you have to admit," Julia said with fear and trembling.

"I don't have to admit any such thing. But I will. I didn't say it wasn't a nice trip. But enough is enough. I wanted to come home. I wanted to check on our addition." She paced. "I offered to stay, but he knew I wanted to come home. Do you know what he did?" She stopped walking and stared at Julia in a way that made Julia feel she was in trouble.

"What?"

"He pouted the entire trip home. The entire trip, Julia. Across the ocean, miles over land and sea, and he pouted the whole way. What am I to do with that?"

Another rhetorical question. Julia waited and sipped her coffee while her mother paced some more. Never mind that her mother cut the trip short. The trip her dad had planned so carefully. "So where do we go from here?"

Mother made the most animated expression. It almost caused Julia to laugh.

"You tell me. I'm not asking him to come home. He's the one who got mad, not me."

Julia held back a groan.

"By the way, why is my picture with Joseph in a different frame?"

A throbbing headache began in Julia's right temple. She had prided herself in finding a frame so close to what she had broken, she was sure her mother wouldn't notice. She should have known better.

"I'm sorry, Mother. I broke the glass on the one Joseph bought you."

Her mother's expression teetered between disbelief and you-better-run. "You what? That was my last gift from him! How could you have been so careless with such a priceless treasure?"

"Excuse me, could I get a drink of water?" Lukas stood in the doorway. In her mother's rant, they hadn't heard him come through the front door.

The last person in the world Julia wanted to see—or to be seen by. Her pajamas and robe were decent enough, but she hadn't run a brush through her hair this morning. She could only imagine what she looked like right at this very moment. Saying nothing of the fact her mother was treating her like a child.

This summer wasn't at all going the way she had planned.

* * * * *

After Julia's walk on the beach in the later afternoon to sort things through her mind, she heard her mother shouting at George and Lukas over something. Julia was mortified that her mother sounded so rude.

In fact, though her mother could be obnoxious at times, the out-of-control squeal didn't sound at all like her.

George stumbled for words of apology while Lukas looked on. The red in his face said he wasn't taking it as well as George.

"Mother, I need to talk with you a moment."

She whipped around and looked at Julia. "What?"

The look on her mother's face would have sent a lesser woman running. "Could we go into the house, please?"

Mother heaved a long, dramatic sigh. Her lips were pursed and her eyes flashing. "I'll be back," she said to the men before she stomped past Julia.

Once they were out of view, hands firmly planted on her hips, Mother turned to Julia. "Now, what was so important that it couldn't wait until I got finished talking with those two?"

Fortunately, Julia's dad pulled up to the house right then and got out of his car. For a moment, a soft glow lit her mother's eyes. Julia was hopeful she'd get her house back.

"I've come for more clothes," her dad said, marching past them.

Julia wondered how many more days till school started.

* * * * *

It did Julia good to get in her car and away from her parents' house later that night. They were feuding and she was caught smack dab in the middle of it all.

The car still smelled like apples from her trip to the grocery store yesterday. She reached for the radio knob and turned it on. Oh, great. Pat Boone crooning "Love Letters in the Sand." Julia listened to the words and thought of how Stefan had vowed he would ever be true and then just totally dropped her. How could anyone do that, without any explanation whatsoever?

Swallowing hard, she tried to shake it off, to forget. Oh, that she could rip him from her heart for good. How she'd like to give him a dose of his own medicine. But her heart told her what she couldn't bear to face. She would never see or hear from Stefan Zimmer again.

With a glance at her paper, she looked at Lukas's address once more. She knew George and some other guys were going to his house tonight to watch a ballgame on TV. Hopefully she could get there before the others showed up.

When she turned down his street, she thought it looked familiar. The closer she got, the more she knew why she recognized the street. Pulling up to his farmhouse, her breath caught in her chest. Lukas had bought Stefan's aunt and uncle's place. Just when she thought she could put Stefan out of her memory.

The crankiness of the car door opening matched her mood. She didn't want to be here. And now that she thought about it, she didn't really want to talk to George and Lukas—especially Lukas. He was bound to be upset by the things her mother had said, and while Julia might agree with his sentiments, she didn't want to hear them from him. Her mother might not be perfect but she was, after all, her mother.

Still, she trudged her way up the walk to the old brick farmhouse that had obviously seen better days. Busted cement left fragments on the aged sidewalk. Tiny green weeds poked through the cracks, though she had to admit the yard appeared neat and trimmed. A neighbor's pig farm scented the air.

With a knock at the door, she waited for him to answer. He didn't. Another knock. Nothing. His car was in the drive, so he had to be there. No one else had arrived yet. Not even George.

She walked over the uneven lawn and made her way to the back-yard. There she could hear his voice carrying from the small red barn.

"Here's dinner, Scooter. How you doin', ole boy?"

She eased around the corner and saw Lukas hunkered down and scratching a dog's scruff with great abandon while the dog responded with twists and turns of sheer pleasure.

Lukas laughed and the dog hobbled around the bowl. That's when Julia got a better look. The animal had three legs. Her heart melted at the sight. What had caused such a thing?

"Oh, what a darling little thing," she said without thinking.

Lukas whipped around. "What are you doing here?"

The sharp tone of his voice startled her. "Oh, I'm sorry. I heard your voice and I followed it. I just—"

"You'd best be careful sneaking up on people like that. You'll get yourself hurt one day."

His comment made her hair bristle. "I wasn't sneaking up. I told you, I was—"

"So why are you here?"

"Well, right this moment, I'm not at all sure why I'm here."

"Am I supposed to understand what that means? If you don't know, how am I supposed to know?"

She gasped. "For the life of me, I don't know why I should ever be concerned about you. You are the most rude, arrogant, selfish—" Just as a powerhouse of mean words gathered momentum to push through her mouth, she realized he stood there, arms folded, eyebrows raised, and with the slightest hint of amusement playing on his lips.

She could not believe her eyes. "You aren't even worth it!" This time she whipped around to stomp off, but he caught her arm.

"Now, hold on. You came to say something. So say it."

Now, hold on? That was something Stefan said to her anytime she got upset. Would she never be free of him?

Hot adrenaline ran rampant through her. There was no way she could apologize for her mother now. "Never mind, it doesn't matter."

His grip tightened slightly. That's when she realized he hadn't let her go.

His eyes pinned hers. "It does matter or you wouldn't be here. I'm sorry I put you on edge. You startled me, that's all."

The adrenaline seemed to slow, her blood pressure settling to a normal level. She stood there a moment, clouded with indecision, wanting to go and wanting to stay.

"I said I'm sorry, okay?" His voice was soft this time. Almost inviting. She looked at him a little longer than she meant to. He looked right back.

"What happened to your dog?" she asked, still not quite wanting to apologize.

Lukas shrugged. "Don't know. He was abandoned. I brought him home."

That little bit of his character surprised her—and warmed her more than she cared to admit. She would never have taken him for the compassionate type.

She reached out to the dog and he snarled and started for her. Julia stepped back.

"Scooter, no! We'd better step out of here while he eats." Lukas guided her, hand still on her arm, out of the barn. "You'll have to excuse his manners. He was most likely abused and doesn't take kindly to strangers."

"I understand." They stepped near his back porch.

"I don't want to keep you. I just wanted to apologize for my mother."

His hand was still on her arm. She knew she should remind him, but somehow his strong grip made her feel dainty and something else she didn't quite recognize.

"No need. I've worked with customers like her before." He looked her full in the face. "I'm glad you came by, though."

Her throat was so dry she could barely move her tongue. "Me too." She took a breath. "So you won't quit on her?"

"It takes more than that to get me to leave a job."

"Make sure George knows I stopped by, would you? I wanted to tell him the same thing," she said.

"I'll tell him." His eyes still held hers.

"Well, guess I'd better go," she said, not wanting to blink.

"Thanks for stopping," he said.

He let go of her arm, leaving her cold and...unattached.

"No problem." She turned to go then swiveled back around. "Oh, one more thing. Did you know the prior owners of this place?"

"Uh, well, uh, I got it through an estate situation."

"Oh, I see. Probably got a good deal then." She smiled.

"A real good deal. Did you know them—the owners, I mean?"

"I had met them but didn't really know them. I knew their nephew."

"Yeah?" he said.

"Yeah. Well, see you later."

CHAPTER ELEVEN

Lukas glanced at his watch then grabbed his bag and climbed out of the car. He still had plenty of time before he had to be at the job site. The air, moist and hot, slowed his steps. On days like this, he was thankful he could walk around the gym track in air conditioning.

A morning walk did him good. Keeping up a brisk pace, his mind wandered to Julia and her parents. Obviously her parents were at odds right now. He didn't know what was going on, but the fact that her dad was nowhere to be seen yesterday, coupled with her mother's anger, made him suspect a problem. Plus, he noticed Julia seemed upset most of the day.

Hopefully they would work through it. The heartaches of a broken family were many. Experience had taught him that much.

"Hey, don't I know you?"

A young woman with dark hair and a wide grin bounced up to him and matched him step for step.

"Isn't that supposed to be my line?" He grinned back.

"On the beach, remember? You ran into me?"

Recognition hit him. "Oh, yeah, I remember."

"Etta."

"That's right." He could sense her obvious interest, but he didn't want to get involved with anyone right now. Time to think things through, get on with his life, that was what he needed. He kept walking.

"So do you come out here a lot?" Heavy breaths lined her words as she struggled to keep up with him.

"Not often. It was just too hot to walk outside this morning."

"Yeah, that's what I thought too. It's unusually hot today. I'll be glad when fall gets here."

Not wanting to be rude, he merely nodded but kept moving, hoping she'd get the hint.

"So, are you married?"

Boy, this girl didn't waste any time. "Nope," he said, wanting to add, "and I aim to keep it that way."

"Me, neither," she said happily.

He picked up his pace.

"Hey, you going to a race or what?"

"Just have to get to work."

"Where do you work?"

Before he could answer, someone called out her name.

"Oh, shoot. I have to go. See you again sometime, Stefan."

The use of his old name made him cringe. If only he could take it back. But how? He would need to give the matter some thought. On the other hand, if he stuck to walking outside, the chances of meeting this woman again were slim.

At least that was his hope. She was nice enough, and even pretty, but he had no interest in anyone...but Julia.

If only he could forget her...

* * * * *

Billowy clouds sailed across the pale June sky. A misty fog blurred the horizon beyond Lake Michigan. Julia cradled the cup of coffee in her hand and took in the scenery. She could hear Elvis singing from the radio she'd turned on in the kitchen. There was something cozy about this sort of day. Unlike the normal sunshine of summer that called for lavish picnics and brisk walks, this hot weather called for a lazy day filled with chilled lemonade and perusing magazines.

"Doesn't look like much out there today." Her mother entered the room dressed in silky pink pajamas. Before Julia could respond, she added, "And don't tell me I need a robe. It's much too hot for that. Besides, the men won't be here for a while. I have plenty of time to get showered and dressed."

"It's your house. Do what you want," Julia said.

"I plan to."

Her mother could use a dash more Pollyanna attitude.

"My feet hurt," she complained, massaging her toes with her fingers.

"Maybe you need different shoes." Julia lamented that her moment of enjoying nature and the morning view was gone. She settled onto the brown sofa.

"I have to be careful. Varicose veins. They run in the family. You'll have to watch for that," she warned.

Of all the things Julia thought she had to worry about these days, she never once considered varicose veins.

"What is with that Elvis fellow? 'All Shook Up,' indeed. He's gotten things 'all shook up,' that's for sure. I've never seen such nonsense."

Julia shrugged. "I think he's cute."

Her mother turned to her. "I've raised you better than that, Julia. I would have hoped your tastes would lean toward more of a gentleman, not some hipster with sideburns."

"Mother. You don't even know the man. Besides, it's not as though I'm longing to marry him, for goodness' sake."

"Well, I should hope not. It took enough effort to get you past that German fellow in your teen years."

The comment shocked Julia. "I don't want to talk about him."

"I don't know why, those days are long past. Unless, of course, you still carry a torch for him." Her mother's eyes studied Julia, but she refused to squirm.

"Did you talk with Dad last night?" Julia asked abruptly.

Mother's chin hiked. "No, I did not talk with your father. Nor do I intend to." She adjusted her seating on the chair. "The man is insufferable."

Oh, how Julia wanted to respond to that—but she knew better. "I don't know what the problem is, but you two have been together too long to let something trivial come between you."

"You're right. You don't know what it is. Therefore, don't try to patch things up, Julia. This is between your father and me."

"Yes, but it affects me."

"How so?"

"He's staying at my house. *My* house. He should be here. With you. And I should be in my own home."

"No one is making you stay here." Her mother pulled a handkerchief from the pocket of her pajama pants and blotted her face and neck.

"What's wrong?" Julia asked.

"I'm hot."

"Please, Mother, promise me you'll call the doctor this morning."

"I'll do no such thing. It's summer. I'm hot. There's nothing at all unusual about that." She stood up, marched into her bedroom, and slammed the door shut.

Julia stared after her. Her mother was in denial, her dad was staying in her house, and Julia had no place to call her own.

* * * * *

Heat slowed Lukas's steps as he walked to the mailbox that evening. He glanced through the envelopes and, with a groan, headed back toward the front porch. More bills from his mother's passing. He wanted to throw away the envelopes, pretend he never got them, hope the hospital would forget. But of course they wouldn't. And it was his responsibility.

Shoving the key in the front door, he turned the knob. Not that he minded. He was thankful for the time he had with his mom. Though they'd all lived in Chicago, he didn't go see his parents much while his father was alive. But once his father died, there had been no reason to stay away. He spent plenty of time with his mother then.

Now, of course, there were times he wished he and his dad had talked things out. While the thoughts tangled through his mind, a thread of stubbornness worked its way to his heart. What was he thinking? It was his dad's fault they'd stopped talking. Why should Lukas waste time feeling bad about it?

By the time he pushed through the front door, Lukas had shoved all thoughts of his dad back to the place in his heart reserved for those uncomfortable things of life that were best kept hidden.

In complete abandon Sauerkraut ran to him, ears winged back as though to take flight, tail sputtering back and forth in a fast staccato. He made a flying leap for the sofa, and Lukas laughed in spite of his troubles.

"With your little legs, it's a good thing the sofa isn't very high," he said, furiously rousing his dachshund.

Ever since he was a kid, Lukas had been drawn to animals—especially dogs. No matter what happened during his day, Sauerkraut, and now also Scooter, always made him feel better. He'd been having way too many pity parties these days. It was time he got a handle on things. One glance at his mail told him it wouldn't be easy, but he could—and would—do it.

The phone rang.

"You want to go to the gym?" George asked.

"I already went this morning before work," Lukas said.

"You did? Good grief, why'd you do that? You're gonna make me look lazy."

Lukas laughed. "Sorry, buddy."

"Guess I'll go it alone tonight. By the way, are you still trying for that discount on your home repairs or have you given up on the idea?" George chuckled.

Lukas had pretty much decided he didn't want to pursue this thing with Julia—regardless of the discount incentive—because he didn't trust his heart. But the bills on his sofa suggested he should reconsider.

"Hello?" George laughed. "I told you it wouldn't be easy to get her to agree to a date."

"And how are things going with Becky?" Lukas asked, irritation rising in his stomach.

"Okay." George took a bite out of what sounded like an apple. "I'm going to ask her out to go skating."

Lukas seriously hoped Becky didn't get a glimpse of George's less-than-polished side.

"Well, I'd better go work out. You'd better get to work on that little girlie. Time's a wastin', buddy." With a fading laugh, George clicked off.

Lukas absently scratched Sauerkraut behind the ears, while letting his mind wander. He'd work on a better relationship with Julia this week in hopes of getting her to agree to a date. All the while, he would pray his heart would stay out of the picture.

His hand stroked the scar along his jawline. One thing he knew, wounds from the war healed easier than the wound of a broken heart.

* * * * *

The smell of fried chicken filled the house. With cooking tongs, Julia lifted the crispy chicken pieces from the pan and placed them on a paper towel and then onto a serving plate. She wiped her hands on her apron and prayed this would work. Her parents had been home a week and she had yet to sleep in her own bed.

Drastic measures were called for.

The only good thing that had come of this week was the change in Lukas. He had seemed downright charming lately. Almost sympathetic with her current situation. More so, it seemed, than Becky—which was saying a lot. Becky only had one thing on her mind these days—George.

Maybe she would talk to Lukas about her parents. He might have some insight into the matter. A girl had to do what she had to do, no matter what the cost. Even if it meant having to spend some time with Lukas. So he might become a friend. No big deal.

She had to get her dad back home—and out of her house.

"It smells good, dear." Her mother seated herself at the table as Julia entered the dining room with serving bowls in hand.

"Thanks."

"I do hope you didn't put too much salt in the mashed potatoes. It ruined them for me when you did that last time."

Before Julia could so much as sigh, the doorbell rang.

"Well, who on earth would be so rude as to call during dinnertime?" her mother said.

"Please, Lord, let this work." Julia knew the Lord didn't owe her any favors, what with her distance from Him and all, but she hoped He would consider this a worthy cause and thus put His stamp of approval on it. Of course, that kind of thinking would get her a reprimand from her mother for being so nonchalant—as she would perceive it—concerning spiritual matters.

"Dad, so nice to see you." Julia leaned in and gave him a hearty hug, which he returned with gusto.

"I'm starving. Something sure smells good. I've been getting by on bacon and tomato sandwiches down at Woolworth's. By the time I add on a Coke and banana split, it costs me about a dollar a meal."

Julia laughed. She wanted to say, "That will teach you to leave home," but she didn't want to provoke him this evening of all evenings. Everything had to be perfect if she was ever to sleep in her own bed again, instead of her old room at her parents' house.

The minute her mother saw her dad, she dropped her fork onto her plate, causing a rattle that seemed to reverberate through the room. Shoving her chair away from the table caused it to grind against the hardwood floor.

"What are you doing here?" she demanded, rising from her chair.

Her father's chin lifted. "My daughter invited me to dinner."

Her mother looked at her as though she were mutinous. "Julia," was all she said. It was enough.

"Now, listen you two. I love you both and I wanted to fix us dinner. As a family."

The last three words seemed to take the fight out of both of them. Their shoulders slumped and though her mother hesitated, she finally dropped back into her chair.

Dad walked to the table with a slight touch of triumph in his step.

"Thank you," Julia said to them. "Dad, would you pray for the meal, please?"

Her mother harrumphed.

Dad was put out. "I think you'd best do the talking to the Lord today, Julia. Your mother and I aren't necessarily in our best form to talk to Him right now."

Julia wanted to point out that she and the Lord were distant friends but thought better of it. Instead, she prayed over the meal and hoped, deep down in the remotest corners of her heart, that they wouldn't choke on a chicken bone.

Amid the delectable smells of chicken fried to a crisp, golden-brown, creamy mashed potatoes whipped to perfection with a dollop of butter, and sweet peas swimming in a creamy, buttery sauce, dishes rattled, silverware clanked, ice cubes danced in glasses. Her father finally found some words.

"So, Margaret, how have you been?"

"Well, how do you think I've been? You've only been gone a week. You think I can't survive that long without you?"

Dad looked at Julia. "Do you see what I mean?" He shook his head and dug his fork into another round of potatoes.

"Just what do you mean by that?" Mother demanded.

Suddenly words hit the air like gunfire in a war zone.

Julia took a gulp of her water then jumped into the fray. "Mother, I saw a dress at the boutique that I'm sure you would just swoon over."

"I don't swoon over anything, much less something like a dress," Mother snapped.

"You might over this dress," Julia said with a smile. She glanced at her dad, who looked like a wounded pup. His gaze rested on his food. He seemed to force himself to take the next bite.

Her mother fell into silence. The rest of the meal.

From the kitchen, before Julia could scoop up the cherry pie à la mode and get it to the table, she heard her mother, loud and clear.

"Well, Frank, just when do you plan to return home?"

That was Julia's signal to get to the dining room and fast. She hoped to hear something positive pass her dad's lips. The meal could have been worse, after all. True enough, they had an explosive moment, but instead of escalating, they had lapsed into silence. That should count for something.

"I will come home once I'm convinced you will act like a civil human being. You refuse to go to the doctor to get checked out, though I'm sure it's probably not a physical matter, but just you being difficult, as usual."

Her mother opened her mouth and Dad held up his hand.

"You let me finish, Margaret Hilton. That trip was meant to encourage and uplift you. I spent a large amount of savings on it—savings that could have been well-spent elsewhere, but I wanted to see that you had a good time. You'd been working so hard. Not only that, but I wanted to romance you, wine and dine you, so to speak. It was our chance to feel young again. Enjoy our time together."

"We're not young, so why would you do that? Such a frivolous waste of money," Her mother rolled her eyes. "Right when we're having remodeling done too. It made no sense."

"Well, obviously one of us is too old to enjoy the good life. I, for one, do not intend to stop living until I no longer have breath in me." With that he threw his linen napkin on the table, walked over to Julia, and gave her a peck on the cheek. "Thank you for a lovely dinner, sweetheart." He turned and walked out, leaving his cherry pie untouched.

At this rate, Julia would never see her house again.

CHAPTER TWELVE

By the time Beach Village was cloaked in twilight, Julia's mother had settled in for the night and Julia took her walk along the beach. Faint stars poked through the changing sky while the sun gave way to the moon. The lake's earlier restlessness had quieted into a whispering roll to and from the shoreline.

The moist night air smelled of earth and lake water. Julia took a deep breath. Probably the first one she'd taken all day. Her parents' problems had become her own, and she didn't know what to do about it. Wasn't it enough that she had to deal with her mother? Now she actually had to live with her.

Where was God in all this?

And all these thoughts of Stefan? True, he had never been far from her thoughts, even after all these years. The least little thing could prompt a memory, an image, a pain in her heart. But lately, it seemed he consumed her thoughts. Why? Was he in trouble somewhere? Or was it that her heart just wanted to revel in the memories once more, torturing her in the process?

She pushed the thought aside for the thousandth time. One day her life would make sense. One day she would find someone. One day…

"Hey, Julia, wait up."

The deep voice sent a surge of excitement through her. She turned around. "Lukas. What are you doing out here?"

"Believe it or not, I come here sometimes just to…think."

"Yeah?" For some reason she liked that he did that. Like an invisible thread, it seemed to connect them.

"Obviously, you do the same." His grin was broad and genuine.

"Yes, I do. I love these quiet nights."

They kept walking.

"I guess I shouldn't bother you. Maybe you'd prefer to be alone?" Their eyes locked and he added, "I hope not."

The stumble of her feet over a rock in her path matched the stumble of her heart.

"No, that's fine. I wasn't thinking about anything in particular." That was true. Her thoughts were a jumbled mess, unable to sort out one particular thread and ponder it.

They walked along the shoreline, allowing the cricket chirps and deep throaty calls of the bullfrogs to fill the silence.

"I hope I'm not out of line here, overstepping my bounds and all that, but I couldn't help but notice your parents are, um, sparring?"

"That's an understatement." Julia chuckled.

"I'm sorry you're caught in the crossfire."

"Thanks." His compassion surprised her. She looked at his profile for a fraction of a second, then turned to the view straight ahead of her—though his profile lingered in her mind. There was something about him....

"I guess my mom felt that way too."

"Oh?"

"Dad and I had an ongoing feud. He had been a World War I veteran, a war hero, in fact. He couldn't have been prouder when I fought in World War II. Until I was, er, uh—" He stopped himself. "I just didn't measure up."

"Sometimes it's hard to live up to our parents' expectations." How well she knew about that.

"That's for sure."

"Have you and your dad patched things up, or is there still a strain between you?" she asked.

"He died a couple of years ago. We never patched things up."

She turned to him and put her hand on his arm. "Oh, Lukas, I'm so sorry."

"Yeah, me too. Guess that's why I wanted to talk to you. To encourage you to do whatever it takes to get them through this with your family staying intact."

His sincerity and concern reached deep into her emotional well. All the anger and frustration she reserved for her mother balled up inside her, resisting his words, while another part of her hungered for them and longed for them to make a difference in her family's life.

"Sorry if I've said too much."

"No, no, you're fine," she said. "I know you're right. It's just so hard to play out sometimes, you know?"

"Yes, I do know."

At this moment, talking on this level, she almost could believe that she'd known Lukas for most of her life. The idea was absurd, of course. Still, she couldn't deny the idea of it. How his words encouraged and soothed her.

"If there is anything at all I can do to help in any way, I want you to know, I'll be here for you."

She looked up at him with a start.

"What is it?" he asked.

"Something about the way you said that reminded me of—of someone I used to know."

"Tell me about him."

"How do you know it was a 'him'?" She was teasing now.

"The way you said it." He smiled.

"He was a guy I once knew."

"I take it he was special."

"Very."

"What happened?"

"I wish I knew," was all she said.

Once they came back to the place they had started, just a stone's throw from her parents' home, Lukas turned to her.

"Do you have to get inside or do you want to sit on the beach awhile?"

"I can sit awhile." Another surge of excitement ran through her. She wanted it to stop. If Eleanor found them out here together, she'd immediately, no doubt, ask Becky for her payoff. She couldn't do that to Becky. But out here, wrapped in darkness, she doubted anyone would spot them.

Not only that, but one glance at Lukas and she decided he was worth the risk.

* * * * *

"So tell me more about your family," Julia said.

Lukas wasn't sure he liked where this could go. "Not much to tell, really. My dad died a couple of years ago, as I said. We had no relationship in those last days. Mom tried to be the peacemaker, but it never worked. It got to the place where I'd only visit her when I knew Dad was gone. Now I realize our stubbornness broke her heart." He picked up a tiny piece of twig and snapped it between his fingers.

"I can imagine that was hard. So many times I want to walk away from my mother, but my love for Dad holds me steady. His love helps me endure her biting words. Still, they leave their mark."

"Yeah, I get that."

"So where does your mom live?" she asked.

"Unfortunately, she's gone too. Died about six months ago."

"Oh, Lukas, I'm so sorry."

"Thanks. She was a wonderful woman." Silence. "Well, enough of that." He could only take so much talk about his parents. Too many regrets still gnawed at him.

"Looks like you're coming right along on the room addition," Julia said.

"Yeah, finally, we got the framing done. Would have been done sooner if not for that storm."

"I know."

"Should get the roofing done and the windows put in this week."

"That's great," she said.

They talked awhile longer about his move to Beach Village from Chicago, though he never shared with her that he had been there before, many times, on nights very much like this one, beneath a moonlight sky, with her by his side....

"Well, I guess I'd better go inside, just in case Mother ventures out of her bedroom to find me gone." Julia stood up and dusted the sand from her hands. "It was very nice to talk with you tonight, Lukas." He rose to face her. "Thank you for your help." She looked up at him with that same sweet smile that had melted him so many years ago.

He grabbed her hand and looked straight into her eyes. "As I told you, I'll be here for you."

As the water rushed to shore, warning alarms roared through his head. This could lead to nothing good. *Turn away from the alluring green of her eyes, the way the moonlight glistens through her hair, the soft feel of her skin, and the invitation on her lips.*

He could almost feel his head leaning toward her, as though he had no control, no way to stop himself.

"Well, good night, Lukas," she said, slipping her hand from his and walking toward the house.

The rejection would have overwhelmed him had she not stopped and turned around. "Thanks again for a wonderful evening."

With that she slipped into the night...and deeper into his heart.

* * * * *

"Oh, this is heaven," Becky said, as she settled onto her beach towel.

"Isn't it? Finally, I'm getting into what summer is all about." Julia sank onto her own towel and adjusted her sunglasses as her head found a comfortable place on the sand.

"Thank goodness there's a breeze today. It's been so hot, I haven't wanted to sunbathe much. This is a perfect day for it." Becky slathered suntan lotion on her arms and legs and rubbed it into her skin. Its tropical scent filled the air between them.

"It truly is. I'm so glad it's Saturday. I didn't want to wear my bathing suit when the guys could see us." Julia sat back up and added a touch more lotion to her shoulders.

Becky grunted. "I don't know why. You have the perfect body. I'm the one who should worry. It's hard to hide the extra cookies I've been sneaking lately."

"Oh, you. You're perfect just the way you are. Obviously George thinks so or he wouldn't keep asking you out." Julia could already feel the sun's heat on her shoulders and was glad she had decided to apply more lotion.

Becky giggled. "We are having fun. I like him a lot. He had dinner at our house last night, complete with my parents and all the siblings."

"This is sounding serious."

"I'll know it's serious if he asks me on another date after that one last night." One more glob of lotion and she snapped the cap back into place. "That's usually where I lose them."

"By the way, how's Etta getting along?"

"She's in love."

"Oh, doggone it. I thought she wasn't going to go back with Jimmie."

"She didn't," Becky said, settling back onto her towel. "She's in love with someone new. Remember that guy she told us about, Stefan?"

Julia's eyes popped open. "Yeah."

"She ran into him again."

"Really? Where?"

"At the gym. You know how she is about signs and all that. She's convinced God wants them together or she wouldn't have run into him again."

"Twice hardly constitutes a sign, do you think?" Julia asked, trying to figure out why the idea bothered her.

"Not a sign in my book, but you know Etta. Besides, I'm glad because it's taken her mind off Jimmie and given her new resolve each time he calls."

That relieved Julia. "Well, then it's a good thing. I just don't want her to get her heart broken again. I hope she'll take her time searching out her next love."

Becky sighed. "Yeah, me too."

A bird cawed overhead. Children's squeals punctuated the breeze and Julia reveled in the moments here with her friend.

"Are your parents back together yet?" Becky asked.

"No."

"Oh, Julia, I'm so sorry. I've been so caught up with George that I didn't realize you were still staying with your mother—or I assume you are?"

"Yes, I am. For now."

"What is the matter with those two? You know they love each other."

"Yes, they do. But they're both being very stubborn."

"So are you just going to wait it out or what?"

"I don't know yet. I tried to make them a dinner—"

"Oh, yeah. How did that turn out?"

"It was a fiasco."

"Oh, dear," Becky said. "I'm proud of you for not giving up on them. I can't believe you're staying with your mother. That's amazing."

"I'm surprised too. But Lukas talked me into staying." Oh, she hadn't meant to tell Becky that.

"Lukas? What does he have to do with it?"

"Oh, I forgot to tell you, we met up on the beach the other night and talked awhile about my parents and their situation."

"Was it like a date?" Becky was sitting up now, alarm all over her face.

"No, why?"

"Oh, no reason. I would just be surprised, that's all. You don't seem like a good match to me." She lay back down.

"No one said we were a match. But I can think of worse things."

Becky sat up again. "You like him, don't you?"

"We just talked, Beck. That's it. Why do you care?" Maybe Becky just needed to bring it all out in the open—that little bet between her and Eleanor.

"Nothing is the matter. I just don't think he's good enough for you."

That made Julia mad. Becky was being deceitful and that wasn't like her. Maybe pride kept Becky silent on the matter, but it still bothered Julia.

"Don't worry, Becky. It's not like that between us."

The sun continued to beat down upon them in the silence. Finally, Julia said, "How is your car doing?"

"My car? Why did you ask about that?"

"I just remembered you were having trouble with it, and I wondered if you'd gotten it fixed."

"I didn't get it fixed, but it's doing much better. No major stalls in traffic recently. Hopefully I'll have enough money to get it fixed one of these days."

"Yeah, you will."

They settled into silence once again, allowing the sun to bake them to a golden brown. The more Julia thought about the bet between Becky and Eleanor, the madder she got. It was enough that her mother tried to run her life, but now her friends tried to run who she did and didn't date? That was too much. Eleanor had pretty much trapped Becky into it, but still. Becky could have put her pride aside and stood her ground. But she didn't. Now Julia was trapped too. If she liked Lukas, it would hurt Becky financially. Julia didn't want to hurt her friend, but the truth was, she did like Lukas Gable.

She liked him a lot.

CHAPTER THIRTEEN

Cotton yarn slipped through Julia's fingers while she knit a headband for Becky's youngest sister. Her mother sat across from her at the kitchen table, reading the newspaper and nursing a cup of coffee. At the sound of footsteps, Julia looked up.

Lukas stood in the kitchen doorway. "Okay if I get a drink?"

"Sure," Julia said, setting her knitting needles aside. "Would you like cold water from the refrigerator?"

She didn't miss her mother's glare.

"No, thanks. Tap water is fine," he said.

"You boys had better be careful not to track in dirt with your work boots," her mother said with a frown.

"Yes, ma'am," Lukas said.

Julia walked over to the sink and filled his glass then handed it to him. After he had his fill of water he glanced at her mother, whose face was turned in the opposite direction. He motioned Julia to follow him out of the room.

"I'm sorry to bother you, but I wondered, uh, I was thinking, maybe you'd want to have a picnic this evening on the beach?"

The tone of his voice gave a hint to his bashfulness, which surprised Julia completely. In all respects he appeared quite the ladies' man. She couldn't imagine him being the least bit shy when it came to women.

He waited for an answer and she remembered Becky's car and the bet and all that. She wanted to say yes, but she couldn't risk getting Becky into trouble.

"Can we do it late? Say, around nine o'clock, when the beach has pretty much cleared out?" Seeing the confusion on his face, she hurried on. "I prefer quiet evenings, away from crowds. Rather than people noise, I prefer the sounds of nature." She smiled, hoping he would agree.

"Sounds great. Nine o'clock it is." With a quick nod, he turned and went back to work.

It felt like she was walking on air when she headed back to the kitchen to join her mother. Did her footsteps even reach the floor? A schoolgirl giddiness swelled up within her and she wondered what on earth was going on. True enough, she hadn't had a date in a while, but it hadn't been *that* long ago.

One thing she knew. She had to be discreet about it. Neither Becky nor Julia's mother could find out. She had to keep it from them, for their own good.

Julia followed the scent of coffee into the kitchen and poured herself a cup. Her mother continued her journey through the morning paper.

"The nerve of that man asking us to get him water. Does he think we're his servants? He's working for me, not the other way around," Mother said.

"He merely wanted a glass of water, Mother. People get thirsty. Especially in this heat."

Mother grunted. "He's scarcely been working two hours. How thirsty can he be?"

Julia didn't know how much more she could take of her parents' separation. If she didn't have Lukas to keep her distracted she most likely would have rebelled from the start. But staying here did have its benefits, whether she wanted to admit it or not.

Julia sat at the table with her coffee. Taking a sip, she studied her mother. Dark circles underscored her eyes. Normally, her hair was immaculate, never a strand out of place, but today several rebellious strays went their own way and her mother didn't seem to notice.

"Did you sleep well last night?" Julia asked.

"Of course I didn't," her mother said. I haven't had a decent night's sleep in months. I keep waking up in the middle of the night for no reason whatsoever."

"Why won't you check with the doctor?"

"It's just life. I'm stressed about your father, that's all."

Compassion tugged at her heart. It was a rare occasion when her mother showed her soft side. Most days, Julia wondered if she had one at all. But right this moment, in the morning's light, her mother looked vulnerable and frail. Almost human.

"I don't know why he's being so stubborn," her mother said.

Julia tried not to laugh. Funny how we tend to see the faults in others but not ourselves. She wondered how many times she'd done that and what flaws she tended to overlook in herself.

"Why don't you kick him out of your house? Then he'd have to come home."

"Mother, I can't do that. It would hurt him terribly," Julia said.

"Well, you don't seem to mind hurting me."

Julia suddenly had an overwhelming urge to hug her mother, something she hadn't done in a very long time. She got up, went over, and did that very thing.

"Don't patronize me, Julia. I will be fine." Her mother rose from her seat, head and chin held high. "It's your father you need to be concerned about." She turned and walked out of the room with an injured air.

Loneliness and sorrow crept into Julia's heart once more.

* * * * *

The black and pink upholstery protested as George and Lukas scooted into the booths. Cindy's Soda Shop was hoppin'. Lukas glanced at his watch. It was still early for the dinner crowd, but he supposed teenagers could eat at any time of day. That had been true of him, anyway.

People were lined up at the jukebox, so they'd have plenty of music while they chomped on burgers and fries and washed it all down with cherry Cokes.

"I don't know why they have to have all this pink," George said. "You can sure tell a woman's in charge."

Lukas grinned. He had noticed that too.

"At least they have great food."

"Ain't it the truth." George leaned back in his seat.

Leaning forward, Lukas looked at him. "I've got something to tell you."

"Oh?" George eyed him. "Good or bad?"

"Good for me. Bad for you."

"Uh-oh, I don't like the sound of that." George leaned in. "Please tell me you didn't get another job."

"I didn't get another job."

George swiped his hand across his forehead in one dramatic sweep. "Whew. I'm glad to hear that. I don't think I could face Margaret Hilton alone."

Lukas laughed. "I don't think anyone could." Blurred memories threatened to surface, but he didn't allow them to take shape.

"So what's the news?"

"You sure you're ready?" Lukas teased.

"I'm ready, I'm ready. Now get on with it."

The waitress placed their Cokes in front of them and George took a drink.

Lukas laughed. "All right. I'm taking Julia out tonight."

George coughed. And coughed. And coughed. By now, everyone in the soda shop was staring at them. George waved and smiled, indicating he was going to live and the diners quickly went back to their own business.

The records flipped on the jukebox and this time the needle on the record played the Platters singing "The Great Pretender," causing Lukas to squirm ever so slightly. He wasn't exactly pretending—well, maybe a little, but for good reason. It was just better for everyone this way. Plus, it gave him time to think things through. No harm in that.

"So you're taking Julia out." George's voice was raspy and raw from coughing. He took another drink of his soda.

"Yep." Lukas sat back in his chair, wanting to enjoy the moment, but instead, there was a growing mixture of pride and shame balled up in his gut. He wished someone would turn off that dumb record.

"How'd you manage that?"

Lukas shrugged. "I just asked her to go for a picnic on the beach."

George nodded. "Nice, very nice." A mischievous twinkle lit his eyes, causing Lukas's shame to grow. If Julia found out about the bet—no, she couldn't. He'd see to that. What surprised him was that no matter how she had treated him in the past, he didn't want to cause her pain. That frustrated him. How many times had he fantasized about getting even with her for the pain she had caused him? There he was, fighting for their country, facing danger at every turn, seeing anguish beyond belief, and she chose that time to dump him, never to give him another word of encouragement or hope. He had wanted so much for her to feel the pain she had caused him. But the other night, looking into those beautiful green eyes, seeing her smile, the way a tuft of her hair fluttered in the breeze, he couldn't do it. He could never break her heart the way she broke his.

"But remember, I said you had to take her out three times. So you'd better make it good, or you won't get the chance again."

"I know, I know. Just don't spread any lies about me and we'll be good."

George brightened. "I hadn't thought of that."

"Hey!"

"Relax. I'm just kidding." George eyed him suspiciously.

"What?"

"Oh, nothing," George said. "I'll be anxious to hear all about it in the morning."

"If you didn't stand to lose some money, I'd be convinced you're trying to play matchmaker here," Lukas said.

"Money or love? Hmm, time will tell." George grinned and slapped Lukas on the back.

* * * * *

Julia carried Beanie into the lobby of the veterinarian's office. Becky rose to meet her.

"Is Beanie going to be all right?" Becky asked.

"Yeah. He thinks she ate something she shouldn't have." Julia paid her bill, thanked the receptionist, and walked with Becky to the Rambler. "He gave her something to help with the nausea. If she's not better in a couple of days, I have to bring her back."

"Poor baby." Becky rubbed Beanie's head a couple of times and Beanie settled into a contented purr.

"Yeah." Julia snuggled Beanie next to her, feeling the soft fur against her skin. "I'm just glad the doctor agreed to see her at quitting time."

"That was nice," Becky agreed. Pulling the car into traffic, she said, "Remember I told you that I started a garden?"

"Yeah."

"Well, check out that bag in the back seat." Becky didn't bother in the least to hide her pride.

Julia pulled open the brown paper bag and spotted several ripe red tomatoes, a couple of cucumbers, and a big bowl full of green beans.

"This is swell, Becky." Julia refolded the paper bag. "You're so ambitious and I'm so, not." She laughed.

Becky shrugged. "You do what you've got to do." She hesitated a moment.

Julia could tell by Becky's expression that something was wrong. "What is it?"

"Well, I haven't had a chance to tell you, but Pop lost his job."

"Oh, no. I'm so sorry, Becky." The hum of the tires on the pavement echoed through the car. "Does he have other possibilities?"

"Not currently, but he'll find something."

Becky, always the optimist.

"Anyway, I'm happy I have the garden. It's not much, but every little bit helps. Mom has a garden, too, so we'll put our goods together for the family. Would you mind if I dropped the bag off at their house on our way home?"

"Not at all."

A wave of remorse settled over Julia—and shame. Becky was so good to her parents, and all Julia wanted was for her dad to move out of her house and her mother to leave her alone. Julia's thoughts rarely went to how she could make things better for them. Selfishness seemed to be at the root of her good deeds.

"Don't worry, we'll be fine," Becky said, misinterpreting Julia's silence.

"Oh yes, I'm sure you will." Julia stroked Beanie's back while the sick feline slept in her arms.

As Becky turned onto the country road where her parents lived, her car started to rattle and clank. Becky turned knobs, pounded here and there, but to no avail. With much effort, Becky guided the car to the side of the road, where it sputtered and coughed, backfired, hissed, then settled into silence beside a weedy ditch.

"Swell. This is just swell." Becky sighed and turned to Julia. "Well, at least Mom and Pop live just down the road," she said brightly. "And Pop has the time to look at my car since he's not working. God takes care of us, I'm tellin' ya."

Not only was Becky optimistic, but her trust in God never wavered. Julia wished she could claim the same, but she couldn't. Life just hadn't been that simple for her.

"Well, how are you girls?" Becky's mom wanted to know. "Here, sit at the table and I'll pour you some coffee. Or would you rather have lemonade?"

Due to the heat and the short, but hot, walk to the house, they decided on lemonade.

"Would you like some pie with your lemonade?" Mrs. Foster gave the pie plate a tempting wiggle.

The girls decided against it. With a glance around the farm kitchen, alive with percolating coffee, kids ranging from eight to twenty-five running hither and yon, the smell of homemade bread baking in the oven, and a fresh batch of blueberry muffins cooling on a rack, Julia soaked in the warmth of a real family. The only time her parents' home smelled this good was when Mother had stopped off at the bakery to pick up pies for a charity.

"Pop, I'm having trouble with my car again. It stalled right down the road. Julia and I had to walk here. Would you have a minute to look at it for me?"

"For you, sunshine, I'd make the time."

"Thanks, Pop."

"Better grab your lemonade and come down with me, though. I may need you to start it while I check out the engine."

"Okay." She turned to Julia. "I'll be right back."

"Don't you worry about Julia," her mother said. "I'll keep her company." Mrs. Foster smiled and slid into a chair at the table. "I know this is hard on her." She watched through the window as Becky walked down the road with her dad. "She tries to keep things secret, but I've seen her passing a dollar here and there to her sisters and brothers." Mrs. Foster dabbed at the corners of her eyes with the tip of her apron. "The good Lord smiled on us the day He gave Becky to us, that's for sure."

While Becky and her dad worked on the car, Julia passed the time listening and laughing at Mrs. Foster's family stories. What the Fosters lacked in monetary value, they more than made up with family.

Things would have been different for the Hilton family if Joe were still alive. Julia was sure of it.

CHAPTER FOURTEEN

Lukas fluffed the blanket into place on the beach while Julia picked up some small, flat rocks.

"What are those?" he asked as they found a spot on the blanket and he opened the picnic basket.

"Rocks."

He laughed. "I can see that. Do you collect them?"

"I make these gifts called Ebenezers. I usually get a wide clear glass bowl or a large vase and fill them halfway with flat rocks—rocks big enough to write on. They represent times of special meaning to the owner. Gifts from the Lord. It might be a baby gift with one rock announcing the baby's birth, another rock dating his first steps, that sort of thing. I normally add a candle in the middle, too, for decoration. You can do almost anything with them. It's a fun and meaningful gift."

"That's a really great idea."

"Yeah, our pastor came up with the idea, and I liked it so much that I decided to make them." Looking over the rocks she had just gathered she said, "These are just the right size for a message."

A slight breeze swirled their way, blowing over one edge of the blanket. Julia smoothed it back in place.

"It's a perfect night for this. Thanks for asking."

"Well, remember you said you didn't want a meal, just dessert. So here we are." He served her a piece of apple pie on a plastic plate.

"Please don't tell me you baked this."

"No, I can't take the credit. The bakery did it."

She pretended disappointment.

"Trust me, you wouldn't want me to make the pie."

She chuckled and he got his own piece of pie then poured hot coffee from a thermos. Once they got down to the business of eating and staring out onto the lake, Lukas wondered how he could approach her, find out why she dumped him—or Stefan, he should say. The need to know grew stronger every day.

"So you never did tell me how you knew the nephew of the prior owners of my house," Lukas said.

"Oh, I didn't?"

"No, you didn't."

"What made you think of that?"

"I found an old abstract of the house upstairs in the attic and it intrigued me. I thought it might be fun to search out more of its history."

"I don't know that I can help you all that much. The nephew's name was Stefan Zimmer. He used to spend the summers with his aunt and uncle in that house many years ago."

Well, at least she still remembered his name. That was something.

"Many years ago. You must have been a kid."

"Pretty much."

"Were you friends or what?"

"Or what." She laughed.

"What does that mean?"

"I'm sorry, do you mind if we don't talk about this?"

"Sore subject?"

"Sort of."

"If he was a jerk, let me at him," he said playfully, with his fists in striking position.

Julia laughed. "I don't think it would help that much now."

"Ah, so he *was* a jerk."

"You're still digging."

"Was he your boyfriend?"

"Still digging."

"Love gone bad."

"Are you a private investigator for him or something?"

He didn't want to push it too far, so he backed off. "Or something." This time he winked. "Want to take a walk?" he asked, wiping their plates with a napkin and putting them back into the basket.

"Sure. The pie was delicious, by the way."

"Thanks. I'll let the bakery know."

All this surface talk when what he really wanted to do was tear away the pretense and tell her who he really was and find out why she dropped him without so much as a good-bye. But he didn't dare. If she knew who he really was, she might not be honest about why she left him without a single word.

A soft glow of moonlight lit the beach while they strolled along. How many times had they walked along this very place, holding hands, talking of a future they would never share? Oh, how he wanted to grab her hand right this minute.

"How are things going with your parents? I still haven't seen your dad around."

"That's because he's staying at *my* house." The way Julia said that told him she wasn't enjoying the arrangement at all.

"Boy, that's tough. There's gotta be some way we can get them back together." They walked along the water's edge in silence. "What if your mom thought he was interested in someone else, would she be more willing to take him back? Or vice versa, maybe he thinks someone is interested in her?"

"Oh my, I've never thought of that." Julia giggled. "It could make or break them—or get me disinherited, I'm not sure which."

"Maybe you don't want to chance it?"

"I didn't say that. I'm desperate, believe me. I'll do just about anything to get my house back."

"Well, well. You just never know who you're gonna run into on the beach at night," a voice said.

Julia gasped.

"Are you all right?" George was staring at her.

"I'm fine. You just startled me, that's all."

"Sorry about that."

"George, what are you doing here?" To say Lukas was irritated was an understatement. George came to check up on him, pure and simple.

"Just out taking a walk, like you." George smiled, but Lukas wasn't buying it.

"Oh, there she is." George looked to his left. Julia and Lukas followed his gaze and spotted Becky.

"Becky, hi. Uh, what are you doing here?"

Julia looked positively embarrassed, as though she had been caught red-handed doing something she shouldn't have been doing.

The question was, why would she react that way? Was she embarrassed to be seen with him? Was it because he was a lowly construction worker? A German? Did she carry on her mother's prejudice? Surely that wasn't the case. The more he saw of this woman, the more he wondered if he ever really knew Julia at all.

Becky looked just as stunned to see Julia with Lukas.

"We're walking on the beach." Becky's gaze went from Julia to Lukas and back to Julia. "Looks like we all had the same idea. Did you two bump into each other out here?"

"Well, not exactly," Julia said.

"We're on a date. Dessert picnic," Lukas said proudly, leaving no room for George to doubt.

"I don't know that I would exactly call it a date," Julia said sheepishly.

"You wouldn't?" Lukas frowned. He wasn't at all sure he appreciated her response.

"You wouldn't?" George looked like a tiger eyeing its prey.

"Well, we didn't go out, per se. We just ate a piece of pie on the beach."

"Yes, but it was prearranged. Isn't that a date?" Lukas pressed.

Becky stood there, staring, gaping, and waiting.

"It's not like that, though. I mean, it's not as though we're"—she gestured with her hands—"'dating.' I mean, we're friends. Friends eating pie on the beach. And now we're walking on the beach. Just like me walking with you, George, or Becky. That's all."

George was clearly satisfied with her explanation.

Lukas wasn't. Why didn't she just knock him to the ground with a punch in the gut and kick him around a couple of times? This woman was a piece of work. He was stupid for putting himself through this. Discount or no discount, he'd get those repairs done. If he did them himself, it might take longer, but he'd get it done eventually.

Julia Hilton obviously had no interest in him. Which suited him just fine.

* * * * *

"I hope I didn't hurt your feelings back there," Julia said once Becky and George had left.

"Hurt my feelings? Not hardly," he said in a Marlboro Man sort of way. "Why would my feelings be hurt?"

His response took her aback a moment. Then she felt stupid. Of course it didn't hurt his feelings. Though he had mentioned he considered it a date, he obviously didn't think it was a big deal.

"Oh, no reason, I guess. I just, uh—"

"No problem." He glanced at his watch. "You know, it's getting late. We'd better head back so your mom won't worry about you, and I need to feed the dogs."

Okay, now that just made the hair on her neck stand up. "I'm hardly a teenager who needs to report to her parents."

"I understand." He made a face. "Just didn't want to cause you more trouble with your mother."

"I'm a big girl, Lukas. I think I can handle it." So caught up was she in their arguing that she didn't notice Eleanor Cooley and some guy coming their way until they were almost within earshot. Any other time, Julia would be thankful for a full moon, but not tonight. It was far too bright, and she knew without a doubt that Eleanor would recognize her with Lukas. Then she'd call Becky to collect her twenty-five dollars. Becky was certainly in no position financially to deal with that. Julia didn't have any money to spare either. She'd made way too many wardrobe purchases lately.

Footsteps headed their way. Approaching closer and closer.

She had to do something—and fast.

"Anyway, I'm sorry," Julia blurted. Then in one swift motion, she reached her hand behind Lukas's neck and pulled his face down to hers and kissed him full on the lips, praying all the while that Eleanor wouldn't recognize them.

While footsteps and a slight chuckle breezed on past them, Julia gave way to the strong arms that now enveloped her and lips that pressed gently upon her own. Everything in her screamed to pull away, but there was something so very comforting and familiar about his embrace. So strong, yet so tender—he held her as though she were fragile—

and yet she could sense he restrained himself, like a starving man at a steakhouse.

What she hadn't realized was that she was starving too.

* * * * *

Lukas hardly knew what hit him.

First, Julia was saying they weren't dating, and the next thing he knew, she kissed him, right in front of God and everybody. This woman was not who she seemed. He knew that was the pot calling the kettle black, but still. What was going on with her?

Right now, with her soft arms around his neck, the warmth of her lips upon his, he could hardly remember his name, let alone sort through all this. His mind was reeling, spinning out of control, and he didn't want to think—not so much as breathe—for fear she would pull away.

After a moment, she did. But one look in her eyes told him what he needed to know—their kiss had changed things—for both of them.

"I'm so sorry," she said. "I just don't know what came over me."

Cement seemed to hold his legs in place. He couldn't move a single muscle. He merely looked at her. She grabbed his hand and pulled him forward. "Come on, we'd better get you to your car and I have to get home, like you said."

Lukas wondered if the planets were in alignment or some cosmic transformation had taken place that caused this…miracle. A shooting star, perhaps? An alien life form had taken over her body? Maybe Orson Welles was back and it had something to do with *The War of the Worlds.* He glanced up at the sky. Whatever the explanation, he hoped it happened again.

When they reached his car, she said, "Thanks for a lovely time, Lukas. I really enjoyed myself. I'll see you tomorrow." Before a regular blood flow could course through his veins, she ran off toward her house.

Lukas watched as she slipped into the shadows of the night then he turned to put the key in his car door. Once he got inside and started the engine, he wondered if he would remember his way home.

* * * * *

"Where have you been?" Mother stood at the door, hair damp and stringy at neck level, eyes shadowed with dark circles, wrinkles setting deeper by the second around her mouth, arms folded across her chest.

Julia took off her sweater and hung it in the hall closet. "I thought you'd be in bed by now."

"I'm hot. Where have you been?"

"I'm not a teenager, Mother. I don't have to answer to you. But if you must know, I took a walk on the beach." She wasn't about to tell her who she took the walk with. In her mother's current mood, she could very well fire Lukas from the job.

Her mother pressed a hand against her forehead and drew out her words with great drama, "How many times have I told you not to walk on the beach alone at night?" She walked over and dropped onto the sofa with a groan. Julia wasn't sure if the groan came from her mother or the sofa.

"What's the matter?" Julia went to her. "Are you all right?"

"I've got a bad headache."

"Why don't you go back to bed and I'll get you a cool cloth for your head. Have you taken anything?" Julia walked toward the medicine cabinet in the bathroom.

"Not yet. I was just getting up to do that when you came in."

Julia picked a washcloth from the linen closet, ran it under cold water, then wrung it out. She plucked two aspirin from the medicine cabinet and grabbed a glass of cold water in the kitchen.

"Here you go," Julia said when she entered her parents' bedroom. Once her mother took the meds, she lay back down on her pillow. Julia folded the cool cloth and placed it across her mother's forehead, then she adjusted the blankets around her, making sure she was warm and comfortable.

"Don't do that. I'm hot." Her mother whipped off the covers.

There were no words to describe her mother's moods these days. Julia envied her dad, sleeping in the comfortable bed in her guest room, enjoying the silence of her home, eating her food.

The coward.

"Well, let me know if you need anything. I'm going to bed. Good night, Mother."

"Thank you, dear."

For a moment, Julia stopped, wondering if she heard correctly. Was her mother having one of those rare moments of tenderness? An out-of-body experience? Was Gabriel calling her home?

"Get your own breakfast in the morning. I'm sleeping in. And don't clang around with the dishes. It annoys me," her mother said.

If it was Gabriel calling, Julia was certain that with that comment, he left without her.

Moments of tenderness in the Hilton household, fleeting and few, taunted Julia's heart with whispers of what could be.

Despite the late hour, Julia picked out a lake rock from her stash and wrote on it. "Shared my first kiss with Lukas." Not ready for anyone to see that, she plunked the rock in a box, wondering if it would one day find its way to an Ebenezer jar....

CHAPTER FIFTEEN

Julia had just gotten her morning coffee and sat down at the kitchen table when she heard the grinding noise of a motorcycle pull up in the driveway.

"What are you doing here?"

Her mother's voice almost echoed the motorcycle engine, loud, irritating, menacing. Julia decided she'd better see what was going on. Grabbing her mug of coffee, she wandered into the front hallway to see who had come calling. No amount of coffee could have prepared her for the vision in the doorway.

Grabbing the bill of his black cap, her dad took it off and stood before them dressed in a black jacket and dark pants. James Dean came to mind.

"I live here," came her dad's response.

Her mother stomped over to the door, glanced outside, and gasped. "Do you mean to tell me that you bought a—a...motorcycle?"

A red flush crawled up her mother's neck and onto her face.

"I did," her dad said, practically rocking on his heels.

Julia had never seen her dad look so alive. She hoped it lasted.

"You can't be serious."

Her mother's voice had reached a pitch high enough to touch the heavens. Julia hoped for her mother's sake that God didn't hear it.

"I am serious," Dad said with a grin. "And I'm having the time of my life."

Another gasp. Julia wasn't sure if it came from her mother or herself. She only knew things were sure to go downhill from here.

"I need to sit down." Her mother headed for the living room, with Dad following behind her.

Out of curiosity—or stupidity—Julia joined them.

"Good morning, Jules," Dad said.

Julia gave him a peck on the cheek. "Morning, Dad."

"Did you see my new bike?" Excitement lit his eyes and his face glowed.

"No, I haven't seen it yet." Julia dared a peek at her mother to see if she was still with them or if she'd gone on to glory.

"You'll have to see it before I leave."

"Why are you here?" Mother demanded.

"I wanted to see how the room addition was coming along."

A flicker of hurt crossed her mother's face. For a fraction of a second, Julia felt sorry for her.

"It's coming along fine, no thanks to you." Her mother's chin could have touched the ceiling. "While you're acting like a teenager, I'm handling the responsibilities of home."

"Margaret, why don't you go to the doctor so he can give you some pills and I can come home?"

"You mean to say I have to have pills before you'll come home?" Her stare pinned him in place.

He sighed. "I cannot stay here if you're the same as you were on the trip. I've never been more miserable in my whole life. And that trip was meant to be a once-in-a-lifetime memory for us."

"Well, it certainly was that," she quipped.

Julia's heart hurt for both her parents. She had to get her mother to the doctor. Something was definitely wrong.

"See what I mean," her dad said with another sigh of resignation. "Guess I won't be coming home for a while."

Mother stood to her feet. "Maybe you'd better not come home at all," she said.

"If that's the way you want it." Julia's dad got up and walked out the front door.

Before Julia could say anything, her mother stomped off to her bedroom and slammed the door. When Julia walked past her mother's room, she heard her soft cries.

* * * * *

"Oh, Becky, it was awful. I wish I knew what to do to help them. Mom won't go to the doctor and Dad won't come home until she finds out what's wrong and deals with it." Julia took another sip from her cherry Coke.

A young girl plunked a nickel in the jukebox and played Doris Day singing "Que Sera, Sera."

"I'm sorry. That has to be tough. For the life of me I can't imagine your dad driving a motorcycle." Becky chuckled and slurped on her chocolate malt.

Julia chuckled too. It *was* pretty funny. "He thinks he's James Dean."

After a coughing spell, Becky put her hand to her chest and laughed. "Oh my, I can't even imagine."

Julia's father was a thin, wiry sort of fellow with a crew cut and black horn-rimmed glasses that did precious little to promote the James Dean image.

"Well, well, well. You just never know who you'll run into at Cindy's Soda Shop."

Julia and Becky glanced up to see Eleanor Cooley with another woman standing beside her. The other woman had piercing blue eyes the size of walnuts and was dressed in the latest fashion in colors that complemented her eyes and long, raven-black hair.

"Hello, Eleanor," Julia finally said. She glanced at Becky, whose face had turned the color of cooked oatmeal.

"This is my friend, Vicki Cramer. You remember her, don't you, Becky?" Something in the way Eleanor said that, coupled with the color of Becky's face, told Julia this was a problem.

"Yes."

"I thought you might." Another syrupy smile from Eleanor.

"Vicki's just moved back to town and I wanted to reacquaint her with as many people as possible as she settles in."

The smile on Vicki's face looked almost identical to Eleanor's. Two Eleanors in the same city—such a cruel possibility made Julia seriously question her faith.

"By the way," the other woman piped up, "Jack turned out to be a real bore. Be thankful I spared you."

Pain shadowed Becky's expression and Julia couldn't imagine what this was all about.

"Well, we'll talk to you later." Eleanor started to lead her friend away from the table then turned back to them. "By the way, Julia, we may stop by your mother's in a couple of days. I'd like for Vicki to meet those cute men who are working on your house. Bye-bye." They turned and strutted out of the soda shop.

Once they left, Julia turned to Becky, who had moved her unfinished chocolate malt aside.

"What was that all about?" she asked.

Becky just sat there a minute. Finally she sighed and leaned in to Julia. "I guess it's time I told you. I had hoped my past would stay there, but it seems it has come back to taunt me."

"What?" Julia had no clue where this was going.

"Before I knew you, I was engaged."

Julia's mouth dropped. She couldn't have been more surprised if President Eisenhower had stepped down from his position.

"His name was Jack Ramsey. Two weeks before the wedding, he told me he had met someone else and had fallen in love. Her name was Vicki Cramer. They left town together, leaving me alone to pick up the pieces and deal with small-town gossip."

Julia reached over and grabbed Becky's hand. "Oh, Beck, I'm so sorry."

Becky dug in her purse for a tissue and blotted the tears on her face. "Isn't this silly. After all these years and I'm still crying about it."

"That had to hurt so very much."

"That's an understatement."

"How cruel for Eleanor to bring her over here. That woman is just plain evil."

Becky shrugged. "Life goes on. It's time for me to let go. In fact, I thought I had let it go years ago, and yet, the minute I'm face-to-face with the past, I crumble all over again."

Julia wondered how she would react if she ever saw Stefan again. She'd probably do the same thing. Though she doubted she would ever have the chance one way or the other.

"There goes George. Once Vicki gets her hooks in him, I won't stand a chance."

"Oh, Beck, that's not true and you know it. George likes you. He'll see right through them."

Becky shrugged. "I'm just glad you aren't dating Lukas. I won't have to worry about you getting hurt."

"Right," Julia assured her, ignoring the rumble of unsettled nerves in her stomach.

"Can we go now?" Becky asked.

"Sure."

They got up and left the table, leaving their tip behind. It hurt Julia to the core to see Becky this way. And though Julia and Lukas weren't in a serious relationship, she wasn't ready for it to end before it even got started. By the time they climbed into their cars, Julia had made up her mind.

It was time to roll up her sleeves and get tough.

* * * * *

Lukas hadn't talked to Julia since their infamous kiss a few days ago. Hammering in a final nail on the board of his boat, he stretched his back and glanced at his watch. When he had gotten home from work, he'd fed his critters then gone to work on the boat, forgetting to eat dinner. He guessed he'd go in the house and grab a sandwich then come back out to finish up. He still had a bit more framing to do on the boat before he would call it a night.

Boat making calmed him. He'd always loved working with his hands. The summers spent building boats with his uncle had given him a love for the work. There was so much more to enjoying a boat than just taking it out into the water.

Walking out of the barn, he headed toward the house. Scooter hobbled alongside him. The three-legged hound seemed to grow more trusting every day and had finally settled in to his new life. Lukas reached down and rubbed the scruff of the golden retriever's neck.

After washing his hands, Lukas cut a slab from yesterday's meatloaf, placed it between two slices of bread, loaded it with ketchup, then put it on a plate with a hefty serving of potato chips.

"Knock, knock, anybody home?" George stood at the back screen door.

"Hey, come on in. Just making myself a meatloaf sandwich. Want one?"

"No, thanks. I had a hamburger for dinner." George sat in a chair at the table. "Why are you just now getting to dinner?"

"Got busy with my boat."

"Oh, yeah, how's that coming?"

"It's coming along all right. The framing is almost finished."

George shook his head. "That's amazing. You really could go into business."

Lukas started to take a bite of his sandwich but stopped to ask, "What brought you over here tonight? Were you bored?"

"Yeah, I guess." George looked up, bright-eyed. "No offense."

"None taken." A bite of sandwich and a drink of iced tea. "You want to help me with the boat?"

"Sure, if you trust me."

"If I trust you? You trusted me with a room addition. Of course I trust you."

"You've done a great job too. Hey, what do you think is going on with Julia's parents? When her dad came over this week, that was the first time I'd seen him."

"I don't know for sure. Julia mentioned to me that they were having some problems, but I don't really know what it's all about."

"After dealing with her mother, I have my suspicions," George said.

Lukas laughed. "Yeah, I know what you mean."

"Can you imagine having to live with that woman?"

"No, I can't." The thought that Lukas should be grateful for his narrow escape from the family occurred to him. Still, his love for Julia had been so strong, he felt sure it could have gotten him through dealing with her mother.

He was positively sure.

Well, pretty sure.

Ninety-nine percent sure.

"I'm not even convinced the money she's paying us for this job is worth what she's putting us through."

"Yeah, she's pretty up and down about it, I must admit," Lukas said.

"It's a good thing Julia isn't like her mother."

"She doesn't appear to be."

"How do you feel about her, anyway?" George asked, helping himself to a glass of iced tea.

Lukas shrugged. "She's all right, I guess." He ate the last bite of sandwich and shoved his plate away from him.

"Just all right?" George grinned. "Looks to me like you two hit it off pretty well."

"Well, I'm not ready to march down the aisle, if that's what you mean." Little did George know how close Lukas had come to doing that very thing. But now? He had no intention of marching down the aisle with Julia or anyone else. Julia had seen to that. She held his heart prisoner, refused to release it, and still held tightly to her own.

"Besides, I could say the same for you and Becky," he said.

"Yeah, she's all right." George's eyes perked at the mention of Becky's name.

Lukas rubbed his jaw and smiled. "Looks to me like she's more than 'all right' in your book."

"Let's just say I'm enjoying the journey, but I'm taking things nice and slow."

"Always a good idea," Lukas said, all the while wondering just where his relationship with Julia would end up. What was he thinking? Nothing good could come from it. She had made that clear years ago. Yet, that kiss would indicate she liked him at least a little—the new him. But why didn't she want other people to know they were together?

That bothered him a lot. And what would she think if she knew who he really was? Not that it was likely, but what if she actually fell in love with the new Lukas? Would he be happy or sad about that? Of course, there was no denying that he had once fallen madly in love with her, but the pain she had caused him built a brick wall that he wasn't sure even she could break through. How could he ever trust her again? The truth was he didn't know if he wanted to trust her. What kind of woman would do what she did—declare her undying love then drop him cold once he went off to war?

Yes, Julia was beautiful. There was no denying that. But he was old enough to know that it took more than beauty to hold a relationship together. He thought he knew her—those many years ago.

Now, he wasn't so sure.

CHAPTER SIXTEEN

Lukas was thankful for the weekend. He grabbed his sandwich and headed for his sofa to kick his feet up on the coffee table and watch TV. Just as he took a bite, he heard a motorcycle pull into his driveway followed by a knock on his front door. Dropping his sandwich onto the plate, he brushed his hands together and went to the door, Sauerkraut nipping at his heels and barking wildly.

"Mr. Hilton. Come on in." Lukas was surprised to see Julia's dad in his doorway.

"Sorry to bother you, Lukas. I went over to George's house, but he wasn't there, so I thought I'd try you."

"Is there a problem?"

"No, no problem. It's just that I didn't get a chance to talk with you two the other day when I was at the house, and I really didn't want to go back to the house right now." Mr. Hilton looked a bit embarrassed. "I wanted to let you fellas know what a great job you're doing, and I wanted to tell you not to worry about what my wife says. She's just not herself these days."

Unfortunately, Lukas remembered all too well his encounters with Mrs. Hilton, and she seemed exactly herself.

"Well, that was very kind of you to come all the way over here to tell me that."

"I saw the door open to your barn, so I checked for you there first and spotted a fishing boat in the making. Are you building it?"

"Yes sir." Lukas couldn't help feeling a smidgen of pride.

"It's a fine boat. A very fine boat, indeed. Is this a side business for you?"

"Not yet. Maybe one day."

"Well, you certainly should consider the idea."

"Thank you, Mr. Hilton."

"Say, I don't suppose you'd consider designing a boat for me? A fishing boat? I love to fish and haven't had near the time to do so...until recently. It's time I had a little fun."

"Sure, I'd be happy to build you a fishing boat. I can't promise how soon I'd be finished with it, since I'm working on your house and plan to start some renovations on my own house, but I can build it."

"That's good enough for me. I won't expect it for this summer, but I can enjoy it next year. Maybe by then I can talk the missus into enjoying it with me."

That comment relieved Lukas.

They walked into the barn and talked about the details for Mr. Hilton's boat. They settled upon a price and Mr. Hilton moved toward the door to leave.

"Hey, I have a good friend who has a boat like the one I'd like you to make. Maybe I could contact him and take you out on it. Would you be willing?"

"That would be swell," Lukas said.

"Okay, I'll be in touch." Mr. Hilton gave a salute, climbed onto his Harley, and drove away.

Life could be strange sometimes. The last thing Lukas considered when he moved here was that he would one day make a boat or work on a room addition for the parents of the woman he had loved—especially knowing how much Julia's mother had hated him.

* * * * *

Julia and Becky walked along the sidewalk, quietly lost in their own thoughts. Julia took a deep breath of the muggy air while hoping she might drop a few calories. That was what she got for indulging in a donut for breakfast.

Her thoughts flitted to the kiss she had shared with Lukas. She might laugh as she remembered the surprise in his eyes when she kissed him, if the idea of it didn't absolutely mortify her. What must he think of her for being so bold?

On the other hand, she couldn't deny the wonder of it. Not just the feel of his strong arms around her, but something in it that felt so...right. It had a certain déjà vu feel to it, though she knew that was silly.

She sensed Becky studying her and decided to probe Becky's thoughts before her friend started probing into hers.

"You're awfully quiet today. Is everything all right?" Julia asked.

"Yeah. Guess I've just got some things on my mind."

"Such as?"

"Oh, Etta is depressed again. She hasn't seen that Stefan guy anymore and she's sulking that she didn't give him her phone number. Never mind that he didn't ask her for it. She's sure he would have called her by now if he had it." Becky sighed.

Julia ignored the twinge of jealousy that twisted in her stomach. How ridiculous. There must be many Stefans out there. This couldn't be *her* Stefan.

"What about Jimmie?"

"He's out of the picture too. Got another girlfriend. Etta ran into them last night at the store. She came home, raided the refrigerator, went to bed, and cried herself to sleep. She thinks she's a loser if she doesn't have a guy."

"Oh, poor thing. If only she could learn to be happy without a guy. That's usually when a good one comes along," Julia said. "And besides, what does that make me?"

"Uh-oh," Becky said teasingly. "What does that make you?"

"Exactly." They took a few paces in silence.

"So what was the deal with you and Lukas the other night—that dessert thing on the beach?"

Julia had known this conversation would happen sooner or later. "Nothing, really. We met up on the beach and he had some dessert, asked me to join him." She wasn't exactly lying, after all. They did meet up on the beach. He did have dessert, and he did ask her to join him. So she left out the part that it was a planned meeting.

"So you're not dating him, right?"

"Right," Julia said.

"Do you think you'd ever want to?"

"Oh, no, no," Julia assured her friend. With Becky's dad off work and their family money problems, Julia didn't want to add to her worries.

"I can't tell you how much better that makes me feel." Becky took a deep breath and blew it out.

Julia couldn't deny the shadow that crossed her heart.

They were almost back to Becky's house when Becky said, "Hey, maybe we could introduce Lukas to my sister—you know, before Vicki Cramer gets her hooks in him."

Julia agreed and smiled, ignoring the twinge of regret that filled her. Becky started up the sidewalk, but Julia glanced over at her own house. "Hey, since Dad's not at my house, I think I'll go over there for a little bit. Maybe pick up a few things."

Becky grinned. "Missing your stuff, huh?"

Her friend's comments about hoarding always irritated Julia. "Something like that. See you later." She turned and walked to her house. Finally a minute to herself without her mother hovering over her.

She walked in the front door and groaned. There was no question that her dad was used to people picking up after him. Her place was a mess. His clothes were strewn about, bowls of leftover popcorn, stray socks, and sections of newspaper dissected from the whole of it littered her living room.

Pulling in a deep breath, she braced herself for the kitchen. The stale scent of neglected food reached her before she arrived. A milk carton with milk still in it, old milk, as in sour milk, sat on her table. The sink bulged with dirty dishes.

This could not go on. She had to get her dad out before he single-handedly destroyed her house. A quick check of the rest of the house didn't fare any better. Bottles of Vitalis cluttered her bathroom sink. What on earth her dad needed Vitalis for, she hadn't a clue. He had a crew cut, for crying out loud. She shook her head. Her mother was right. He was an easy prey for advertisers.

Julia spent the next hour washing dishes and straightening her house. As much as she hated to admit it, seeing her house in disarray this way made her realize just how much clutter she had of her own. Maybe Becky was right. She did hoard things.

With a glance toward the attic, she realized it had been ages since she'd been up there. True, she brought her Christmas tree down from the attic once a year, but she never really looked around at the other boxes.

The next thing she knew, she was up in the attic, going through old, dusty boxes that held memories of her childhood. Her Raggedy Ann doll and her Madame Alexander dolls, a ballerina doll, babies—even her Scarlett O'Hara doll that she got when she turned fifteen. Another box had all her paper dolls impressively stored away in impeccable shape. She remembered how she loved playing paper dolls, but now, from the looks of them, she wondered how much her mother let her really play with them.

After rummaging through a few more boxes, she realized it would take her days to go through everything. Maybe she'd come back later and take a stroll down memory lane.

A car door alerted her to her father's arrival. She guessed he wasn't in the mood to ride his motorcycle today.

After she closed the boxes, she carefully made her way across the attic floor and headed downstairs. Suddenly realizing her car was still in Becky's driveway, she decided she'd better let her dad know she was there. She edged her way toward the living room then heard him talking on the phone.

"Hey, listen, we need to keep our meetings discreet. You understand. Till the time is right. See you soon." He hung up the phone.

A wave of nausea hit Julia. Was Dad making a date with someone? Her breathing came in short, shallow puffs. She had to do something. But what?

She drew in a ragged breath and eased around the corner.

"Hi, Dad."

He turned to look at her. "My goodness, Jules, you could give a fella some warning before scaring him like that."

"I'm sorry."

"What are you doing here?" he asked.

What was *she* doing here?

"I live here."

He chuckled. "Oh, that's right." He glanced around. "That's why it's so clean."

No mention of "I'll be leaving soon. Oh, I'm sorry, honey, I'll get out of here before you know it."

"Dad, what is going on?" She sat down beside him on the sofa where he was now cracking open peanut shells and popping the nuts into his mouth. Shells dropped into a bowl with occasional misses scattered along the floor.

"What do you mean?" He popped another one.

Her dad was normally a patient, gentle, organized, and somewhat tidy man. Julia didn't know this man who sat beside her, making the room smell like a peanut factory.

He threw a peanut in the air and maneuvered his mouth into position to catch it on its way down. Once he claimed it, he chomped heartily and gave a closed-mouth triumphant grin.

Julia's parents were starting to frighten her. "Dad, are you listening to me?"

He threw another peanut higher and had to work a little harder to get his mouth in position. He missed. It lay to rest with the others on the floor. He snapped his fingers and went back to business.

When he turned his head, all air squeezed from Julia's lungs. "Are you growing—are you growing sideburns?"

"Are they even? I told my barber to make sure they were even." His eyes held worry.

There were no words. In her brain. Anywhere.

He cracked open another shell. "It's all the rage, you know. That Elvis fellow started it." He turned to her and grinned. "Bet you didn't even know I knew about Elvis." Another chomp on peanuts. "Bet you didn't know your dad could be cool."

She thought this thing between her parents was a passing thing. That they'd be over it in a few days, but with the way her mother was acting and now her dad, she didn't know what to think. Her earlier compassion evaporated.

She rose to her feet, crossed her arms across her chest, and tapped her foot on the floor. "Dad, when are you going home?"

Now he looked worried. He stood up. "I'm sorry, Jules. You're not going to make me go home yet, are you? I just can't take your mother's ups and downs right now. I'm tired. She tosses and turns all night, I can't sleep." He put his hands on Julia's arms. "Just give us a little more time, please, Jules? I'm trying, I really am. I figure it will get better once the remodeling is finished."

Everything in her screamed for her to tell her dad to go home, but one look in his sweet, gentle face, and she couldn't do it. He had done so much for her over the years, loving her when she felt her mother didn't, how could she not do the same for him?

He took the fight right out of her. "All right. But please promise me you'll get things worked out with Mother soon. I want to come home."

He gave her a soft kiss on the forehead. "I promise, sweet girl. Just help me work on her, to get her to go to the doctor." He thumped down on the sofa. "Whether it's menopause or something else, she needs to be checked out. I suspect she's concerned too, and that makes her cross."

"Well, then why doesn't she go?"

"Jules, you know your mother." He popped another peanut into his mouth. "She thinks if she ignores a problem, it will go away. If the doctor doesn't tell her there's a problem, then she doesn't have one. Do you see?"

"I see." Julia sighed. "Well, I'd better go. I'll talk to you later." She gave him a hug good-bye. Just as she opened the front door, she turned to him. "Please, be careful. Don't do anything—anything—well, just be careful. Mother loves you in her own way."

"I know."

A fifty-pound weight seemed to slow her steps to the car. A couple more months and she could go back to school where life was normal.

CHAPTER SEVENTEEN

After church Julia got a bite to eat and went back to her house. Her dad said he would be gone today. She thought maybe he was meeting with the mystery person he talked to yesterday. If only she knew where they were going, she would have followed him there to find out if he was meeting another woman.

This was her life. Reduced to snooping. She sighed and shoved the key into her front door and pushed it open. Surprisingly, her dad had cleaned up the littered peanuts. The living room actually looked clean and inviting. He must have felt guilty when she came over and caught the place in such a mess. Good. Maybe he'd be more careful from here on out.

She pulled her suitcase into her bedroom, emptied out the dirty clothes, sorted them, and threw them in the washer. It was silly, of course, for her to bring dirty clothes home and wash them when she could do it at her mother's. Still, she preferred to use her own machine. It gave her another reason to stick around her house awhile. And her mother couldn't see Julia's clothes and complain about them.

She poured a generous amount of Tide into the washer and closed the lid. Then she went back into her bedroom to pull out some clean clothes for the week. If her parents didn't patch things up pretty soon, she'd go crazy. Living out of a suitcase was no way to live.

Unmentionables jammed her drawers full. When Julia started to pull out what she needed, a tangled heap tumbled to the floor. When had she collected so many clothes? She didn't wear half of the things in this drawer. She eased open the next drawer. More of the same. Clothes for when her weight shifted, tops she never got around to wearing, some out of style now. Some she wondered why she ever bought in the first place. Why did things look better at the store than they did at home?

She poured the contents of that drawer onto the floor too. Kneeling, she sat back on her haunches and surveyed the mountain of clothes. Many of them her mother had purchased for her. She and her mother didn't share the same fashion tastes. Which would explain why she had never worn them.

Thoughts of her parents' latest struggle crowded Julia's mind while she sorted through the clothes. They had had a decent marriage up till now. How could things have gotten so out of hand? Had something happened on their trip—something they weren't telling her? She knew her mother could be difficult, but that was nothing new. Her dad had lived with that for years. Now, all of a sudden, he couldn't take it anymore. She didn't get it.

An unpleasant thought jolted through her. If there was another woman, it would explain why he no longer wanted to deal with Mother's complaining.

Another woman.

The very idea sickened Julia. If there had been one thing she could always count on, it was her parents' relationship. Her dad had never wavered in his responsibility to Mother or to Julia.

Unbidden tears fell from her eyes onto her cheeks. The more she tried to wipe them away, the more they fell. It was as though a storm had gathered without warning and wreaked havoc on her emotions. A torrential rainfall had come out of nowhere and flooded her cheeks. Tears for her parents, tears for the relationship she wanted with her mother but didn't have, tears for the loss of her brother, tears for the one true love she had and lost, tears for Becky's dad and his job loss. Tears, tears, tears.

"Please, God, help my parents through this—this—whatever 'this' is. Help them to work things out." She grabbed a handkerchief from her pile of clothes. With great resolve, she walked over to the lake rocks she had in her bedroom closet, pulled one out, and wrote, "God heard my plea for my parents." She eased it into a jar—her Ebenezer jar. No better time than the present to start one for herself—though she still wasn't ready to put in the rock about her kiss with Lukas. Maybe one day…

By the time she dried her tears and sorted through the clothes, she figured there was enough for Becky's sisters to fight over. Most likely Etta would get most of them, which was fine with Julia. She wanted to help in any way she could.

Once the laundry was done and her fresh clothes were packed in her suitcase, Julia had a couple of boxes of clothes to take to Becky's. She packed it all in the car and headed to her friend's to drop off the boxes.

"Hey, girl," Becky said when she opened the door.

Julia stumbled into the door with the first box. The sweet aroma of oatmeal cookies baking drifted through the house.

"What's this?"

Dropping the box on the floor, Julia stood and dusted her hands together. With a wide grin she said, "I thought your sisters could use these clothes. I haven't worn them in a long time or they're the wrong size or whatever. Anyway, if they want them, they can have them. If not, feel free to give them to anyone who can use them."

Becky stared at her.

"What?"

"You look like Julia. Your voice sounds like Julia. But the Julia I know never parts with anything—ever."

"Well, there's a first time for everything, right?" Another grin. Julia just couldn't help herself. There was no denying how good it made her feel to share her things and clean her house at the same time.

"Truly, I'm proud of you. This is a big step."

"Thank you, Dr. Foster," Julia said with a curtsy. "I'll be right back. There's one more box out in the car." Julia ran to the car and brought in the second box and gave it to Becky.

"This is really sweet of you. Thank you." Becky put the box on the floor with the other one then turned back to Julia.

"So are you going to offer me some of those yummy cookies baking in the oven?" Julia said with a grin.

"Sure. Come on into the kitchen." Becky led the way and grabbed some glasses from the cupboard. "Oh, doggone it, I'm out of milk. Will you check the milk box on the porch to see if the milkman has come yet?"

"Yeah." Julia stepped out the front door, opened the lid to the milk box, and pulled out a fresh carton of milk. "Here you go."

"Wonderful." He must have just come.

"I never knew they would deliver on Sundays."

"They don't. His wife was sick yesterday and he stayed home. Asked me if he could bring it today and I told him he could." Becky poured the milk, placed some warm cookies on a plate, and took them to the table.

"Thanks," Julia said.

"Hey, how come your eyes are red? Are your allergies bothering you again?"

"Oh, just concerned about my parents," Julia said, deciding she wasn't confiding any more than Becky already knew.

Becky covered Julia's hand with her own. "I'm so sorry, Julia. Things aren't any better?"

Julia swallowed back fresh tears and shook her head.

"They'll come around. You know your parents love each other. I wonder if your dad is going through some kind of age crisis."

Julia looked at her. "Do you think so?"

Becky settled on the sofa and motioned Julia to a nearby chair. "It's possible. I've heard of things like that before." She took a bite from her cookie.

"Me too. Though I must admit I hadn't thought of that." Julia dunked her cookie in the milk then carefully bit off a piece. "You know what else he's doing?"

"What?"

"Growing sideburns."

Becky's eyes were about as large as the cookie she held in her hand. "You don't mean it."

"Yes, I do. He blamed it on Elvis."

Becky started laughing and couldn't stop herself. Despite her own sorrow, Julia joined her. It seemed her emotions were going from one extreme to another today, so she just gave in to them and enjoyed a good fit of laughter.

"Oh my, that was so funny. You know, Julia, maybe you should talk to Lukas or George about it. They already know there's a problem, and maybe they could help you from a guy's perspective. What do you think?"

"I've talked to Lukas about it a little, but not a lot."

"Just an idea."

Julia felt sure she could talk to Lukas about it some more. Friends could talk about most anything. And they were friends, weren't they?

* * * * *

"Brought you guys a drink," Julia said, placing a tray of cookies and glasses of iced tea on a worktable away from the insulation and sheets of drywall that littered the room addition.

"You're a doll," George said.

"You don't know how happy I am to hear that." Lukas stepped off the ladder and swiped his arm across his forehead. "Hey, cookies too."

"I need to get some more turpentine for these brushes," George said. "I'll be right back."

He stepped outside and Julia edged over to Lukas, her heart pounding, nerves gnawing at her stomach.

"Um, Lukas, do you think you could meet with me after work today?" she asked him.

To say he looked surprised was an understatement. First she kissed him, then she asked him to meet with her. What kind of woman would he take her for?

"I need to talk to you about something, if you have the time." There. Now he would know it wasn't a date or anything like that. Relief touched his face. She didn't know if she liked that or not.

"Yeah. I don't have anything going on tonight."

Did that mean if he had something better to do, he wouldn't meet with her? The more she stood there, the more annoyed she got.

"Great. How about we just meet down at the beach where we met the last time? You know, near that old boulder?"

Was it her imagination or did she see a shadow cross his face?

"Yeah, I remember. I'll be there. What time?"

"Is nine o'clock too late?"

"Nine o'clock is fine," he said.

"Thanks." Julia turned to see George standing in the doorway. She hoped he hadn't heard anything or he would tell Becky. Wait.

Becky was the one who suggested she talk to one of them. She would understand this. It wasn't a date.

"See you guys later." Julia edged out the door and hurried off to the house. Though why she hurried, she didn't know. Her mother awaited her inside.

* * * * *

"You dog, you. How do you do it?" George looked at Lukas with pure awe in his eyes.

Lukas knew what he was thinking, that this was a date. George hadn't really given him a definition for the term "date." This could very well be considered a date by some. Who was he to argue?

Lukas shrugged.

"This is number two, isn't it? Double-dating doesn't count." George grabbed his iced tea and slumped against the drywall that was yet unpainted.

"I guess it is at that," Lukas said with a grin. Evidently, George had decided to count the date on the beach, despite Julia denying it was a date. "Looks like I'll be getting that deep discount on my house."

"You're not there yet," George said, between bites of his cookie. "Three times, that was the deal."

"No problem."

George shook his head. "I don't get it."

"What do you mean?"

"No offense, but Becky told me Julia wasn't interested in dating you."

Lukas's eyes darted to George. "What? How did that come up? Did you tell her about our bet?"

"Oh, no, no. I was just trying to dig out Julia's feelings for you, you know, to see if she would date you again. So I asked Becky what she thought. Then she told me that Julia said she liked you as a friend, but that was it. She wasn't interested in you that way."

"Well, evidently my charms are getting to her." Lukas forced a teasing grin, but George's comment had stripped the fun mood right out of him. Was she stringing him along—again? Reaching for the bag of insulation, he hauled it up the ladder.

He was too close to turn back now. He'd get her to agree to one more date for George's benefit and for his own benefit financially. By then he'd be done with their room addition and he could get away from Julia Hilton for good.

* * * * *

When George and Lukas finished work for the day, they stacked the drywall, put away their tools, and loaded up George's truck. Just as they were prepared to leave, a pink Cadillac pulled into the driveway behind them.

"Well, hello, boys." Eleanor exited the car on one side, while another beautiful woman exited on the other. "I was hoping to catch you before you left I wanted to introduce you to my friend, Vicki Cramer. Vicki is new to town. Well, she used to live here, but that was a long time ago, so I'm reacquainting her with people."

"Hi," Lukas said, taking in Vicki's long black hair and blue eyes. Her beauty was undeniable. Still, he'd given his heart away a long time ago.

"This is George and Lukas."

Vicki shook George's hand then Lukas's. He started to pull away and she held it a little longer, batting her eyelashes for emphasis. He smiled politely and eased his hand from hers.

Julia stepped out the front door looking none too pleased, but when the others turned around she smiled. Maybe she and her mother had been arguing.

"Eleanor, Vicki, what are you doing here?"

Something in her voice made Lukas wonder what was wrong.

Eleanor explained that she wanted Vicki to meet the guys.

"By the way, boys, I'm throwing a little party tonight, so Vicki can meet people, and I thought you might want to come along. George, you can bring Becky. Lukas, maybe you could keep Vicki entertained?"

Vicki looked at him as though he were a hamburger and french fries. He shifted on his feet. One glance at Julia and a vision of her with a bow and arrow popped into his mind—and he was the target. What was that all about? She'd only been out here a few minutes. He couldn't have done anything wrong already.

"Oh, and of course, Julia, you'll come. You're a part of the group. You won't need a date. I won't have one either. You can help me hostess." Eleanor acted as though she'd just given Julia the best news.

Lukas wasn't sure Julia saw it that way.

"How about it, Lukas?" Eleanor said.

"Well, Julia and I—"

"Sure, we'd all love to come," Julia said.

"Great. I'll see you all around five thirty." Eleanor gave a wave and she and Vicki got back in their car and drove off.

Lukas turned around to ask Julia about their "date," but she was already gone.

He wasn't at all sure what just happened.

CHAPTER EIGHTEEN

The last thing Julia wanted to do was show up at Eleanor's little party without a date. That woman made her feel like such a loser. Still, she would show Eleanor it didn't bother her one bit that Lukas was with Vicki and she was, well, dateless.

Had she imagined it or did Lukas light up when she came around to the backyard where they were all mingling? One glance at Vicki, and she doubted it. Vicki was a total knockout. The latest fashions enhanced her body in all the right places. What guy wouldn't be crazy about her? Before Julia could reach the others, her mood had already swung south.

Lukas looked at her with a grin and opened his mouth to speak. Unfortunately, before he could utter a single sound, Eleanor seemed to swoop down upon them like a hungry gull.

"Julia, so glad you could make it," she said in a syrupy voice. She linked her arm into Julia's. "After all, I didn't want to be the only one without a date."

So kind of her to point that out.

Eleanor's house overlooked the lake. Large windows flanked the back. A large patio beckoned guests to linger and visit. Julia was less than impressed; after all, she had grown up in such an environment, even though her own little house wasn't nearly as elaborate. She had refused her parents' help to buy a "better" place. For years her heart had been fixed upon her current home, and she'd never considered another place. Lakeside or otherwise. She and Stefan had seen so much potential in it.

There he was again, popping into her mind when she least expected it.

Oh, Stefan, why didn't you write? I loved you so much. Were we too young? I miss you still.

"Don't you agree, Julia?" Vicki asked.

Julia blinked. Everyone stared at her. "I'm sorry. I guess my mind was elsewhere."

Becky tossed a sympathetic glance her way.

"I was just saying how glad we are that Lukas has come to town." Vicki clutched his arm with undeniable ownership.

"Oh, yes."

Vicki smiled. "I thought you of all people would agree."

Julia's blood pressure ignited. "Why is that?"

Vicki gave a dramatic pause and blinked. "Well, because of the room addition, of course."

"Of course," Julia said with a smile.

"How is that coming along, by the way?" Becky asked before anyone could get hurt.

Julia looked at George and Lukas. "Your turn," she said.

While the burgers cooked on the grill, they discussed the progress of the room. Once they sat down to dinner, Julia felt bone-tired. Keeping herself guarded was exhausting. She'd eat, stay long enough to be sociable, then leave. She could hardly wait.

"So Luke—is it all right if I call you that?" Vicki asked, looking up at Lukas with wide eyes and…longing.

"I guess," he said, before taking an ambitious bite of his hamburger.

Julia wished she could read him. What did he think of Vicki? Was he enthralled with her beauty? Her mood continued on a downward spiral.

"Eleanor told me you were in the war?" Vicki asked.

He looked at Julia. Touchy subject. Vicki had better watch herself.

"Yeah," was all he said, as though it didn't bother him in the least.

Julia crossed her legs and kicked her top one back and forth, back and forth.

"So tell me about it, Lukie."

He stared at her a minute. The name would have struck Julia funny if her temper hadn't been swelling with the gray clouds overhead.

Lukas shoved corn around on his plate with his fork. "Nothing to tell. I served in the war, fought like everyone else, came home."

Vickie sighed in a dreamy sort of way. "You're so brave."

"I don't know about that." Lukas looked uncomfortable with the compliment.

Vicki turned to Julia. "Didn't your brother fight in the war?"

The question sent a sharp pain through Julia's chest. "Yes. How did you know that?"

Vicki waved her hand. "I can't remember. Someone mentioned it to me."

"Julia's brother died in the war," Becky said in solemn defense.

"Oh, I didn't know. I'm sorry."

Julia didn't hear the sorrow in Vicki's voice, but at least she apologized. "Thank you. We still miss him."

"What happened—if you don't mind telling us," Vicki said.

Julia shrugged. "All we know is they said he was killed in the line of duty. Someone saw a German near him."

Vicki gasped. "Oh my. Did the German get away?"

"He was severely wounded. Not sure if he made it or not."

"Well, I hope he got what was coming to him," she said.

Julia shrugged. "Death brings pain, no matter who a person is."

Lukas stared at her, his face unreadable. Had she said something out of line? Maybe he held a grudge against the Germans because of the war. She hoped she hadn't offended him, but the whole evening was so stressful, she was almost too tired to think about it.

All she wanted to do was go home and go to bed.

* * * * *

Lukas wasn't sure what to think of Julia's comment. Maybe she didn't hold her brother's death against the "German," as they put it. It intrigued him they never once considered the German had been fighting for the Americans. There were plenty of immigrants who had done so.

Julia had never been prejudiced in the past, obviously, since they were planning to get married. But then again, once he left, everything had changed. So he wasn't sure if her mother's prejudice had washed off on Julia.

While the women cleaned the table and fussed over the dishes, Lukas walked over to the lake's edge and stared out at the water. He took in a deep, calming breath. Vicki might be nice to look at, but she was driving him crazy, hanging onto him every moment, laughing at things he hadn't meant to be funny, watching his every move.

Women were so confusing. Why had Julia told Becky that she had no interest in him? When they were together, her eyes suggested otherwise. And what about that kiss? Despite the growing feelings he had for her—that he chose to ignore—being with her seemed to calm him, most of the time.

"Lukas, sorry to bother you."

He turned around and found Julia standing there, moonlight glistening on her hair, eyes shining. She looked so vulnerable, so beautiful. How he wanted to take her into his arms—no! He had to stop thinking like that. If only she hadn't kissed him that night. The thing was, he had no idea why she did that. Afterwards, nothing had changed. Still, if she wasn't interested, she wouldn't have kissed him. Oh, how he wanted to take her into his arms. If only—

"George and Becky asked that I come and get you to come back to the party." Julia lifted a smile that said she understood his need to get away.

"Thanks."

Julia started to walk away and Lukas grabbed her hand. "What was it you were going to talk to me about tonight?"

"Oh, I just thought I'd get a guy's perspective on what my father is going through."

They started walking back towards the group.

"I'm not sure I'm the one you should talk to. Remember, I told you I didn't do so great with my own father."

"It's so hard. Mother refuses to get medical help, and frankly, Dad seems to be having a good time at my house." She lifted a weak grin.

"That has to be frustrating—being away from your own house and all. Might be a good time to get things fixed between you and your mom, though."

The look she gave him said she didn't think that was a good idea at all.

"I don't seem to make much headway there. It's as though we take two steps forward and three steps back."

"Yeah, I understand that."

"Did you have a good relationship with your mom?"

"Yeah, I did. I miss her a lot." Thoughts of the updated hospital bill he received in the mail today taunted him. He'd get the money somehow. He had to. He refused to complain or worry. Well, he'd try not to complain or worry.

A dog howled in the distance.

"Goodness, that sounded like a wolf," Julia said.

"Yeah, it kind of did. Do you get scared easily?" Lukas asked.

Julia straightened. "No."

"Great. How about you go with me to see *I Was a Teenage Werewolf* on Friday night?" Date number two. That was the only reason he asked her. Two more dates. He'd get that discount and be done with it before his heart got broken again.

"Well—"

"You're not afraid, are you?"

"No, I'm not afraid," she said, almost adamantly. "All right, I'll go."

"Good."

They reached the others and Lukas couldn't help noticing that even though she'd done nothing all night long but laugh and flirt with him, Vicki's eyes were now shooting daggers his way. Women. Would he ever figure them out?

* * * * *

"I like the fir plywood on this deck," Mr. Hilton said as they rowed the boat farther out on the lake.

"It's nice," Lukas said.

"I'm not looking for a fancy sailboat or yacht, I just want a good fishing boat." He watched his oar as it lifted then dipped down into the water. "Yep, a man's got to get out of the house once in a while and do manly things." He grinned.

Lukas wasn't at all sure how to respond to that.

"Well, the boat you want sounds simple enough. You want it similar to this one, but with a modest price?"

"You got it there, my boy," Mr. Hilton said. He stopped rowing. "Listen a minute."

Water dripped from his oars as Lukas lifted them from the lake and listened. A serene quiet followed them as the boat drifted lazily upon the lake. The sun beat down hard, warming the wood beneath his arms and feet. In the distance a fish jumped into the air and made a splash, leaving a ring on the water's surface.

"There's nothing like this, is there?" Mr. Hilton asked.

"No sir, there isn't."

It had been a long time since Lukas had stopped to listen to nature sounds and drink in creation around him. He had to admit at times like these, he had no doubt there was a God who was in charge of it all. A twinge of sadness tugged at his heart as his thoughts drifted to better days when he trusted God with his needs, his wants, his life. But somewhere along the way he had taken it all back. He wasn't sure when or where, he knew only that it had happened. Yes, he went to church on a regular basis, but most decent folks did. It was more or less expected in polite society.

But right now, sitting here in this boat with nothing but the sound of a light summer breeze stirring upon the water, he realized anew that a true walk with God was so much more than that. He realized, too, that some days he missed that relationship.

"A man can find peace on the river like nothing else," the older man said, his eyes taking on a dreamy, faraway look. "Guess that Huckleberry Finn fella had it right, didn't he? Living on the river, one lazy day following another."

Lukas laughed. "You don't think that would get old?"

Mr. Hilton's expression grew somber. "People get old, Lukas. It happens so fast, you hardly know you've been hit, until you wake up one morning with an ache here and a pain there, and you suddenly realize you've given all your days to fixing up a fine house and passed up a good many fishing days that you can never get back."

Lukas had a suspicion that there was a lot more going on with Mr.

Hilton than anyone knew. But he couldn't tell Julia, or she'd ask questions about why he was with her father.

"So you think you can do it?"

Mr. Hilton's question pushed into Lukas's thoughts. "Yes sir, I think I can."

"Great." Mr. Hilton slapped his knee and grabbed up his oars once again. "Like I said, if I could have it by next summer, that would be great."

"No problem," Lukas said, wondering if he was doing the right thing to lock himself into a year's stay in Beach Village. But then, it would most likely take that long to get his house ready for sale, what with winter coming upon them.

"Remember, I don't want anyone to know about this. As you know, my wife and I are already on the outs with one another. If she finds out I've bought a boat, I'll be put out with the fish." He laughed at his own joke.

Lukas wasn't sure what to do.

"So that means don't tell Julia."

Lukas looked up at him.

"What? I'm not stupid. I know you two keep company."

"Only a couple of times," Lukas said.

"Is that so? Something tells me there are more times ahead." A teasing glint lit Mr. Hilton's eyes.

Truth be known, Lukas had always liked Mr. Hilton. Still, the plan was to get the house fixed up, sell it, pay off the medical bills, then get out of town. No one was going to change that plan.

Two more dates with Julia to win the bet. Just two.

As much as he hated to admit it, he could think of worse things.

CHAPTER NINETEEN

With her dad shopping and getting things from his house for his week-end fishing trip, Julia could take her time getting ready in her own home for her date with Lukas. She sat on the edge of her bed. Date? Was it truly a date? She thought a moment while her hand moved absently across Beanie's back. The cat purred and leaned in to Julia. It was a date, Julia realized with a start. He'd asked her to a movie, he was driving her in his car. It was a full-fledged date.

She stood up. Her cheeks flamed and her hands reached up to cover them. How long had it been since she was on a real date? Yes, she'd gone out with other men, but this was the first time that it actually... mattered.

Running to her closet, she spread wide the door and rummaged through one hanger after another. She needed a dress with flare, with color, but not too much, something that said she was happy to be with him—but not too happy, lest he become overconfident.

Hangers screeched on the steel bar as she shoved through one out-fit, then another. She spotted clothes she hadn't worn in quite some time and yanked them off the bar, throwing them on the bed. Her church had an outreach program for women in need, and they might have some use for these outfits if Becky's sisters didn't want them.

As she pulled out the unwanted items, she was surprised how the extra space gave room for her remaining clothes to hang without the crush of other items against them. Then she spotted just the dress she would wear. How long ago had she bought it? With a bit of embarrassment, she realized she had forgotten about it. Amazing what a little decluttering could do.

Over the next couple of hours, Julia primped and preened herself with a luxurious bath, lotions, and perfume. Spending extra time on her hair, she made sure every created curl was perfect and laughed at herself in the mirror for making such a fuss.

Still, one look at Lukas's face when he picked her up told her it was worth every minute.

"You look beautiful," he said.

She couldn't help noticing the change in his voice, low and romantic. It sent a chill through her. Must be the night air. Then again, it was mid-July, and the temperatures hovered in the eighties, so she doubted it.

"Thanks."

As they walked to the car, she glanced up at him, taking in the strong set of his jaw, the hairline scar that traveled alongside it. She noticed he rubbed it a lot. She wanted to ask him about it but didn't want to embarrass him, so she decided against it.

"So where's your dad tonight?"

"He's been out shopping, and I suppose he stopped at his house to pick up some things for a fishing trip with his buddies. They leave in the morning. Not sure what he's doing tonight." She hoped whatever it was it didn't include another woman.

"It'll be a good day for fishing. Nice weather."

Julia nodded.

"I hope you like steak. I thought we'd go to Bunker's Steak House."

"Oh, I love that place."

His face held surprise. "That's probably where all your dates take you, huh?"

What was that she heard in his voice, disappointment?

"I've only been there a few times." She wanted to put him at ease.

He smiled. "Good. I want it to be special." As soon as he said the words, he looked uncomfortable.

She smiled and touched his arm. "This is nice. Really, Lukas."

He cleared his throat then turned on the radio.

Once they reached the restaurant, they settled in at their table, placed their orders, and sipped from their glasses of iced tea.

"Did you have a nice time at Eleanor's the other night?" she asked.

He shrugged. "It was all right. Nice of her to invite me, though I'm not completely sure of her intentions." He grinned.

Julia wasn't sure what to say to that. She only hoped he hadn't fallen for Vicki, and yet it bothered her that she felt that way. She was falling for him herself, no question about it. But it seemed something held her back, apart from Becky's bet with Eleanor. Of all the guys she had dated, none had come close to making her feel the way she had felt with Stefan. But Lukas, he was different. There was something about him that reminded her of Stefan—his mannerisms, his occasional comments, the sound of his voice now and then. She had to stop reading things into it. It wasn't fair to Lukas to compare him to Stefan.

"Do you think your mother is happy with the progress on the room? We'll be finished soon."

"Yes. Despite her complaining, she does like it. I can tell."

He let out a long breath. "I'm glad you can tell. Some days I wonder if we've done anything right."

"It's just Mother. She speaks her mind, no matter what."

He laughed. "I've picked up on that one for sure."

"I bet you'll be glad to be done with it so you can start on your own home repairs."

"Yeah, I'm ready to get started. Up to now I've just been working on my boat."

"Your boat?"

"Oh, yeah, I don't think I told you about that. I'm building a boat, in the barn."

She laughed. "Seems I remember another story with farm animals and a boat. Have you been told to build an ark?"

He chuckled with her. "Not that big. No one told me to build it. It's all on my own."

"Oh, good. I didn't know you made boats. You are a man of many talents."

He shrugged, as though uncomfortable with the remark.

"The owner of your home also worked on boats. I guess when you live around a lake, there's a natural draw to the craft."

"Yeah, I guess." His eyes stayed pinned to hers.

A warm sensation crept up her face and she turned away. It was then Julia spotted her parents in a booth across the room. Though she was glad to see them together, she didn't want her mother to see her with Lukas. In her mother's book no one seemed to measure up, and Julia just didn't want to hear her droning on about it—especially since Julia was staying with her…for now. Hopefully they were patching things up and she could move back home to her own privacy, her own life.

"Is something wrong?" Lukas looked at her with concern.

Julia held the menu in front of her face. She was visible only from the eyes up. He pointed at her.

"Oh, this." She reluctantly put it down and turned her head away from her parents. "Just thought I'd make sure I didn't miss anything else I might want, for dessert or something."

"You'll have another chance to order dessert, I'm sure, after the meal. Though you may want to save room for popcorn."

"Oh, yeah, that's right." She glanced back toward her parents, and her mother wasn't in the booth. Julia's gaze darted around the room.

While she looked to the left, her mother approached their table from the right.

"Well, hello, Julia, Lukas."

Julia's heart zipped straight to her throat. Time swept her back to when she was seventeen and her mother had found Stefan's class ring in her jewelry box. It was a night she had wanted to forget.

"Hello, Mother."

"What are you two doing here?"

"Having dinner," Lukas said with a mischievous grin.

Her mother's eyebrow quirked. She was not amused.

"Who are you here with, Mother?" Though Julia already knew, she wanted to steer the conversation away from her and Lukas.

"Your father." Her mother studied Julia. "You needn't look so surprised. We are still married, and we do need to eat."

That was Mother's cue to let the matter drop.

"Will you be home this weekend?" her mother asked. "And yes, I know about your father's fishing trip in the morning."

"I was planning to stay home. I need to get some things done around the house."

"Fine. Well, you two enjoy your dinner." She looked at Julia then at Lukas, lingering a tad too long on him, with a subtle glance of disapproval.

Fortunately, just as her mother walked away, the waitress came with their dinners, so the matter of her mother was dropped. They eased into more conversation about her teaching and their past lives, both of them picking and choosing the highlights to share. Listening to him, she watched the sparkle in his eyes, the way his jaw twitched now and then, the movement of his strong hands as he told a story. He mesmerized her.

With the flip of her heart, she decided this would be a wonderful evening, despite the fact that she had to watch a werewolf on the big screen. Something told her she'd hardly notice. Her mind would most definitely be on the man beside her....

* * * * *

After her date with Lukas, Julia went to her bedroom at her own home and pulled out a lake rock. She wrote, "Lovely date with Lukas Gable, July 19, 1957." Then she reached for another rock, wrote the date, and then, "I'm learning to declutter."

Smiling, she eased the rocks into her Ebenezer jar then tucked it safely back into her closet. The rocks were monumental moments in her life. Her pastor said the rocks were also to represent God's work in her life.

When was the last time she'd considered that?

* * * * *

"So the prodigal decided to come home," Mother said the minute Julia stepped in through the door on Monday morning.

"Good morning, Mother."

Julia thought it was her mother. It sounded like her. But the woman now sitting on the sofa sipping coffee looked nothing like the mother she knew. Bare toes peeked from underneath her housecoat that lay haphazardly around her, with the belt fallen from the last loop and hanging low to the ground. Charcoal shadowed her eyes. Pout lines gathered around her mouth and pale cheeks. Curlers capped her head.

Julia dropped her bag and walked over to the seat beside her mother.

"Did you and Dad have a nice time Friday night?"

"We ate dinner," her mother said in a flat tone.

"You didn't talk about things?"

"What's to talk about? He's at your house, I'm here. He's the one who left. It's up to him if he wants to come back." Chin lifted, pride in place.

"Are you all right?"

"I wish everyone would stop asking me that," Mother said, with a snarl to her voice.

Mother's reaction suggested there were probably more problems between her parents than Julia knew.

Her dad had come to Julia's house late last night and gone straight to the guest room that he now called "his room." Despite that, he had been in a great mood this morning before he left for work. Whatever the problems between her parents, they didn't seem to bother her dad.

If he kept this up, Julia was going to charge him rent.

Julia knelt down beside her mother. "Don't you think it's time to call the doctor? You're not yourself these days. The doctor can tell you if there's something going on physically."

"I know."

Two words, but the way she said them and the look on her face shocked Julia to the core. For the first time in her life, Julia saw the woman before her—this woman who never, ever let her guard down—as truly vulnerable.

"Would you like me to call him for you?"

"No, I'll do it when I'm ready," she said, bristles back in place.

Julia sighed. "I'm worried about you."

"I appreciate it, Julia, but I'll be fine. So let's talk about you now."

Julia pulled herself up from her kneeling position and fell back onto the chair. This could take awhile.

"Yes?"

"What were you thinking, to go out with that Lukas fellow?"

Julia stared at her. "Lukas is a nice man."

"He's not your kind, Julia. And you know what I mean."

"No, I don't. I have no idea what you mean."

"Do you even know what part of town he lives in? What do you know about him?" Her mother crossed her arms in front of her.

Sometimes her mother's pride surprised even Julia. "I happen to know where he lives. It's a very nice older home, as a matter of fact."

Her mother's eyebrows lifted, obviously wanting to know more. "Oh?"

Julia raised her chin. "He bought the place where Stefan's aunt and uncle used to live." Just speaking Stefan's name, letting it drop from her lips, brought an ache to her heart.

Her mother's eyes widened, and her face turned ashen.

"What is it, Mother?"

"What if he's related to those Germans," her mother whispered, as though a profound secret had just come to light.

"Why do you say that? Anyone can buy a house."

Her mother didn't respond.

"I don't know if he is or not. But it wouldn't matter to me one way or the other. The war is over, Mother. You can't blame the Germans forever." Julia stood and started to walk away.

"And he's poor."

Julia whipped around. "Is that all that matters to you? Race and money? I feel sorry for you. I really do. Your superiority toward others causes you to miss out on so much."

"Don't feel sorry for me. You mark my words, daughter, you'll regret living a life with little money. And don't come crawling to me when you have nothing."

Julia's breath caught in her throat, along with a choking sadness. "I wouldn't ask you for a dime."

"You resent me when all I've tried to do is spare you what I—"

"You what? What you perceive as a bad relationship? You might have tried that when I was a kid, but now I'm thirty-four years old. I think I can handle my choices." Julia stomped into the hallway toward her bedroom. Passing the kitchen, she spotted Lukas getting a drink of water. She could only pray he hadn't heard their conversation.

* * * * *

The water ran into the glass and overflowed, bringing Lukas to his senses. He shut off the faucet. Was that what Mrs. Hilton thought of him? Obviously, old prejudices still haunted her—and him. He'd been an idiot for coming back. And a bigger idiot for getting involved with this family all over again. Was that what had happened with Julia the first time around? Her mother started in with her control methods and talked Julia out of seeing him? He wiped his hands on a towel and put the glass in the sink.

George was running late this morning, but as soon as he got there, Lukas would let him know he'd taken Julia out on Friday night. Then one more date and he'd get that discount and be done with it. That was all he cared about anyway. Though he couldn't blame Julia for her mother's ways, he'd be a fool to think he could love her and not be affected by her mother's influence. It would always be there.

The more he thought about that the more he realized just how fortunate he had been the first time around that it hadn't worked out between him and Julia. Maybe that was why he had come. He needed to see for himself that it wouldn't have worked. Mrs. Hilton would have always stood between them, interfering, conjuring up problems.

He'd walk, no, run, from this situation for good. The very idea, as though a long-time matter had finally been settled, should have made him feel better.

Most likely, he just needed time to get over the shock of Mrs. Hilton's words. Then he'd feel better. In fact, he'd probably feel great. Something told him it was time to celebrate.

CHAPTER TWENTY

Julia punched her pillow into place for the hundredth time, causing Beanie to stir. The feline lifted her head, stared at Julia through large, emerald-green eyes, blinked, then lowered her head and curled her paws around her face.

How dare her mother imply that she should not see Lukas anymore. For crying out loud, Julia was not a child. She had to get out of that house and back into her own home—and fast. Enough was enough. She had been more than patient with her parents, but this was getting ridiculous. Why, summer would be over soon, and she had wasted most of it staying with her mother!

Oh, why was her pillow so uncomfortable? Another fold and repositioning of her head.

She prayed Lukas hadn't overheard her mother's ramblings.

Prayed?

Now, there was a thought. And it seemed that thought was coming to her more and more these days. It could be the Ebenezer stones of remembrance that stirred her slumbering spirit. Was God nudging her back on track, or did it just mean that her life was out of control? She suspected it was more of the latter.

Not that her mother had anything to worry about. Lukas hadn't even tried to kiss her after their date. Maybe he decided she wasn't his type or something.

Her stomach gurgled. Her thoughts were not getting along with her spicy dinner. Maybe a glass of milk would help. Julia threw off the covers and grabbed her robe. Beanie refused to follow her at this late hour.

A light rain pattered on the rooftop as Julia made her way to the kitchen. Grabbing a glass from the cupboard, she opened the fridge to get some milk. One glance inside the chilled container reminded her they hadn't taken the milk out of the milk box this afternoon. Fortunately, the day had been unusually chilly with the pending storm that was just hitting them.

Tightening the belt of her robe, Julia tiptoed through the living room and gently opened the front door. Stepping onto the porch, the cold concrete beneath her feet sent a chill through her. Quickly she opened the milk box and pulled out the carton. She looked up in time to see someone sprint from their yard to a car in front of their neighbor's house. Squinting, she could just make out the color and model of the car, thanks to the amber glow of the streetlights.

What was her father doing sneaking around his own house?

* * * * *

Lukas sat at his kitchen table, coffee mug beside him, and worked on the specs for the boat Mr. Hilton wanted. Once the plans were made and he received approval, he'd order the planking, set aside his own boat, and get to work on this one. He was so busy these days, he wondered if he'd ever get around to working on his house so that he could get away from Beach Village.

His fingers worked the pencil across the page, putting in this detail and that. It came easy to him. His heart seemed to soar when he worked on boats. Though he loved small-town living, he knew he couldn't stay here. Aside from Julia, he still had memories of the prejudices of war that followed him. Good people who couldn't see past his lineage to befriend him or his family.

Though his father had accused Lukas of being weak and ashamed of his German heritage, Lukas knew it wasn't true. He had changed his name out of anger toward his father. He knew that was the one thing he could do to fight back. How many times had his father's words cut him to the core? But even more than that, the way his father had treated his mother made Lukas turn his back on the man.

Still, Lukas regretted that he hadn't made his peace with his father before he died. Unfortunately, there was no going back. Being "right" about something just didn't seem to matter now. He longed to hug his father and apologize for hurting him with the name change.

Did people realize the power of their words? Did Julia's mother realize how she was cutting her daughter to little bits with her biting comments and controlling ways? Maybe he'd tell her. What would it hurt? It wasn't as though there was a future for him and Julia. But if he could help her before he left, he could walk away feeling like he had done something good with what he learned from the heartaches shared with his dad.

The more the pencil flew across the page in long strokes and tiny dots of details, the more he realized that was exactly what he would do. When the opportunity presented itself, if it did, he would let Mrs. Hilton know just what she was doing to her relationship with her daughter. Julia's mother had never liked Stefan, and obviously she wasn't all that wild about him as Lukas either.

He would do this. For Julia. So she didn't have to live with the same regret he did.

* * * * *

What in the world had her dad been doing home at this late hour, Julia wondered as she climbed back into bed. This time, Beanie didn't bother to move at all, let alone acknowledge Julia's presence.

Julia lay still in the quiet of the night, staring at the ceiling that glowed with the shadows of moonlight. A soft rain continued to patter against the windowpane. The room had seemed a tad stuffy before bed, so Julia had slid the window open a crack, causing a slight breeze to whisper through the room and cause the sheers to respond with a ghostly dance. Julia loved the smell of a summer rain.

Though nature had lured her into a moment of calm, Julia couldn't stay there. Her thoughts kept going back to her dad. She couldn't imagine why he would be sneaking around his own house in the middle of the night.

Had he slipped in to spend time with her mother? Sneak something from his home office? Check on something? None of it made sense to Julia, and she had to admit the way her parents were behaving frightened her a little.

Fortunately, it didn't keep her awake for long. The gentle rains soon lulled her into a semi-restful sleep where all thoughts of her parents were gone and the only person who filled her dreams was Lukas.

* * * * *

Julia spent the next morning shopping. She needed a few things for the new school year, and Mildred's Corner Boutique was having a sale. Why not reward herself for cleaning out her closet? Though with the packages at her side, she couldn't help feeling a tad guilty, knowing Becky was struggling so.

Walking toward the middle of town, she wasn't really hungry for lunch, but decided on such a hot day as this, ice cream sounded good.

So she stopped in at the Beach Village Five and Dime, at their ice cream counter.

"What can I get you?" a woman with long auburn hair asked before turning around.

Julia lifted some money from her purse then snapped the clasp closed before looking up. "I'd like a strawberry—Becky! What are you doing here?"

Becky looked just as surprised as Julia felt. Then she laughed. "I work here."

"What?"

"Why not? I have the summer off from teaching. I may as well get another job and make some extra money." Her auburn curls bounced on her shoulders as she talked, moving her hands with her words. "Strawberry sundae?"

"Yeah." Words didn't come easy for Julia right now. She tried to shove her purchases under her chair.

"So what have you been doing?" Becky asked good-naturedly.

"Oh, you know, just out and about."

"You've been shopping?" Becky laughed, scooping strawberry ice cream into a cup and adding the topping.

Julia made a face and shoved her chin into her palm.

"You know you can't hide that from me. Besides, why wouldn't you want me to know?" Becky passed her the sundae, took Julia's money, and rang it up. Then she wiped her hands on a towel.

No other customers sat on stools at the counter, so the two friends were able to visit a few minutes.

"Well, here I am spending money while you're working. I feel like a total birdbrain," Julia said.

Becky laughed again. "Stop. You are not a birdbrain. I want to do this. Besides, I'm helping Mom and Pop."

"That's what I mean. You're always thinking of others, Beck. I love that about you."

Becky smiled and patted Julia's hand. "You're too hard on yourself. You do things for others all the time. Besides, this is kind of fun. Get to see lots of my friends. George hasn't been in yet, though." She wiped the counter with a washcloth.

"Does he know you work here?"

Becky finished the wipe down then rinsed the cloth at the sink before turning to Julia. "Yeah. But this is only my second day, so he hasn't had much time to get here."

Julia felt a stab of jealousy. "You mean you told him you were working here before you told me?"

"Oh, come on, that's not fair. We haven't talked the past couple of days."

"You could have called me," Julia said.

Becky winced. "You know I don't like to call your parents' house. Your mom makes me nervous."

"Tell me about it," Julia said, plunging her spoon in for another scoop of ice cream.

"So how are things going? Do you think you'll ever get to move back home?" Becky had a teasing glint in her eyes, but she had no idea how the question scared Julia. She wondered if it would ever happen.

"Honestly, Becky, I don't know."

"You're serious?"

"Yes."

"Isn't today when your mom is supposed to go to the doctor?"

"Yeah."

"Are you going with her?"

"No. She won't let me." Julia stirred the melting ice cream in her bowl. She didn't really want to talk about her mother. "How's Etta doing?"

"Not well. She's gained weight and she mopes around the house all the time. She's starting to work here tomorrow, so we'll see if that helps."

"Do you think she'll go back to Jimmie?"

"No. He's moved on. Not even in town these days."

"Oh, poor Etta."

"It's a good thing for her. She'll snap out of it and move on with her life. I just pray she doesn't wait too long."

"Yeah, me too." Julia waited a moment. "No more run-ins with that Stefan guy?"

Becky shook her head. "Guess it wasn't meant to be."

"Guess not."

Just then the bell over the door jangled. The girls looked up to see George walk in with a big smile. Lukas was beside him. When he spotted Julia, he smiled too.

"What are you two doing here? Aren't you working today?" Becky asked.

"Ever heard of lunch break?" George winked.

The guys settled in at the counter and placed their orders of cheeseburgers, fries, and Cokes while they discussed the final stages of the room addition and the next upcoming project at another house.

"We've also got to get started on your house," George said to Lukas.

"Oh?" Becky said. "What are you doing there?"

"He's doing all kinds of upgrading around the farm so he can make a better sale," George answered for Lukas and slapped him on the back. "A real businessman, this one."

"You're trying to sell already?" Becky seemed surprised to hear the news and glanced at Julia.

Lukas shrugged. "Well, it's too big for me to live there by myself."

"Well then, why did you buy it in the first place?" Becky looked confused.

Julia wondered why Becky didn't just drop the matter. The conversation depressed her.

"Oh, uh, well, there weren't a lot of houses available. You know how it is, the economy and all."

Before anyone could respond, the bell jangled over the door once more.

In walked Eleanor and Vicki. Great. Just what they all needed.

Everyone said their greetings and instead of scooting onto stools, Eleanor and Vicki stood behind Lukas.

"Fancy running into you," Vicki said, putting her hand on his shoulder as though she owned him.

"Uh, yeah." He looked uncomfortable, which gave Julia an inkling of satisfaction.

"So nice to talk to you last night," Vicki said, looking over at Julia to, no doubt, make sure she had heard her.

Lukas lifted an uneasy smile but Vicki didn't seem to notice.

"We saw the movie, by the way," she said.

"What did you go see?" Becky asked.

"We went to see *I Was a Teenage Werewolf*." She gave a dainty laugh. "Crazy movie. But Michael Landon is so dreamy."

"Hey, Lukas told me you and he saw that movie together," George said to Julia.

Though she was glad he had pointed that out in front of Vicki, she wasn't glad that Becky and Eleanor heard it.

Eleanor raised an eyebrow and glanced at Becky. "Oh, is that so? Did you enjoy the movie?" Eleanor directed the question to Julia but her glance kept darting to Becky.

"Uh, yes, it was fine. We just happened to bump into each other," Julia said, trying to help Becky out.

Becky looked relieved. Surprisingly, so did Eleanor.

Lukas, on the other hand, did not. She'd have to explain it to him later.

While they all discussed the movie together, the bell over the door jangled yet again. Julia glanced over and in walked Etta. Her depression appeared wiped clean with the smile that replaced it.

She walked straight over to the group, looked directly at Lukas, and said, "Stefan, we meet again."

CHAPTER TWENTY-ONE

Scrambled thoughts plagued Lukas all the way home. How had he made such a mess of things? First, Vicki made a big deal out of him calling her. He had wanted to point out that he had just returned her call regarding a boat matter so Julia wouldn't misinterpret things, but he didn't want to sound rude. Though after Julia's comments about running into him at the theater, he wished he had said something. What was that all about? Why did she keep talking as though their meetings were accidental? It didn't make sense at all and he planned to find out exactly what was going on with her.

Then Becky's sister came in and called him Stefan. Would Julia put two and two together? He had kept his identity from her till now, but with staying at his uncle's house and being called Stefan, he wasn't sure he could hide it anymore.

As he drove home, he moved ideas around in his head, trying to come up with an explanation for Julia. Though he couldn't rationalize her comment that she'd bumped into him, he didn't want her to find out the truth about him—especially not this way, and not before he found out the truth of why she had never answered his letters.

What had everyone thought when he fumbled around for an explanation to Etta as to why he said his name was Stefan? Stating that he didn't want to give his real name since he didn't know her, and he'd chosen Stefan because he'd just seen the name on a billboard advertisement was hokey even to him—hokey and untruthful. Obviously he hadn't the time to think things through. Etta had laughed it off. So did everyone else—everyone except Julia.

The way she stared at him had made him nervous. The very memory of it made him squirm in his seat even now.

He felt like a hypocrite. He'd acted so offended when Julia avoided the truth with her mom, and he was behaving far worse.

As he sat at a stoplight, he smacked the palm of his hand on the steering wheel. Why did everything have to be so complicated? Once the light switched to green, his foot hit the accelerator and his thoughts kicked back into gear.

By the time he arrived home, he'd made up his mind. He would not leave Beach Village until he knew the truth of what happened between him and Julia those many years ago.

Once he found that out, he'd leave. Never to return.

* * * * *

After Julia was showered and dressed, she headed toward the kitchen. She had spent the previous evening cleaning her own house, and her mother was in bed when Julia had finally gotten to her parents' house for the night. She still didn't know how the doctor visit went. Most likely, everything was fine, but Julia couldn't deny the nerves bubbling in her stomach.

Coffee perked on the kitchen stove, pulling Julia in with its strong scent. A scent that always wrapped around her with warm memories. Before leaving home, she'd had lovely times of sitting at the table with her dad, sipping coffee and sharing sweet conversation.

"Good morning, Mother." Julia walked over and planted a kiss on her mother's cheek. Quite unexpected for both of them. Reaching for a mug, she poured herself a cup of coffee and joined Mother at the table. "So tell me how your doctor's visit went."

Mother's eyes were shadowed with unrest. Deep lines that Julia had never noticed before trailed from her mouth, giving her the appearance of a puppet. In short, her mother's appearance both startled and frightened her.

Staring into her coffee cup, Mother stroked the side of it as though a magic genie would appear and make everything go away. Finally, she looked up.

"You were right. I'm going through"—she leaned in and whispered ever so quietly—"menopause."

Relief washed over Julia. Menopause she could handle. Her mother didn't have some dreadful disease. She was merely going through the change of life. Surprisingly, Julia wanted to shout for joy.

"Oh, that's wonderful." Julia reached for her mother's hand to give it a reassuring pat and she yanked it away.

"Wonderful? What's so wonderful about it?" Mother said. "Once you get here, you won't think it's so wonderful. It's dreadful. Hot flashes, flushes that burn my neck and face, restlessness, sleepless nights. There's nothing wonderful about it, young lady."

Julia stared, speechless, at this woman. Maybe menopause wasn't a better option.

"I'm sorry," was all Julia could manage. And indeed she was. Not only for her mother, but for everyone within a fifty-mile radius. "Is there anything you can take that will help?" *Please, say yes.*

"Something called hormones or some such thing."

"You're taking them, right?" Julia could hardly wait for school to start.

"Yes. And don't tell your father what's wrong with me."

Julia looked at the frown on Mother's face. "You can't mean that. He has a right to know you're okay—er, um, that it's not life-threatening." Well, at least not for her mother.

"I will tell him," she said. "It's not your place." The look in her eyes was downright unchristian.

"Yes, Mother."

At least her mother would tell her dad. By the look on Mother's face, Julia hoped she would tell him soon—before he had her committed.

* * * * *

Julia's stomach churned as she stepped through the yard, making her way to where George and Lukas worked. She stepped around the corner to see them putting their tools away for the day.

"Hey, Lukas, when you get finished, could I talk to you for a few minutes?"

"Sure." He brushed the sawdust from his arms and followed her outside.

"Everything all right?'

"Everything is fine. I just—" She cleared her throat and told herself to quit staring at the way his biceps bulged beneath the sleeves of his T-shirt. "I, um, just wanted to explain why I told the group that I had bumped into you at the movies."

Instead of telling her she didn't need to or that he hadn't noticed, he looked at her intently. "Yeah, I wondered about that."

"Do you have to get right home or could you walk with me on the beach?"

"Yeah. Let me just tell George." Lukas slipped back into the room addition while she waited outside.

George and Lukas both stepped outside. George pulled his truck keys from his pocket. "You kids behave yourselves," he said with a wink.

Julia could feel the heat creep up her neck and wondered if that was how a hot flash felt. They waved good-bye to George then headed toward the beach.

"I know how you dislike lying or deceit, and I thought I should explain my comment about bumping into you at the movies. The problem is, Eleanor sort of forced Becky into a bet."

"Oh?"

Julia told Lukas about the bet and how she had to stay away from him. From time to time she stole a sideways glance to see his reaction to it all. His face didn't so much as twitch.

When she had finished telling him, Lukas scratched his jaw, right around the scar area. "Well, I understand that you were trying to spare Becky any trouble. That explains a lot. I was beginning to think you didn't want anyone to know you were out with me."

"Oh, no, not at all." Her voice held more urgency than she had intended. She sounded desperate, as though she wanted him to know without a doubt she was interested in being with him. The very idea made her face burn all the more. She was beginning to understand her mother.

"I'm glad," he said, grabbing her hand.

He linked his fingers with hers and she couldn't swallow to save her life. They walked this way in silence until they were away from the sunbathers and near the large rock. Their rock. The one where she had met Stefan the night he went away.

"Let's sit over there," Lukas said.

Once there, Julia closed her eyes and lifted her face toward the sky, allowing the gentle breeze to lift her hair and refresh her skin. She just wanted to bask in the moment.

"It's a perfect evening," she said. When she opened her eyes, Lukas was staring at her.

"Yes, it is," he said.

His eyes refused to blink and seemed to hold her captive as his head leaned closer and closer. The wisp of a breath escaped her just before his lips touched hers, oh, so gently. He pulled her to him, his strong arms enveloping her as his mouth craved for more. Everything in her surrendered to his kiss with a passion she had thought long gone. A kaleidoscope of colors twirled and danced beneath her eyelids, her mind thick with the intoxication of his kiss, his touch.

A déjà vu enveloped her. She'd been in this place, felt like this before. With Stefan, yes, but something about Lukas reminded her so much—she had to stop. Maybe her mind ran to Stefan because she hadn't cared about anyone in this way since Stefan. Still, it wasn't fair to Lukas that her mind kept comparing the two.

Odd how he had even called himself by that name when he met Etta. It was as though someone was playing a cruel joke with her heart.

Breathless, she pulled away, frightened by the emotions running through her.

His eyes, so familiar, so warm, were glazed and cloudy, like someone awakened from a deep slumber.

"Let's walk," she said, grabbing his hand.

The sound of lake water rushing to shore accompanied their footsteps, but they kept silent. Julia felt sure their relationship had reached a crossroads. The kiss seemed to release a torrent of emotion for both of them. Had he been holding back, trying not to love her, just as she had tried to do the same? Had Lukas a lost love—a part of him shadowed with pain that refused to become involved with someone?

One kiss. No words. Yet so much was said.

As water lapped at her sandaled feet, she thought how ironic it was that she would share such a memorable moment with Lukas in the same spot where she had pledged her love to Stefan. Oh, how she had loved him. This wasn't Stefan and yet, when he held her in his arms, she couldn't help feeling she was back home. Safe. Secure. Loved. Still, one question plagued her.

How was it her heart could let her be at home in the arms of another man?

* * * * *

Though he had tried with everything in him to keep Julia at arm's length, Lukas knew it just wasn't possible. He loved her then and he loved her now. No matter how hard he tried to convince himself otherwise, he realized there was no use fighting it.

The way she kissed him back told him plenty. She was just as interested in him as he was in her—no matter what she told Becky. But it was Lukas she cared about, not Stefan. He blew out a sigh. He didn't even know who he was anymore. His fingers stroked the scars on his face. She'd never asked him about them. They had faded somewhat and the doctors had tried to make them discreet. They didn't seem to bother her. In fact, no one he'd ever dated seemed to mind... but he did.

If only the doctor hadn't found that picture of Doug Spencer and his girlfriend in Lukas's pocket, assuming that picture was of him. With all the chaos of an enemy strike, who had time to worry if he had the right nose or chin? So now he wore the face of a stranger.

The question was, who did he want Julia to love, Stefan or Lukas?

* * * * *

The next morning, Julia had made up her mind. No more playing games. She would tell Becky the truth, and Becky would have to figure out how to handle Eleanor. Julia had lost one man she loved; she wasn't going to lose another.

"Where are you going?" her mother asked when she spotted Julia by the front door, purse in hand.

"I'm meeting Becky for breakfast." She hesitated when she saw her mother fanning herself. "Will you be all right?"

"I'll be fine. I'm just hot."

Julia nodded. "See you later then." She slipped through the door before her mother could heat up some more.

When she met Becky at the diner, they settled into a booth and quickly ordered breakfast.

"So glad you thought of this," Becky said, breathless. "I needed a chance to get out of the house."

"Me too," Julia admitted. "Mother is not herself these days." She thought a moment. "Well, come to think of it, maybe she is." She chuckled.

"What did the doctor say?" Becky asked.

Julia explained about the menopause.

"Oh, dear. Something tells me if we have another war, God forbid, all the United States would have to do is send your mother and she'd take care of it single-handedly."

Julia laughed. "Poor thing. I know she's miserable, but she isn't exactly making it easy to help her." She sighed.

When the waitress brought their breakfast, Becky said a prayer for their food and they began eating.

"Listen, Becky, I wanted to meet with you this morning to tell you something."

"Oh?"

One look at Becky's face and Julia lost her nerve. "So, how is your car holding up?"

"You didn't bring me here to talk about my car, did you?" Becky asked with a grin.

"Well, how is it?"

She shrugged. "It'll be fine. It has to be. Mom and Pop need me."

Julia noticed the dark circles under Becky's eyes and her heart ached for her friend. "What can I do, Becky?"

"Just pray." Tears filled Becky's eyes but she quickly turned away. She sniffed. "So tell me, what was it you really wanted to tell me?"

"Oh, nothing really." The last thing Julia wanted to do was burden Becky with the news of her love for Lukas. She'd get the money for Eleanor first, and get it to Becky in such a way that Becky wouldn't feel it was charity. That would be the only way she would accept it.

"Hey, isn't that your mother?" Becky asked, pointing to a woman who got out of her car and crossed the street.

"Yeah," Julia said, perplexed. "She didn't mention she was going out this morning. I guess she doesn't have to answer to me, though." She turned her attention back to her eggs and bacon.

"Well, who is that?"

Julia looked out the window once more in time to see her mother getting into another car...with a man who was not her father.

CHAPTER TWENTY-TWO

Once the kitchen was clean from lunch, Julia walked to her bedroom. She hadn't been sleeping well lately and decided to take a nap. Yet, knowing her mother was with a strange man, Julia wondered if she'd be able to sleep.

George and Lukas were busy filling in drywall seams, sanding, and painting. A big job from what Julia could see. She settled onto her bed and Beanie curled up beside her. Just as Julia's eyes grew heavy and drifted to a close, she heard a loud thump overhead. Her eyes shot open.

"What on earth?" She waited, breath lodged somewhere at the base of her esophagus. Another thump.

Panic soared through her. Someone was walking around in their attic. But who? Her mother was gone and the guys were working on the room addition. She took a moment to calm her nerves. She was over-reacting. She needed to get a grip on herself.

Another thump.

Quietly, she eased out of bed, grabbed her umbrella from the closet on the way out, and tiptoed toward the attic stairway. She could go get Lukas and George, but by the time they got back, the intruder could have escaped—or worse, the intruder could be a squirrel and they'd have a good laugh—at her expense.

The attic door was dropped, the ladder of stairs touching the floor. Julia tugged on the steps and slowly, quietly, inched her way upward, wincing with every creak. Her pulse knocked hard against her temples. White-knuckled, her fingers clutched the umbrella.

When she reached the top step, she spotted the culprit. The umbrella slipped from her fingers, thumped its way down the stairs, and made a bang once it hit the floor.

"Dad, what are you doing here?"

He jumped and turned around to face her. "Would you quit sneaking up on me?"

"I hardly did that. Didn't you hear the umbrella drop to the floor? It could've waked the dead."

"I didn't hear it," he said with an edge of grumpiness.

"Well, you scared me. I was trying to take a nap and heard you thumping around up here." She climbed the rest of the way up and heaved herself onto the floorboard. Brushing her hands off she asked again, "What are you doing up here?"

"Just going through some things."

Julia spotted an envelope in his hand.

"Oh, Dad, please tell me you aren't clearing out your things." Julia's heart sank with the possibility. Her parents couldn't be that bad off, could they? A little menopause couldn't separate them for good, could it?

He cleared his throat. "Um, no, no. Just looking through some things." He tucked the envelope into a book he was holding.

Though Julia was curious as to what was in the envelope, she didn't feel it her place to ask.

"So where is your mother?" Dad asked.

"I have no idea," Julia said, meaning it. She wanted to ask her dad about that man, but she didn't want to upset him. Julia felt confident that her mother would explain it all and it would make sense. But the waiting was hard.

Her grandma had always told her that trusting came in the waiting. A lot of good that did her. She had waited for Stefan and he never came back.

He glanced at his wristwatch. "Well, would you look at the time? I'd better get back to work," he said, heading toward Julia. He stopped and dropped a kiss on the top of her head. "Have a good day, sweetheart."

* * * * *

After dinner, Lukas went to the barn to work on his boat. Very soon he would have to put this project on hold so he could start work on Mr. Hilton's boat. With the mounting medical bills, he had no choice. His own boat would have to wait. But until then, he would try to get some more work completed on it.

The bottom board was in place and he now worked on the ribs of the boat, sanding along the way. As his hands worked the wood, his mind fought to keep thoughts of his growing love for Julia at bay. This wasn't part of the plan. He had come here to take care of business and get home, back to a life void of pain. He knew from experience Julia equaled pain.

Lukas maneuvered the wood and spread the epoxy to hold the plank in place. As crazy as it seemed, it bothered him to think Julia loved him…as Lukas but not as Stefan. What would happen once she found out Lukas and Stefan were the same man?

Oh, why had he come?

Most people would be thankful for an inheritance. Not that he didn't appreciate his aunt and uncle's kindness to him. The money would definitely come in handy once he sold their home—if he ever sold it.

But now that his heart had betrayed him and fallen into the same old trap of loving Julia, he didn't know what to do. His muscles tightened and ached, from working with the wood or his thoughts, he wasn't sure. Lukas stretched in an attempt to relax his muscles. But there was so much to think about, to work through.

He couldn't imagine where this would all lead, but the deeper he fell, the more certain he was it wouldn't work between them. Knowing how Mrs. Hilton felt about him—her prejudice toward him, how could he be in their family? Not only that, but once Julia discovered who he really was, he doubted she would have anything to do with him anyway.

Still, he couldn't deny his heart's yearning. He was tempted to run away from it all, start over. But he'd tried that...for the past seventeen years. Other women had come and gone in his life, and no one, not one single woman, could make him forget Julia.

* * * * *

Julia sat cross-legged on the floor of her old bedroom, sorting through a box of old pictures. The photos had no organization to them whatsoever. They were thrown in a heap with all the patience of a high school girl. Now she wished she had taken a little more time to make sense of them all. Presently, with no place to call her own, she just might have the time to do it.

"What on earth are you doing?" Mother's imposing figure stood in the doorway.

"Hello, Mother. I found this box of pictures in the attic and decided to organize them." Julia picked up a photo of her and a classmate and placed it in a pile.

"Whatever for?"

Julia looked up at her.

"I mean, why now? Are you feeling nostalgic because of staying here?" While that comment from most mothers might be followed by an endearing look or hug, her mother's voice seemed to imply Julia had a weakness.

"I just wanted to do it."

If push came to shove, Julia had a few questions of her own for her mother, as in, who was that strange man I saw you with?

"Don't be so sentimental, Julia. Your emotions can get you into trouble, remember?" Her mother started to walk away.

"Are you referring to Stefan?" Heat crawled from Julia's belly and worked its way upward.

Her mother stopped and turned to her. "As a matter of fact, I am," she said without hesitation. "He was a mistake from the start, but you just couldn't see it."

Pain swept through Julia. "I loved him," she whispered, looking at a photo of the two of them together.

"He was not good enough for you," her mother said.

"How would you know that, Mother? Are you really that prejudiced?"

Her mother's chin hiked. "I'm not prejudiced in the least. I knew his family. I wanted better for you."

"Because they were poor?" Julia's stomach knotted. "Does love mean nothing?"

"Love." Her mother spit out the word as though it tasted bad in her mouth. "It takes more than love to hold a marriage together, young lady. All that fairy-tale mumbo-jumbo you see on the movies means nothing. When you find yourself knee-deep in dishes and babies and no money to put food on the table, tell me how love will sustain you then."

"Are you saying that if Dad hadn't had money, you wouldn't have married him?"

Her mother stared at her. "One day you will thank me, Julia."

"Thank you for what?"

Her mother blinked. "For—for holding you steady. For teaching you not to follow your every whim but, rather, to consider your future. Love sounds all cozy and wonderful, but the reality is you need to eat." With that she turned on her heel and walked away.

But what if the lost love takes your appetite away, Mother? What then?

* * * * *

The next day Julia decided to go over to the school and check on her room. In no time, she'd have another class and be full-swing into a new year. She sorted through boxes, wondering why she had kept some things, tossing here and there. This must be the week for it.

"Hey, Julia, how are you?" Bob Chesterton, the biology teacher, stood in the doorway.

"Hi, Bob. Guess we had the same idea. I thought I'd get a head start on things."

"Yeah, me too. Mr. Small is interviewing potential teachers today, so if you see any strange people roaming the halls, that's what it's about."

"Thanks for the heads-up. Have you had a nice summer?"

"It's been a blast," he said. "I made a little extra bread working at the golf course."

Julia smiled. This was Bob's second year of teaching—no family, no major responsibilities yet, ducktail hairstyle still in place.

"That's cool."

"Well, I'd better get back to work. Someone is coming down the hall."

Julia smiled, watching Bob slink off as though he might get into trouble for talking to her. Sorting through her box once again, Julia barely noticed the sound of heels clacking against the shiny tiled floors.

"Well, hello, Julia. Fancy meeting you here."

Julia looked up to see Vicki standing there in all her glory. Her long raven hair was now bobbed and curled toward her face, accentuating her blue eyes all the more. She wore a blue-and-black-checked dress with a red flower pinned to it, her lipstick matching the cherry shade.

"Vicki. What are you doing here?"

"Trying to get a job," she said with a broad smile. She walked over to Julia. "So is this your room?"

"Yes." Julia didn't want to be friendly, knowing the pain this woman caused her best friend. Becky. If Vicki got a job here, Becky would be miserable.

Vicki leaned in and whispered, "Hey, put in a good word for me with the boss."

Julia just looked at her and lifted a slight smile. No way would she put in a good word and she couldn't lie about it. An awkward moment grew between them.

"Well, I just thought I'd stop in and say hello." Vicki inched backwards.

"Yeah, um, I'm glad you did," Julia said.

"I'll see you around. Maybe Eleanor will have another bash we can all go to."

"Yes, maybe."

Vicki gave a little wave and walked away. A smidgen of guilt fringed the edges of Julia's heart. She could have been friendlier. Still, there was Becky to consider. The more she thought about it, the more Julia decided she'd better warn her friend, just in case Vicki got the job.

* * * * *

When Julia arrived at Becky's parents' house, the place was hoppin', as usual.

"Come on in," Becky's oldest brother said. "Beck's in the kitchen with Mom."

Julia thanked him and walked into the kitchen. The ammonia smell was so strong, Julia wanted to pinch her nose. Becky's mom's head hung over the sink, while Becky squirted permanent solution over individual curls.

"Hi, Julia." Mrs. Foster's muffled voice came through the towel she held over her nose and mouth.

Julia laughed. "Don't try to talk."

"Pour yourself a glass of iced tea from the fridge," Becky said. "Mom will never forgive me if I don't offer." She laughed.

"Thanks." Julia poured the tea, thinking how much like a second home this place was to her.

"Mom, is it okay if I go to Tricia's house?" Becky's sister Katie asked.

"Can I use the car to go to the record store?" her brother Pete asked. "I can drop her off at Tricia's if you want me to."

Their mother agreed to both and finally stood when Becky sopped the last curl and wrapped her mother's hair in a plastic cap. Putting her hand to her back, Mrs. Foster stretched. "Oh, dear, I'm afraid I'm getting old," she said with a half grin. "You girls come join me at the table."

She grabbed her own glass of iced tea and settled in at the table with Julia and Becky. As Julia watched their family interact with one another, she longed all the more for such a family. She could count on one hand the times she and her mother had sat down together for sweet conversation. The only time her mother sat with Julia was when she wanted to give her advice and see to it that Julia followed it.

"So what are you up to today, Julia?" Mrs. Foster asked.

"Not too much. I was out at the school today, checking on my room, cleaning out some things."

Becky looked at her in wide-eyed wonder. "You were cleaning out some things? What has happened to my friend? I don't know this person." She laughed.

Mrs. Foster stifled a chuckle. "Now, Becky, you be sweet. I've taught you better than that."

Julia laughed. "I'm afraid she's right. I don't know what's happened to me either. But it's true. I'm getting rid of things, at home and at school. I hope I stop myself before I give too much away."

"I don't think that will happen," Becky muttered before taking a drink from her glass.

"Hi, Julia." Etta bounced in all perky and happy.

"Well, hello. You look happy."

"I am happy," Etta said. "I've decided to go to college."

"Really? That's wonderful, Etta," Julia said, marveling at the change in her friend's sister.

"Yeah, I'm excited. Pops is helping me fill out the paperwork, and I hope to get started this semester. Don't know why I wasted all this time waiting around for Jimmie. Sis convinced me I don't need a man to be happy," she said, winking at Becky. "Though you do notice that she has a boyfriend now." She shrugged. "But that's okay. I'll snag a man one of these days. I hear there are plenty to choose from on the college campus." She gave a wicked grin and bounced back out of the room, leaving them to laugh at her comments.

Mrs. Foster shook her head. "That girl will be the death of me."

"I'm excited for her," Becky said. "She's finally let go of Jimmie and the dream of that Stefan guy."

"You mean Lukas," Julia said, smiling.

"Whoever he is. Lukas, Stefan, whatever."

Becky and her mother turned their attention to the weather and the starting of school being just around the bend while Julia pondered Becky's comment about Lukas. For some reason it unsettled her, having Lukas and Stefan's names lumped together once again. She couldn't say why, but the whole thing gnawed at her.

When Mrs. Foster left the kitchen to check on the kids, Becky turned to Julia. "I can't help feeling there's another reason you came over here. Normally, you would wait to see me when I got home. Is something wrong?"

Julia chewed her lower lip for a moment. "I'm not sure yet."

A crease formed between Becky's eyebrows. "What is it, Julia? Your mom? Your dad?"

"No, no, nothing like that." She looked at her fingers, wondering how she should say this. "I told you I went to school today."

"Yeah. So?"

"So I saw someone there interviewing for a job."

"I heard we had a couple of openings. Is that a bad thing?"

"Depends on how you look at it." Julia shot Becky a glance. "I met the woman interviewing."

"Anybody I know?"

"Becky, it was—"

"Time's up," Becky's mother said, standing in the kitchen doorway. Becky and Julia stared at her.

"My hair. Got to rinse off this stuff." Mrs. Foster whipped off the plastic cap and drooped her head into the sink once again.

"I've got to get going. I'll talk to you soon, Becky." Julia slipped out of the kitchen, telling herself that maybe, just maybe, Vicki wouldn't get that teaching job and Julia wouldn't have to tell Becky anything.

CHAPTER TWENTY-THREE

"Did you scrub the bathroom sink like I asked you to?" Mother asked Julia as they sat in the living room the next afternoon.

Julia felt her back bristle. "Yes, I did."

"You know how I hate toothpaste residue in the sink," Mother mumbled as she worked a crossword puzzle.

"There was hardly any residue at all, but it's completely gone now." Julia picked up her knitting needles and began to knit.

"I need to get my shoes polished before church in the morning. Are yours polished, dear?"

Julia clenched her teeth in an attempt to pause before speaking something that was sure to be disrespectful. "Yes." She noticed the tension in her knitting was a little tighter than usual. She tried to relax.

"Good. Make sure you keep them by the front door, so our floors will stay clean." Her mother filled in some squares on the puzzle. "By the way, what are you wearing to church in the morning?"

The question made Julia flinch. "I haven't thought about it, why?"

Her mother shrugged. "Just wondering." She made another notation on her puzzle, giving Julia time to squirm. She knew her mother's manipulative moves well. "Your black sheath last week was a tad snug. Perhaps you were unaware?"

Julia attempted to squelch the growing anger inside her. "I've been dressing myself for quite some time now, Mother. I will continue to do so." She tossed aside her knitting, stood up, and stormed out of the room.

"Of course, if it was your intention to look that way…"

Julia's heart thumped in her throat as she exited the front door. Her stomach went into that old pattern of churning that she had semi-forgotten. She kicked off her shoes and walked down to the sandy beach, tears stinging her eyes. Would she never get away from her mother's critical tongue?

With the back of her hand, she wiped her face and tilted it toward the sun, soaking in the warmth of its rays. Her toes sank into the soft, wet sand where she stood. Cool lake water rolled toward her and washed the sand from the tops of her feet. Closing her eyes, she listened to the soothing ebb and flow of the water. Oh, that life could be so calming, so refreshing.

But her mother would have none of that.

From the time Julia could remember, her mother had always had a biting tongue toward others, including her family. Bitterness seemed to chart her course, even before Joe's death, though Julia couldn't imagine why. Her mother had most everything a woman could ever hope to have in this lifetime. A husband who had always adored her and given in to her every whim—until now. Her lifestyle was the best that money could buy. Julia's father had seen to that. Everything he had done, he had done for Mother.

Julia resented it. Not out of jealousy towards her mother, but that her father could work so hard to please her and yet her mother had only criticism to offer in return. She wouldn't blame her father if he didn't come back.

Though she knew her mother deserved it, the very idea saddened her more than she could say. Even with all her mother's faults, Julia didn't wish ill on her. In fact, she loved her. More than she cared to admit, even to herself, most days. Still, she couldn't deny her sense of emptiness when she watched Becky and her mother interact.

As Julia's footsteps carried her farther from the house, lake rocks hot beneath her feet, a deep sense of loneliness wrapped around her like a black cloak. She tried to tell herself she was overreacting to her mother's comments. After all, she'd grown up with them. They were nothing new. But for some reason, right now, this moment, they bothered her in the deepest part of her soul.

Maybe she was acting like her mother. Didn't she have much for which to be thankful and yet here she was feeling sorry for herself? She had parents who loved her—though her mother most definitely had control issues—and she had the potential of a growing relationship with Lukas. Yet part of her held back for fear he would leave Beach Village. Hadn't he made it clear that was a possibility? She'd been left behind once before by the man she loved. Could she survive it again?

As her thoughts wandered and tangled through a maze of what-ifs, Julia felt a cool drop of rain on her arm that shook her free from her mental meanderings. She looked up to see dark clouds gathering and headed back toward home.

By the time she reached her parents' home, it had just started to rain. Grabbing her shoes at the door, she slipped into the house and quietly placed them on the floor. She hoped to tiptoe to her room without her mother knowing so she could have some more time to herself.

As she edged her way down the hall, she heard her mother's voice, talking softly. "All right, I'll meet you for lunch, but on Monday, not tomorrow. It's hard for me to get away after church. And we must be careful so my husband doesn't find out. What time? Eleven thirty. No, no, not there. Too many people. Let's meet at Rick's Café just outside of town. No one will see us there. Very well. Good-bye."

Julia's breath caught in her throat. First her dad, and now her mother? What was going on with those two?

Upon hearing the sound of approaching footsteps, Julia quickly tiptoed into her room and gently closed the door.

* * * * *

Lukas put his coffee mug down when he heard the motorcycle pull up outside his house. It had to be Mr. Hilton. He didn't know anyone else with a motorcycle. He wondered what he needed on a Sunday.

He pushed open the screen door and stepped outside. "Hello, Mr. Hilton."

"Oh, please, call me Frank."

"All right, Frank."

"I hope I'm not bothering you. It's such a beautiful day, I thought I'd stop by and see if you'd started work on the boat design." He held up his hand. "It's absolutely fine if you haven't, I just thought I'd check."

"Come on in so we can talk," Lukas said, holding the screen door open for him.

Once they were settled at the table, drinking coffee together, Lukas presented the plans he had made for the boat. They discussed some minor changes then set the plans aside.

"You're going to do a fine job," Frank said with a smile.

"I appreciate the opportunity, sir," Lukas said.

Frank eyed him. Lukas almost thought he saw the light of suspicion in his eyes. He hoped Mr. Hilton—Frank—trusted him. He would do the best job he could. After all, he was Julia's dad and the truth was, Lukas had never had a problem with Frank. It was Mrs. Hilton who had talked down to him those many years ago.

Frank leaned back in his chair. "So what's your story, Lukas?"

The question jarred him. "My story?"

"Yeah, your story. A nice-looking man your age, not yet married, working construction, with a passion for boats and an interest in my daughter." Tiny lines crinkled at the corners of his eyes when the older man smiled.

Lukas heard a gulp and was pretty sure it came from him. By the look of amusement on Mr. Hilton's face, he was right.

"Not much to tell, really. I lived in Chicago, decided to come here, and—"

"Why?"

"Why what?"

"Why did you come here?"

"Oh, um, our family had visited a few times when I was a kid. It's a nice town." He shrugged. "I just thought, why not? I have no ties, nothing to hold me in Chicago."

"No family?"

"My family is gone. Here, let me get you some more coffee."

Frank put his hand over his cup. "No, no, thank you."

He paused a minute and Lukas hoped he wasn't trying to come up with more questions.

"You know, son, sometimes people make decisions that affect others, but they don't always do it out of meanness. Sometimes they think they're helping."

Lukas had no idea what the man was trying to say.

Mr. Hilton's gaze held his own. "I'm just saying, if you have people in your life who hurt you, try to let the pain go and forgive. People who can't forgive, well, they become bitter, that's all."

Lukas wondered if he looked as confused as he felt by Frank's words.

The man laughed. "Listen to me. An old man rattling on about the lessons of life." He stood up and pushed his chair in. "That boat is going to be first-class, yes sirree. Thank you, Lukas. I'm thankful you came to this fair city of ours." Frank gave Lukas a hearty handshake and walked out the back door. Scooter hobbled out of the barn to check on their visitor.

With a wave, Lukas watched Frank ride off. He reached down and patted Scooter on the head. "Wonder what that was all about?"

* * * * *

"Julia, I have a few errands to run. I'll be back sometime this afternoon," Mother said, inching on her gloves and adjusting her hat before grabbing her purse. She opened the clasp, checked something inside, then snapped it closed. "The paint fumes are giving me a headache. It will be good to get away for a while."

Julia nodded. "Have fun."

Her mother studied her a moment then turned and walked out the front door.

Easing the curtains back, Julia watched her mother drive away from the house. From a glance at the clock, she knew her mother was meeting whoever was on the phone with her Saturday. Though she had hoped to snatch a few minutes alone with Lukas, her curiosity got the better of her. She had to know who her mother was meeting and why.

Julia checked on Beanie and spotted her curled up on her bed. Grabbing her purse, Julia headed for the door, taking one last glance behind her to make sure Beanie didn't follow her and get out of the house. In her dash for the door, she had no time to stop herself when she turned back around and plowed straight into Lukas's strong chest.

"Whoa," he said. "Are you all right?"

All right? His thick arms wrapped around her and held her steady, while a healthy heart beat inside his hard, muscular chest. What could possibly not be all right about this?

"Oh, I'm so sorry," she said. Maybe she lied, but a lady would never admit it.

"I'm not," he said with a smile and an ornery glint in his eye.

She smiled back.

"Listen, Julia, about last week, when we—"

"Yes?" She prayed he wouldn't say he regretted their kiss, that it was all a mistake.

His eyes held hers.

"Hey, where's that water?" George's voice broke them apart. He stepped into view. "I figured you might have gotten sidetracked." He grinned.

Julia felt heat climb her face. "Did you need something?"

"Oh, man, you didn't even ask her for the water yet? I'm parched."

"Uh, yeah." Lukas's gaze never left hers for a moment. "Could you get us a drink of water? We didn't want to track paint inside."

"Oh, uh, sure," she said. "Be right back." On shaky legs, she walked to the kitchen, heart trying to push through her chest. What was he going to say to her? Did he regret kissing her?

Oh, George, why couldn't you have stayed where you belonged?

Julia grabbed two glasses, filled them with ice cubes and water, and carried them to Lukas and George just outside the front door. "Here you go," she said.

"Thanks," Lukas said.

"Come on, Lover Boy, we've got work to do," George said, already making his way to the room addition.

"Talk to you later." Lukas turned and followed George.

Julia sighed and glanced at the clock. There was still time. Her mother was eating lunch with whomever, after all. Julia could get there before lunch was over—if she hurried.

Just then the phone rang.

"Hello?"

"Vicki is trying to get a job at our school," Becky shrieked.

"I know."

"What? And you didn't tell me?"

"I tried the other day, Becky, but you were giving your mom a perm and all that. She came in when I was trying to tell you. I'm sorry."

"Julia, I can't stay there if she starts teaching at the school. I just can't do it. She ruined my life. Absolutely ruined it."

"I know she hurt you, Becky, but you have a new life now. A better life, don't you?"

Silence.

"Becky, do you still love Jack?"

"No, of course not."

"Then she actually did you a favor, right?" Julia was trying to get her to see the positive side, but she also knew she had to be careful.

"I guess." She said it as though she wasn't sure. "I just don't want to be reminded daily of what she did, you know?"

"Yes, I know."

Becky sighed. "If she gets hired, you will have to help me through this, Julia. It's one thing to forgive, it's another to be confronted with it day after day."

"I understand. Just keep reminding yourself she did you a favor. If he would leave you like that, he would most likely have done it after you were married."

"You're right." The fight had seeped out of her like the slow release of air from a balloon. "Thanks, Julia. You're my hero."

"Why is that?"

"If you can forgive Stefan for what he did to you, I guess I can forgive Vicki. Thanks."

"You're welcome." *Thanks for the reminder.*

Julia wanted to tell Becky about her growing feelings for Lukas, but one glance at the clock told her there wasn't time if she wanted to catch her mother with her lunch date. Instead, she quickly ended the call with barely enough time to make it to the café before her mother was sure to leave. Against Julia's better judgment, she had to speed in order to make it. Unfortunately, just as she pulled into the café and spotted her mother's car, it was pulling out at the opposite end of the parking lot, going in another direction. She was alone, Julia could see that much, which relieved her. What had she supposed she would find? Two lovers secretly meeting, away from prying eyes? Julia shook her head. She had let her imagination run away with her.

Just as she shoved her car into gear to back up and pull out of the parking lot, another car drove toward her. She had to wait for it to pass before she could turn her car around. Just as it rolled by, she got a good view of the driver.

It was the same man she had seen with her mother before....

CHAPTER TWENTY-FOUR

Rain pounded the roof as Lukas sat in his living room, reading the paper. A lazy Tuesday. Sauerkraut snoozed quietly at Lukas's feet. Lukas peered over his paper toward the kitchen where Scooter sat on his haunches watching him. For some reason, Scooter refused to stay out of the rain and in the barn, so Lukas had mercy and let him come inside. Lukas smiled at the dog and shook his head before turning his attention back to the paper.

He'd already eaten dinner and was too tired to work on Mr. Hilton's boat. The painting would be done soon on the room addition and their job there would be finished. He wasn't sure how he felt about that. No more whining from Mrs. Hilton. Unfortunately, he also wouldn't be around Julia as much—unless he did something about that.

With a sigh, Lukas folded the newspaper. No point in holding it if he couldn't read it. Too much going on in his head.

Shoving himself out of his chair, he walked over to the bookshelf. His aunt and uncle's books were still there. He hadn't had the time to clear them out. A rainy night like this one beckoned him to read. He wasn't an avid reader; he was much too active for that. But every now and then he enjoyed a good book.

Quickly, his eyes scanned the titles until he came across a Bible. He thought it strange that it would be tucked between the novels, so he pulled it out. The leather was frayed and worn from obvious use. Gently, he opened the pages. It had belonged to his uncle. Penned comments marked up the margins. Passages were underlined, pages dog-eared. Lukas took the Bible over to his chair and sat down.

He'd read through the passages that had obviously meant something to his uncle, comments that revealed his spiritual journey. A somber mood settled over Lukas as he browsed through the pages. His own Bible collected dust each week, which he merely brushed off for Sunday's meetings. Lukas walked into his bedroom and grabbed his Bible from the nightstand then walked back into the living room and sat down.

Flipping through his own Bible, he saw nothing inside that would indicate a spiritual journey. Nothing on the pages or tucked between them. Which, come to think of it, pretty much summed up his spiritual growth at the moment.

There was none.

With a sigh, he reached for his uncle's Bible once more. He carried it back to the bookshelf. This was a treasure he hoped to search through again in the days ahead, but for now, he would tuck it away and keep it safe. When he took one last glance inside, a small folded piece of blue paper drifted to the floor. Lukas bent down and picked it up.

Worn with age, the fragile paper had no crinkle left when he gingerly opened it. What seemed a harmless note before opening, now held two words so powerful, they rendered his feet immovable and his tongue parched.

The note read simply, "I'm pregnant."

He wasn't sure how long he stared at those words. The profound impact they had on him could not be understated. There was much more to them than the announcement of a growing child. He remembered his mother's words, explaining how much his aunt and uncle loved him and that he was the son they never had. And now he remembered her saying something else. Their being childless wasn't by choice. His aunt and uncle had never been able to have children.

* * * * *

"Thanks for inviting me to dinner, Dad. This is nice," Julia said, breathing in the smells of sizzling meat and oven-baked bread at the restaurant.

"Well, I wanted to spend a little time with my girl." He winked. "I know things have been crazy this summer, and I'm sorry. You most likely are ready to move back to your own home."

Julia stopped shoving the pork chop around on her plate with her fork and looked at him with a smile. "Well, the thought had occurred to me."

"I'm sure it has. But I figure you aren't in a real big hurry—at least until the room addition is completed." Another wink.

Julia was speechless.

"Oh, come on. Don't act so surprised. Your old dad isn't as dumb as you might think. I see how you and Lukas are around one another." He whistled quietly. "Sparks are flying."

She laughed. "You're starting to over-dramatize, like Mother."

"Ouch," he said.

"How are you and Mother? I mean, are you going to work through this?"

He put his fork down and let out a breath. "I think we'll be all right. We just have a few things to work out. I want her to realize how ungrateful she can be at times. I have to be honest, I put a lot of work into that trip, and it hurt me deeply that she complained the entire time and didn't even try to enjoy herself."

"I'm sorry, Dad." Julia squeezed his hand. "I'm sure she didn't mean it. She's just going through that menopausal phase."

He let out another whistle. "Men should be warned."

Julia laughed. "I don't think it hits every woman that way. I've heard some sail right through it."

He grunted.

She sobered a moment and looked at him. "You still love her, right?"

He sighed. "Right. But sometimes people just have to learn."

"I know."

"Listen, Julia, your mother has made a lot of mistakes—we both have—but you remember, everything we've ever done concerning you, we've done out of love."

"Why do I get the feeling you're trying to tell me something?"

"I am. I'm telling you that no matter how things may look, we love you and have always wanted nothing but the very best for you."

"I know that, Dad."

He grabbed the cloth napkin from his lap and placed it on the table. "Good. Don't ever forget it." He smiled and called for the check.

* * * * *

On Friday evening, Julia leaned against the boulder on the lake, lost in thought.

"Hey, you're hard to catch up with, did you know that?" Lukas walked over to her.

His presence startled her. "Oh, I'm sorry, did you need something?"

"Well, not really, just wanted to talk to you a minute. Mind if I join you?"

"Not at all," she said, settling her gaze straight ahead where the sun, in a passionate display of colors, dipped toward the distant horizon.

Lukas edged beside her. A slight breeze sent a whiff of leather and wood, a very masculine scent, her way. She closed her eyes and drank it in. Didn't Stefan use a similar cologne?

"It's nice out here," Lukas said.

Julia drank in another deep breath. "Yes, it is. I love the calming effect the lake has on me."

"Do you need calm right now?"

She turned to him and saw the teasing sparkle in his eyes.

She sighed. "In case you haven't noticed, my mother can be a real pill sometimes."

"I've noticed."

They both laughed.

"I'm sorry. I hope she hasn't made you too miserable with the room addition," Julia said.

"Nothing I can't handle."

They stood there, side by side, for a few minutes, wrapped in the warmth of the sun, the gentle breeze, and the presence of each other.

"This boulder is a nice meeting place," he said, surprising her.

If he only knew.

"Yes, it is," she said simply.

"Where are we taking this?" he asked, jolting her with his question.

"Taking what?"

"This. You. Me. Us."

She looked at him. "I don't know. Where do you want to take it?"

His eyes bored into her, as though looking into a deep dark corner of her soul, but he said nothing. She waited, heart hammering against her chest, palms sweaty.

"I want to see where it leads us, but I don't want either of us to get hurt."

As he said this, something flickered in his eyes, as though he had been burned by a past love and didn't want it to happen again. The idea of him loving someone else bothered her. She turned and faced the lake once again.

"Have you ever been in love?" he asked.

She swallowed. Hard. "I was once."

"What happened?"

"It just didn't work out."

"Did you just stop caring?"

She turned to him. "No. He did."

Her comment seemed to surprise him. "What about you? Ever been in love before?"

"Yep."

"What happened?"

"Guess she changed her mind." His hand absently reached up and rubbed the scar along his jawline.

"I'm sorry."

"Yeah, me too."

She looked at him.

"Well, I was sorry. I'm not now," he said, quickly.

She smiled.

He reached for her hand. "I think we have something between us, Julia," he whispered, his voice thick and heavy.

"I do too." She tried to keep the emotion from her voice, but she felt so close to him, she allowed all the love to flood her heart, love that had been dormant and bound up inside her for so long.

"But the question is, can our love weather the storm? Life isn't easy. There are surprises and twists and turns at every bend."

"What is it, Lukas? Is there something you need to tell me?" Fear crept into her joyous heart and crumbled it to pieces.

"I don't know how to say this, but—"

"Hi, Julia. Stef—I mean, Lukas." Etta strolled up beside them with a friend at her side. "This is my friend Amy. We've both signed up for school in the fall."

Julia and Lukas greeted them and they discussed Etta going back to school.

"So what are you two doing here?" Etta asked. "I didn't expect to see you together, what with the bet and all."

"You know about the bet?" Julia asked, surprised that Becky would tell Etta about her bet with Eleanor.

Lukas cleared his throat.

"Sure. Becky told me."

"Well, I think we've worked that out," Julia said, knowing she and Becky planned to have a cookie bake sale to earn the money she needed to pay off Eleanor.

Etta smiled at Lukas. "Looks like you get that discount."

Lukas coughed.

"Discount? What discount?" Julia asked.

"You know, from the bet," Etta said.

Julia was confused.

Etta sighed. "You know, if Lukas got you on three dates, George said he would give him a discount on his home repairs." She smiled, obviously unaware of the bomb she had dropped on Julia.

Etta's friend Amy looked as uncomfortable as Julia felt. The sun had gone down and twilight had swooped in upon them. It had lost its romance, though. A couple argued in the distance. Julia could feel her mood plunging.

"Oh, yeah, that's right," Julia said with a laugh. She struggled to keep her balance. Bile rose in her throat and her legs trembled. She leaned against the rock for support, trying with everything in her to hold herself together, to get through this without anyone seeing her pain.

So their relationship was all based on a bet? How could she have been stupid enough to let this happen? Obviously, some people were meant to find love and others were not. She would live her life out in her home—the home she had dreamed of sharing with Stefan—alone. That was that.

She could feel Lukas's gaze on her, but she refused to meet it. If only Etta would leave.

"Yeah, I thought it was pretty funny," Etta continued. "Evidently, George thought no guy could get you. But Lukas here proved him wrong." She laughed. "Looks like maybe it turned out different than you both planned. Haven't you already met the three-date qualification?"

Lukas cleared his throat again. "Listen, Etta, I don't mean to be rude, but I have some things I need to discuss with Julia. If you wouldn't mind—"

She held up her hand. "Say no more. We can take a hint, right, Amy?"

Her silent friend nodded.

"Well, see you two lovebirds later." With that, the two girls continued their walk along the beach.

As soon as they turned to go, Julia took a moment longer to steady herself.

Lukas put his hand on Julia's arm. "Listen, Julia, it's not what you think."

"Would you please let go of me," she said through clenched teeth. "I've heard quite enough for today, thank you."

"Julia, don't go."

"I said let go of me! You've had your fun. Too bad you didn't make it to three dates to get your discount."

Julia turned to storm off and Lukas ran beside her.

"You don't get it. Things may have started out that way, but obviously, things have changed. You mean more to me than any bet. I love you!"

She wanted to believe him. Oh, how she wanted to believe him.

Tears streamed down her face. "I can't do this right now, Lukas. With this, my parents' problems, everything. I just can't do this. I'm sorry."

Julia turned once again and ran up the hill toward her parents' house, leaving Lukas to watch after her.

* * * * *

A lone lamp lit the area around Lukas's chair that night. He turned the paper over in his hand. The words "I'm pregnant" taunted him. He had to know who it was from and why his uncle had it in his Bible.

It was so hard to concentrate on the mystery after the blowup with Julia. He had hoped that she would think it through and come around, realizing their relationship may have started with a bet, a dare, whatever they wanted to call it, but that love had developed between them and kept them together.

Just like years ago.

Maybe it was time for him to tell her who he was. Maybe that was the only way he would find out why she stopped writing to him. Or maybe she would leave him once again? She was mad at him right now, but he didn't think she would call it quits between them—yet. He wasn't sure he could risk their relationship—still, he knew she would find out the truth about him sooner or later. If he didn't want to lose her, and he didn't, timing was everything.

His thoughts went back to the slip of paper. If it were unimportant, say, from someone just letting his uncle know her good news, he wouldn't have kept the paper. It wasn't in his mother's handwriting, so it wasn't a family note of good news. No, there was something about it. If Uncle Clay hadn't wanted Aunt Catherine to know, would he have put it in his Bible? A Bible is a personal thing. Maybe he thought she would never look there?

If it were something he didn't want her to know, would he have kept it? Just two words, but they were powerful words. If she had seen it, how would he have explained it?

Sauerkraut jumped up in the chair beside him and Lukas scratched the hound's head.

He was probably making something out of nothing. No doubt he should just toss the piece of paper and forget it. Yes, that was what he would do.

Rising from the chair, he walked over to the trashcan and lifted his hand to drop the paper in it. But something stopped him. He just couldn't throw it away and act as though it had never existed. He had to get to the bottom of it. And he would. He didn't know how or when, but he would find out why Uncle Clay had kept that paper.

It was just the thing he needed to keep his mind occupied while Julia searched her heart for her own truth.

CHAPTER TWENTY-FIVE

Julia tossed and turned in her bed. She could still smell the liver and
onions her mother had made for dinner. Julia had never liked liver and
onions. It was as though the smell was roaming down the hallway just
to find and nauseate her. She covered her nose. The movement caused
Beanie to roll on her back and kick her paws in the air.

"It's no fair that you can sleep through it." The sheet over her nose
muffled the words. Not that it mattered. Beanie slumbered on.

The house was quiet until the grandfather clock in the living room
struck two. Why didn't her mother turn that thing off at night? Normally, Julia could sleep through it, but tonight, she'd heard every stroke
of every quarter hour. Then she tried to hurry up and force herself to
get to sleep before it struck again. Just about the time she'd drift off, it
would strike and wake her all over again.

She turned impatiently to her side and plumped her pillow. Her
neck hurt. She turned again and once she got her head settled into place,
she tried to move her leg, but Beanie was in the way and wouldn't budge.
Julia tried to scoot Beanie over without waking her, but it wasn't happen-
ing. Julia fumed and tried for the umpteenth time to get comfortable.

Thoughts of Lukas and George and their bet would not leave her
alone. She wanted to be angry about it. In some ways she felt used,
betrayed. Still, things turned out all right between her and Lukas. But
what if things had gone sour—if he hadn't enjoyed her company and
she found out about the bet, say, on their third date, what then?

She sighed. Maybe she should just be thankful. After all, how could she stay angry, since the bet had brought them together?

Another fluff of her pillow. The more she thought about it, the more she decided the bet wasn't enough to keep her apart from the man she loved. And she did love Lukas. She knew that now more than ever.

After she had settled the matter in her mind, she sank peacefully into her soft pillow, allowing her eyelids to grow heavier and heavier… until the clock struck three.

* * * * *

Once Lukas had stopped stewing over his uncle's note, the situation with Julia came back to him with urgency. He paced the floor. He was too upset to sleep. Just as he and Julia were about to get serious, Etta stirred up trouble.

"We were right at our boulder," he said to Sauerkraut, causing the hound's ears to perk and his head to tilt. "I had plans—and those weren't it."

More pacing.

Sauerkraut cowered. Lukas saw him and hunkered down to his dachshund. "Come here, boy." Sauerkraut cautiously edged over and Lukas scrubbed the hound behind his ears. "I'm sorry. It's been a rough day." Sauerkraut seemed to understand and relinquished total surrender of himself to his master, reveling in every scratch and belly rub.

Lukas laughed then stretched back to his feet. He walked to the kitchen and made a pot of decaf coffee. It was late and he needed to go to bed, but it wasn't going to happen any time soon. Once he had his mug in hand, he sat in a chair at the table and allowed his thoughts to skim over the day, which brought him back to the paper. He'd just get his mind over one problem and the other one would pop up. Finishing the last drop of liquid from his cup, he got up, rinsed the mug at the sink, then headed up to the attic. Since he couldn't sleep, he decided he might as well look for clues about the note. It would give him something to do to keep his mind off Julia and their future—or lack of one.

One by one, he searched through boxes of pictures, old clothes, books and such. The dusty air made him sneeze. The floorboards beneath him creaked as he inched along from one box to another. After pouring over hundreds of old photos, his back ached and his legs began to cramp. He needed to stretch in the worst way.

Just as he was about to close the box he was currently rummaging through, he spotted a photo of his aunt and uncle that caught his attention. His aunt looked a little different in this picture. Upon closer inspection, he realized why. It wasn't his aunt.

The woman looked familiar, but he couldn't put his finger on her identity. It could have been anyone. It wasn't as though the picture were taken yesterday. And he hadn't lived there all his life, so how could he possibly know who she was? And even if he found out who she was, what did it mean?

The fact his uncle had his arm around her and was smiling at the camera really didn't mean anything. She could have been a long-lost cousin or something. It didn't mean they were in a romantic relationship.

Then a thought occurred to him. Maybe he could ask a few people around town what they knew about his uncle. And if anyone remembered him—which he was sure they would since it was a small town—maybe they'd also remember the woman. And if that didn't work, maybe Julia could help him.

If she was still talking to him.

* * * * *

The next day George showed up at Lukas's house and asked him to go to lunch, so they went to the diner to eat. Once they settled into their booth and placed their orders, Lukas noticed George squirmed a bit in his seat and cracked his knuckles nervously.

"Is something wrong?" Lukas asked.

"Uh, no." George paused.

"What is it? Don't tell me Mrs. Hilton has another complaint about the addition?"

"No, no, nothing like that."

"Well, come on, man, out with it."

"I asked Beck to marry me." Panic flickered in George's eyes.

"What's wrong? Aren't you happy about it?"

"Yeah, I'm happy. Just scared to death."

Lukas stretched his arm on the back of the booth and laughed. "Is that all?"

"You think that's normal?"

Lukas raised an eyebrow. "Probably. So I take it the little woman said yes?"

"Yeah."

"That's great, man," Lukas said, meaning it.

"You don't think I'm crazy?"

"Sure I do, but she said yes anyway."

George lifted a slight smile.

"So when is the big day?"

"We haven't set it yet. We're going out tonight and we'll talk about it some more."

Lukas shook his head. "What happened to that 'I'm going to take it slow' idea?"

"Well, I guess when you know you've found the right one, why wait?" George's full grin was now in place, his fear obviously easing.

The comment echoed in Lukas's ears. *When you know you've found the right one, why wait?* He'd found the right one, but she didn't wait on him—at least not back then. But now? And what will she say once she finds out...the truth? The bet was a small deception in comparison to the truth of his identity.

"George, I've been meaning to talk to you about something."

"Oh? Don't tell me you're ready to pop the question to Julia?" The light in his eyes said he would be pleased if Lukas did tell him that.

"Um, no, it's not about Julia."

"Oh." George looked disappointed. "What is it then?"

"Well, I'm not sure how to tell you this."

Just then the waitress came up to their table, delivering hamburgers, fries, and drinks.

When she walked away, George closed his eyes for the prayer then said, "Go ahead." He took a huge bite from his sandwich.

Lukas wondered if he'd picked the right time to go into it. Then he decided it was as good a time as any.

"It's like this. My name used to be Stefan Zimmer."

George stopped chomping and looked at him.

"I've had a name change. It's a long story."

"Are you in trouble with the law?"

"Oh, no, nothing like that. My dad and I didn't get along. I changed my name to hurt him. He was very proud of his German heritage. I picked my mother's maiden name. She wasn't German."

"Wow."

"Yeah."

"So why are you telling me now? It doesn't really change anything. I mean, your name now really is Lukas Gable, right?"

"Right."

"Okay, then, no problem." He picked up a french fry and started to put it in his mouth.

"Well, not exactly."

George put the fry back on his plate. "I'm listening."

"I was injured in the war. The enemy attacked. There was chaos on every side. I had a picture in my pocket of a friend and his girl, a picture the medical personnel assumed was of me and my girl, I guess. They tried to reconstruct my facial features to look like him. I ended up looking like neither one of us. Even my closest buddies didn't know me.

"I was released from the service and my dad couldn't seem to handle that I was wounded and 'let go,' as he put it. He had a lot of pride when it came to serving his country. He fought for the United States in World War I. Yes, he was proud of his German heritage, but he'd lived here all his life and was happy to fight for the country where he was a true citizen."

By this time, George had completely forgotten about his sandwich and fries. No small matter, to Lukas's way of thinking. He hadn't touched his own plate of food.

"So you changed your name?"

"Yeah. I wasn't exactly happy to be back home living with my parents. My dad wasn't happy to have me there. We had a huge blowout. I set out on my own and eventually changed my name. Never talked to him much after that, though Mom and I stayed in touch."

"That's too bad. Sorry to hear that." George picked up his sandwich.

"There's more."

George put his sandwich back down.

"When I was Stefan Zimmer, I had plans to come back and marry the woman of my dreams. But she stopped writing to me. At first I thought her letters just didn't get forwarded to me, but I received letters from other friends with no problem. It was then I realized she must have lost interest."

"Oh, man, that's rough." George grabbed a fry and stuffed it in his mouth as though he wouldn't get the chance if he didn't hurry.

"There's one more thing."

"I was afraid of that."

"You know the woman."

"I do?" George gave up, shoved his plate aside, placed both arms on the table, and leaned in. "Who is she?"

"Julia Hilton."

* * * * *

Julia opened her front door and saw her dad on the other side.

"Dad, what are you doing here? I thought you were going out this evening." Julia had her hair pulled back in a ponytail and was dressed in green pedal pushers and a white shirt with green polka dots.

"You look all of sixteen today," he said with a sweet smile and a touch on the tip of her nose with his finger. He stepped into the house.

"Don't I wish," she said with a laugh. "Would you like something to drink?"

"No, thanks. I was hoping you'd be here tonight, because I thought maybe…"

He held a motorcycle helmet in his hand. "I was thinking it might be fun if you'd go for a ride with me on my Harley."

Julia whirled around. "Are you kidding?"

"No. What better thing to do on a Saturday night?"

She put her hands on her hips. "Dad, are you bored?"

His shoulders drooped. "A little."

Her heart squeezed. She walked over and gave him a hug. "Okay, I'll go."

He brightened. "You will?"

She grinned and nodded. "But I get the helmet."

"Deal. I'll even take you to get a malt."

"Now that's a deal I can't pass up. Let me grab a sweater?"

"All right."

Julia followed her dad out to his motorcycle. Tucking her hair into the helmet, she pulled it on and settled onto the back of the bike while her dad settled onto the front seat. He gave her instructions on how to lean with the bike on turns and to keep her arms around his waist. She couldn't deny her anxiousness, but she also felt a twinge of excitement over her first motorcycle ride.

"You ready?" he asked.

"Ready."

Her dad started the motor, kicked the stand, and off they went. The wind blew against her face and the thrill of the ride invigorated her. By the time they arrived at Cindy's Soda Shop, her heart was pumping, adrenaline ran through her veins, and she let out a whoop.

"That was fun, Dad."

A wide grin brightened his face. "You liked that?" It was obvious he was pleased that she enjoyed it as much as he did.

"I sure did."

"Maybe you can talk your mom into trying it out with me sometime."

They edged toward the door of the soda shop just as Julia's mother and a man walked outside, nearly bumping into them. The same man Julia had seen her with twice before.

"Margaret?"

The look on her dad's face made Julia heartsick.

"Frank. Julia. What are you two doing here?" Mother asked.

"We could ask the same of you," Dad said, looking at Mother then turning to the man.

"Oh, Frank, this is Robert Brown."

The man looked to be in his sixties, salt-and-pepper hair, an honest face. He extended his hand toward her dad.

"Mr. Brown," Dad said, without shaking his hand.

"Robert is—" Mother hesitated, as though she didn't want to finish her comment. She lifted her chin and said, "Well, he's a private investigator."

Surprise lit her dad's face. "A private investigator?"

"Yes," Mother said, as though she'd just introduced the mailman.

"Well, I'll leave you folks to your discussion," Mr. Brown said. "My wife will be waiting for me."

In silence, Julia, her dad, and mother all watched Mr. Brown walk away and drive off in his car. Finally, her dad turned back to Mother.

"Margaret, we need to talk."

"Yes, we do. And Julia, you need to be in on this."

Julia couldn't imagine what this would have to do with her.

"Let's go back to our house," Mother said. She looked at Julia and must have noticed the obvious confusion on her face. She said, "This concerns Lukas Gable."

CHAPTER TWENTY-SIX

Once Julia and her parents got to the house, they all went into the living room and sat down. Though the furniture was stylish, the room lacked warmth. Julia prided herself with fluffy pillows and warm colors—delicate touches here and there that gave her house what she hoped was an invitation to guests to sit and visit awhile. Her mother's home, on the other hand, had imaginary signs scattered about in the form of stiff cushions, stark stands, white walls that said, "Let's get down to business."

Julia and her dad sat on the sofa. Her mother sat on a Queen Anne's chair across from them.

"What's this all about, Margaret?" her dad asked, appearing no more comfortable than Julia.

"Well, as I said, this has to do with Lukas."

Julia ignored the churning in her stomach. She just wanted to get this over with. Next week, once the room was finished, she could go home for good, and her father would do the same. That was the deal, and she aimed to see that they all stuck to it.

"As I said, Robert Brown is a private investigator. I hired him to watch Lukas Gable."

"Why would you do that, Margaret? Lukas is a nice young man. I see nothing suspicious about him," Dad said.

"Well, of course you don't. You never see anything in people beyond what they want you to see," Mother snapped. "Something about him reminded me of someone else, and I couldn't put my finger on it. I just couldn't get past the feeling that we knew him."

"This is ridiculous," Julia said, though she couldn't deny she'd had the same feeling herself, many times.

"I do believe you'll want to hear this, Julia."

Mother said that in such a way Julia knew she'd better listen.

"It seems our young employee has lived in Beach Village before."

"I know that," Julia said. "He told me he'd visited here. So what?"

"So, you knew him very well when he lived here before," Mother said. Julia was taken aback. "I didn't know him."

"Oh, I assure you, you did. Quite well, in fact. The thing is, you didn't know him as Lukas Gable."

"Margaret, you are making absolutely no sense."

"You knew him as…" Mother's dramatic side kicked in and she paused for special effect, "Stefan Zimmer."

Julia's heart zipped from her chest to her throat. "What? You can't be serious. I think I would know Stefan if I saw him again. A person doesn't change that much in seventeen years."

"He does when he's been wounded in battle and had plastic surgery on his face. And when he's legally changed his name to Lukas Gable."

Julia stared at her mother. Could it be true?

"Are you quite certain, Margaret?"

She nodded. "According to Mr. Brown, Stefan came back because he inherited his uncle's estate."

"Why would he cover up his identity?" Julia wondered out loud.

"Who knows?" Mother said. "He obviously didn't want you to recognize him. Maybe he was concerned you would try to light the old flame. Maybe he's married."

Mother's words cut deep. "That can't be true. Otherwise, he wouldn't have dated me in the first place." Julia thought of Lukas's—Stefan's bet with George and wondered why he would need the money to fix up the house if he had inherited the estate. There had to be some money there. And why would he keep his identity a secret? She didn't get it.

"Well, I don't see as it matters, either way, Margaret. Lukas or Stefan, he's a fine young man, and there's no denying he's done a good job on our addition," Dad said.

Mother's chin hiked. "Maybe so. But don't you think it's a bit strange that he would disguise himself—"

"I hardly think plastic surgery from battle wounds constitutes disguising himself," Dad interjected.

"Well, he certainly didn't tell us his real name," Mother said. "I don't trust him." She paused a moment. "Oh, and there's one more thing. He was the 'German' who left our Joseph to die."

Julia gasped.

"I find that hard to believe," Dad said.

"Believe what you will," Mother said. "The fact remains he saw Joseph wounded and just left him. Stefan Zimmer is a coward."

"That's ridiculous. Stefan isn't like that. He and Joe were friends," Julia said.

"I'm telling you, Julia, we don't know this man. There's more to him than we see."

Julia hated the way her mother spread seeds of doubt about Lukas, bringing his character into question.

"Stefan is merely back here to sell his uncle's property. Then he will leave again. Maybe he kept his identity a secret to avoid entanglements," Mother said.

Julia cringed. Could her mother be right? Lukas had said he planned to sell the property. Julia couldn't think straight. Right now, she hurt all over. Why had he come to her, asked her out, started things

between them? She couldn't believe it was all for money. Was he playing her for a fool...again?

She stood up. "Dad, since I came with you on your bike, will you
take me back home?"

"Don't you want to hear anymore?" Mother asked.

"I've heard enough. I have a headache."

"Sure, Jules. I'll take you home."

"You mark my words, there's more to this man than meets the eye.
You'd better stay clear of him, Julia."

Mother's words pounded hard against Julia's temples. She didn't
know what to think about anything anymore.

Just when she thought she could love again...

* * * * *

"Are you all right?" Becky asked when she stepped inside Julia's house.

"Becky, thank you so much for coming over. I'm just so confused
and I need to talk to my best friend." She hugged Becky and they walked
into the living room.

"Oh, honey, what's going on?" Becky sat on the sofa beside her.
"Please tell me it's not about the bet between the boys."

"No, no, that's not it."

Becky took a deep breath. "I'm so relieved. I was worried about that."

Julia rubbed her temples then proceeded to tell Becky about her
mother hiring a private investigator and what they discovered about
Lukas's true identity.

Becky whistled. "Oh, what a tangled web we weave..."

"Exactly. I don't know what to make of any of it. Why would Lukas
keep his true identity from me?"

Becky shook her head. "I have no idea. It doesn't make sense."

"Do you think George knows the truth?"

Becky thought a minute. "If he does, he hasn't mentioned it to me, and I think he would. Maybe not, though. I guess guys can keep secrets too."

Julia nodded.

"Maybe he wanted a second chance with you and thought he wouldn't get it if he was Stefan, since he didn't write and everything," Becky said.

"I suppose that's true. You know, there were times he seemed familiar, but I never once thought he was actually Stefan. I just thought he reminded me of Stefan because I cared so deeply for them—both. Still, it's odd I didn't know him."

"Well, plastic surgery does change the way people look."

"Yes, but it doesn't change the heart. How did I not recognize his heart?" Julia couldn't understand it.

"Well, you just said he seemed familiar. And just yesterday, you told me you thought you were in love with him." Becky smiled.

"So you think my heart recognized him?"

Becky nodded. "It's possible."

Julia dared to hope that was true. She wanted to think she had a deeper connection to Lukas than just the superfluous physical side.

"Okay, so let's say he was afraid I wouldn't go out with him and let's say I did fall in love with him all over again because of who he truly is inside, what do I do with the fact he hasn't been honest with me?"

Becky made a face. "You got me there. I'm not sure. Maybe he was waiting for the right time to tell you."

"Maybe. I don't know, Becky. Honesty is important to me." She paused. "Oh, my goodness."

"What is it?"

"He gave me this big speech about being honest when I told Mother there was no damage to her house after that storm, remember?"

"Yeah."

"Well, he has some nerve!" She gasped and her hand flew to her mouth.

"What?"

"He even met me at 'our' rock, knowing all the while it was the place where Stefan and I met the last night I saw him." Julia put her face in her hands. "Oh, Becky, I'm so confused."

Becky scooted over to her friend and put her arm around her. "I know, but it's going to work out. I just know it will. Don't worry, Julia."

* * * * *

Feeling restless, Lukas decided to swing by Julia's house. Hopefully, her dad wouldn't be there. He wasn't even sure Julia would be there. It was a Saturday night, after all. But with any luck, he would find her there.

He needed to explain about the bet with George and assure her that was not the reason he was dating her. Though he'd told her as much already, he wanted to convince her—to leave no doubt in her mind as to his feelings toward her. He'd made up his mind; he couldn't lose her again.

Picking up the picture of his uncle and the strange woman, he tucked it into his pants pocket and gave it a pat for good measure. Might as well ask her about that while he was at it. Lukas headed out to the driveway to his car.

Within a few minutes, he'd pulled up to Julia's house. It still took his breath away when he pulled up to the house they had vowed would be theirs one day. It had to mean something that she would buy it on her own. Would she have done that if she truly cared nothing for Stefan?

After he pulled the car into her driveway, he cut the engine, checked his hair, and climbed out of the car. Julia's car was there but her dad's motorcycle was gone, so hopefully, that was a good sign that he would have her to himself.

Lukas glanced up at the evening sky. Another cloudy summer's night. They'd had a couple of rain showers lately. He couldn't complain, though. The farmers needed it for their crops.

Julia's roses perfumed the air with sweetness. Just like her, he thought. Their relationship was growing—or at least he hoped it was, depending on if she'd forgiven him over the bet.

He knocked on the front door and waited. Nothing. He knocked again. Still nothing. Just as he was about to give up and walk away, he heard footsteps inside growing louder as they came toward the door.

The door cracked open. Julia stood on the other side, looking as though she'd been asleep or crying or something.

"Are you all right?"

"I'm fine."

They stood looking at each other for about fifteen uncomfortable seconds.

"May I come in? I wanted to talk to you about some things." His heart pounded hard against his ribs. By the look on her face, it could go either way. Her hesitation didn't assure him any.

Finally, she opened the door and he stepped aside. He followed her into the living room. She didn't offer him anything to drink; she simply sat down on the sofa and pointed to the chair for him to sit. Obviously, she wasn't feeling all that social tonight.

Tucking her legs under her, she looked at him. "What did you need to talk about?"

The way she looked and acted seemed almost professional, like she was talking to a boss about a business matter. Clearly, she wasn't going to make this easy on him.

"Julia." He paused, hoping the right words would crowd his mind to make this conversation run smoothly. "I'm sorry about the bet. I truly am. If I had it to do over again, I wouldn't."

"I understand," she said, stiff-lipped.

"Then I'm forgiven?" His heart seemed to pause.

"For the bet? It's fine," she said, as though it wasn't fine at all.

Why did she say "for the bet"? Was there something else for which he needed forgiveness? Maybe she needed a few days to mull it over. He'd leave her alone a bit and give her time to cool off.

"Well, that's all I wanted. Just wanted to explain that it was meant to be a harmless bet, a guy thing that in no way reflected on you—or at least it wasn't intended to. I enjoyed every time we were together. I'm glad I asked you out and that you accepted." He smiled. "I was stupid to ever make the bet."

"Forget it," she said. Her manner still seemed cold, unforgiving.

He wanted to hug her but had a feeling if he tried, she'd whack him one.

"Well, I'll be going then." He stood and walked toward the door then he remembered the picture. "Oh, one more thing." He went back over to her and pulled the picture from his pocket. It had already been a tad crinkled, and being in his pocket hadn't helped.

Julia stood up.

"I found this picture in my house. That man was the owner—"

"How do you know that?" she asked, catching him off-guard.

"Well, I, um, he, um, I just assume so."

"Why?" she asked.

"Well, who else would it be?" Now, she was irritating him.

"It could be anybody," she said with a challenge in her voice.

"Okay, maybe so. I'm just trying to get a little history on the place. Thought I'd try to find out who some of the people are in the pictures the owners left behind."

She seemed satisfied with his response and glanced toward the picture.

He shoved it under her nose before she changed her mind and decided not to look. "Do you know either of these people? Particularly, the woman?"

"The man is Mr. Zimmer," she said without skipping a beat. Then her eyes traveled to the woman. And the woman is…" A gasp escaped her.

"What? Do you know her?" he pressed.

She stared a moment longer at the photo before speaking.

"Julia? Do you know her?"

With a dazed look in her eyes, she looked up at him. "Yes, I know her. She's my mother."

He tried not to make anything of it. Yes, his uncle's arm was around her, but that could have been a friendly gesture and nothing more. Still, why hadn't Julia's mother or his uncle mentioned that they knew each other when Stefan and Julia had dated?

"Can I borrow this? I'll give it back. I just want to show it to my mother."

He nodded.

"Thanks." She walked toward the door, making it clear their discussion was over.

He had a feeling so was their future.

CHAPTER TWENTY-SEVEN

The choir music and sermon did little to ease the chaos in Julia's stomach. For one thing, she couldn't concentrate. Rambling thoughts refused to untangle and make sense. She wanted to confront Stefan—wait, he'd legally changed his name to Lukas—but she needed time to sort through it all.

And then there was that picture of her mother and Lukas's uncle. If the picture of her mother had been with another man, it would have been no big deal to Julia. Could have been an old friend. But her mother's attitude toward Germans made the picture so...confusing. And why hadn't her mother told her she knew Lukas's aunt and uncle? Everything in Julia's world was turning upside down.

"Julia, I'd like you to come over for lunch," her mother said when she approached her in the church vestibule.

Julia's mind scrambled for an excuse, but her mother saw right through her.

"We need to talk. Please."

The sincerity on her mother's face was a rare sight. It tugged at Julia's heart.

"All right, I'll come."

"Thank you, honey."

Her mother's demeanor, the sweet sound of her voice, touched Julia in a surprising way. Maybe she and her mother would have a decent, meaningful conversation today. One could always hope.

Julia watched as her mother talked to a friend nearby. The shadows in her eyes, the long breaths, all made Julia sorry for her. Yes, her mother could be contrary, obstinate, stubborn, and hurtful, but despite all that, there was something deep inside her that few could see, though Julia saw it from time to time. A soft side. A side she assumed her dad also saw, but a side that had been harder to see in the last few months.

What could have made her so hard and rough around the edges? Julia didn't know a lot about her mother's family. Her grandparents were gone before Julia was old enough to know them. Her mother didn't talk about her family much.

Once they were seated at her mother's table for lunch, eating chicken and mashed potatoes, her mother took a deep breath and Julia braced herself for her mother's reason for inviting her over.

"Listen, Julia, I didn't mean to hurt you when I told you about Lukas. I was just concerned that he not hurt you again."

That was the closest thing to true concern her mother had ever voiced to her. Julia had long ago accepted that her mother wasn't a huggy, sappy kind of person. Prickly would be a better term. Still, that was who she was, and somehow through it all, Julia still knew her mother loved her.

"I know," was all Julia said. She thought about the picture Lukas had shown her. "Mother, I have a question for you."

"Yes?"

"Did you know Lukas's uncle Clay? I mean, other than through my relationship with him. Did you know him before Lukas—Stefan at the time, and I met?"

A startled expression touched her mother's eyes. She fidgeted with her fork and almost toppled her water glass. "Whatever would make you ask such a thing?"

"I saw a picture of the two of you together."

Her mother busied herself tidying the table. She didn't look up. "Could I get you some more chicken, dear?"

"No, thank you, I'm fine." Julia studied her a moment. "Mother, you didn't answer my question. Did you know him?"

"I think I can answer that for you." Julia's dad walked into the room.

"Frank, what are you doing here?" Mother asked.

He ignored her question and turned to Julia. "I think this may shed some light on things." Her father pulled a piece of folded lavender stationery from his pocket and handed it to her.

Her mother gasped. "Where did you get that?"

"Buried in the attic," he said. "Guess you thought I wouldn't find it."

The look on her dad's face scared Julia. Something was desperately wrong. She looked down at the letter and began to read. It was written to her brother...by her mother.

"Give that to me," Mother demanded, trying to snatch the letter from Julia.

"Leave her be," Dad said, grabbing her mother's hand.

Mother dropped into a chair and said, "I didn't mean for you to know." Tears began to spill down her face.

As Julia read through the letter she wondered if she was caught up in some sort of nightmare. She finished reading and looked at her mother through tears of her own.

Her mother looked at her dad. "I never meant to hurt you, Frank. It was before you and I started dating. I thought I loved him." She twisted a handkerchief between her fingers. "We had a night of indiscretion. He dropped me when he met Catherine. By the time I found out that I—I"—she swallowed hard—"that I was pregnant, they were engaged."

Julia sat speechless, having no idea what to say. The world around her seemed to spin out of control.

"Frank, you had just come along."

"You saw me as your way out," her dad said in an angry but low voice Julia had never heard come from him before.

More tears from her mother. She took a deep breath. "In some ways, that's true. I knew you could provide for our baby."

"Your baby," he spat. "You let me believe all these years that we had a honeymoon baby. That Joseph was mine. You never loved me. You used me." Dad turned to leave and Mother got up and grabbed him by the arm.

"Don't go, Frank. It's not true. I have loved you—and still love you."

"At least Joe never knew the truth." He jerked his arm free and stormed out of the house. Julia watched through tears of her own and went over to her mother and put her arms around her. No matter what her mother had done, Julia couldn't abandon her right now, especially when she looked so broken, so vulnerable.

Her mother wept in Julia's arms. "Oh, what have I done? What have I done?"

* * * * *

No one could help Julia right now. All she could do was walk and keep on walking until she sorted through everything. Joseph was Lukas's half cousin. No wonder her mother had been against their relationship from the start. As she had said to Julia through her sobs, she couldn't have stood being thrown together with family gatherings, knowing her secret.

Still, in her mother's defense, she didn't tell Uncle Clay about his baby, because he was already engaged and had moved on. Mother hadn't wanted to destroy that for him. At the same time, she hadn't meant to keep the secret from Julia's dad, but he loved her and she couldn't bear to tell him the truth. He was so proud of Joseph, how could she ever come between them that way? She had gotten in too deep to tell anyone by then.

She had lived with her lie all these years. So many regrets. And now Dad knew. This just added more pain to an already hurting relationship.

The lake water to her left churned and rolled along with Julia's emotions. Gray clouds flanked the evening sky. The cool air and blowing sand told her a storm was coming, but she kept walking. She couldn't go back, not yet. Too much to think about and sort through.

In just a few days, her world had turned completely inside out.

No wonder her mother had been against Stefan. First his uncle got her pregnant and then Stefan, her mother believed, caused her son to die. How could Julia ever have a relationship with the man now called Lukas? Yes, his uncle was gone, so she might have been able to work past the pregnancy, but believing that Lukas caused Joe's death? Her mother would never get past that. Not ever.

And now Julia had to go home and face her dad, knowing he had heard the news and his heart was now breaking.

The first drop of rain fell onto Julia's arm, then another and another, until a full downpour caused her to run back toward her car. Heavy weights seemed to pull her feet deeper into the spongy sand, making it hard to run. The frustration of it—of her entire day, the previous weeks—caused her tears to mingle with the rain. By the time she reached her car, she had cried more tears than she ever thought possible.

Would this nightmare ever end?

* * * * *

When Julia arrived at her parents' house the next day, she braced herself to meet her mother.

"Is he all right?" her mother asked the minute Julia stepped into the house.

"Who, Dad?"

"Yes."

The worried look on her mother's face squeezed Julia's heart. She wished she didn't have to tell her the truth.

"He didn't come to my house last night."

"Oh, what have I done?" Her hands covered her face.

She fell in a heap onto the sofa. Julia ran to her side. "He'll be back, Mom."

With tears in her eyes, she turned to Julia. "You've never called me Mom." She put her arm around Julia and pulled her close. "I'm so, so sorry…for everything. I've asked God to forgive me. Can you forgive me as well?"

"Of course I forgive you."

As her mom embraced Julia, the two women cried away tears of regret and pain.

"I prayed last night too," Julia said. "I've been away from God far too long. It's time I came back."

"That goes for me too." Mom wiped her face with a handkerchief. "I don't know where to look for your dad."

"I'll find him. Don't worry."

Mom listed off some of his favorite places for Julia to check. They talked awhile longer then Julia left in search of her dad. Before she went to her car, she walked around to the room addition to give Lukas his picture back.

"Thanks for letting me use this," Julia said, though now she wished she'd never seen it.

"Was that your mother in the picture?" he asked.

"Yes." Julia turned to walk away. She couldn't tell him more without betraying her mom.

"So where do we stand?" he asked, his blue eyes calling her to him, his strong arms waiting.

Looking at those eyes, Stefan's eyes, she wanted to tell him she knew who he was, talk it out, but now was not the time. "I'm sorry, Lukas." Julia turned and walked away from the only man she had ever loved.

Again.

* * * * *

Later that night, Lukas's jaw clenched as he thought about Julia's words to him today. She was sorry? That was it? No explanation, just, it's over? That silly bet with George could hardly merit Julia's reaction. If she was willing to give it all up that easily, he didn't want her anyway.

He slammed the book in his lap closed, causing Sauerkraut's head to lift and his ears to perk. Lukas stood up, grabbed his keys, then laid them back on the stand. He turned on the television then turned it back off. Enough thinking about Julia.

Reaching for the photograph in his pocket, he looked at it again. After Julia walked away from him, he hadn't given the picture much more thought. His eyes narrowed as he studied Julia's mother with his uncle. The more he scrutinized the two of them together, the more he decided they stood together like an item. He glanced at the ring on her finger. A class ring of some sort. No doubt it was his. Maybe that was the problem. Her mom didn't like his uncle or something and didn't want Julia with him. But that would be a stupid excuse. Julia wasn't seventeen anymore. She could make her own decisions.

He threw the picture down. So much for thinking things would work out with her. Fine. If that was the way she felt about it, so be it. His phone rang.

"Hello?"

"Is this Lukas Gable?"

"It is. Who's this?"

"My name is Steve Gallagher. I own a small company in Chicago. We build boats. I've lost one of my builders, and I've been told you're a fine craftsman. Wondered if I could talk to you about a job?"

Lukas considered Frank's boat but quickly decided he could finish that no matter where he lived. Then he thought of Julia, and how she had walked away from him.

"I'd like that," Lukas said.

* * * * *

Julia wrote the news of her renewed commitment to God and her healed relationship with her mom on lake rocks and put them in her Ebenezer jar. Strengthened by prayer, she walked out to the kitchen and approached her mother. She had aged ten years in the last two days, and Julia's news would only make matters worse. But her mother had the right to know.

"I went to Dad's work this morning," Julia said while her mother stared into her coffee cup. "He's taken off two weeks for vacation." She tried to quiet the rumble in her own chest upon saying the news out loud.

"I know," was all her mother said. "I called them."

"He'll be back, Mom. He just needs time to think, to sort through everything. It's a lot to digest."

"I know that too." Through red-rimmed eyes, she looked at Julia. "But what if he doesn't come back?"

"Now, don't borrow trouble, isn't that what you always say? He'll be back." Julia prayed it was so.

"I have myself to blame. No one else," she said, practically in a whisper.

"It'll blow over. What's done is done. You meant no harm."

"I kept the truth from him, Julia. Don't sugarcoat it."

"Yes, you did. That was wrong. But wallowing in that won't make up for it. We have to go from here. Figure out how to make it better from this point on."

Her mother continued to stare into the distance with glazed eyes.

"It's helped me to learn the truth, Mom." Julia covered her mom's hand with her own. "I always thought you loved Joe and not me."

Her mom looked up. "Why would you ever think that?"

Julia shrugged. "Who knows why kids think what they do?"

"I truly loved Clay. If I favored Joseph, which I never meant to do, it may have been because he was my only link to the man I once loved."

The words cut through Julia. "Does that mean you've never loved Dad?"

Her mother blinked. Then she smiled. "It doesn't mean that at all. Clay was my first love, but I grew to love your father in a way I never thought possible. My life has been far better than I could have ever deserved, thanks to him."

Relief washed over Julia. There was hope for her parents, she just knew it. There had to be.

"I'm sorry I made you feel that I favored your brother, Julia. I've always loved you and been proud of you. My mother was always harsh with me, expected only the best from me, and I guess I just passed that on."

A knock at the door caused them both to look up.

"I'll get it," Julia said.

"Hey," George said when she opened the door. "I just wanted to let your mom know the carpet will be laid today, and I hope to have the final inspection by the end of the week."

"Thanks, George. I'll let her know."

"Guess you know Lukas went back to Chicago for a job interview."

Alarm shot through her. "He did?"

"Yeah." George's expression revealed his disappointment.

"Who's watching his dogs?" she asked, hoping he'd offer more information.

"I am."

"Oh." She wanted to ask him why Lukas left and the details of the job but didn't want to sound desperate. "Thanks for telling me." Not even Becky knew what was going on in her family right now, so at least she didn't have to worry about George knowing.

Julia gave her mother George's message and went to her room. They both needed time to think, pray, and wait on Dad to return. Tears wetting her cheeks, Julia curled up on the bed with Beanie.

She had made it through the last seventeen years without Stefan. And now she had to start grieving all over again.

CHAPTER TWENTY-EIGHT

"Thanks for meeting with me, Julia," Becky said, as she and Julia walked along the lakeshore. "Seems like every time we've tried to get together lately, something has come up."

"Yeah, I know. I'm sorry about that. Things have been a bit crazy with my parents."

"Forgive my selfishness for bringing this back to me, but if I wait any longer, I'll explode."

Julia stopped in her tracks and turned to her friend. "Becky, what is it?" The light in her eyes, the glow on her face, pretty much told Julia what was coming next.

"George asked me to marry him!"

"Oh, my goodness, Becky, that's wonderful!" Julia pulled her best friend into a warm, congratulatory hug. "I'm so happy for you."

Tears filled Becky's eyes. "Me too." She laughed. "I can still hardly believe it."

"So tell me about it."

Becky explained how George took her to a fine restaurant in the next town over then walked her to a moonlit spot on the beach and proposed.

"That is so sweet," Julia said, meaning it. She was truly happy for Becky. There was no denying the look of love on her face, the sparkle in her eyes. "So when is the big day?"

"We're looking at next spring."

"Wow, you're going to be busy."

"I know, isn't it so exciting?"

Julia smiled at her. "I love seeing you this happy, Beck. You deserve it."

"Thanks, Julia. You'll be my maid of honor, of course."

"But what about your sisters?"

"They understand. They'll be bridesmaids. But they want you there too. We've already discussed it. Besides, you're practically a sister."

The very idea of Becky's family giving Julia such a prominent place in so important an occasion warmed Julia clear through. "I love your family," she said.

Becky gave her a sideways squeeze. "They love you too."

The two best friends talked of wedding colors, flowers, and ceremony. Julia smiled as she watched her friend's eyes glisten and her face shine with happiness. Once they'd discussed all they could about the wedding, they continued walking for a few minutes in silence.

"I'm sorry about Lukas. George told me he went to check out a job offer in Chicago."

"Yeah." The mere mention of it caused a heavy weight to bear down on her shoulders. "Oh, well. Que sera sera."

"Still, I know you liked him."

Julia thought of all that her mother said and how her life had changed in a few days. Yes, she liked—no, loved—Stefan—Lukas. She loved him. But once again, she had to let him go.

"What is it, Julia? I can tell something is wrong."

"It's just that whole thing with Lukas's identity and all that."

"Let's go back to my car," Becky said.

With every step, fatigue took over Julia's body. The evening sky, thick with clouds, punctuated her dreary world. Taking a deep breath, she scolded herself for the self-pity. She would get through this. She had to.

"So Lukas came back for his uncle's estate," Becky said, once they pulled their car doors to a screeching close.

"Uh-huh."

"It still makes no sense that he would go back to Chicago, not when you two were just—"

"Well, there's a little more to it." Julia hesitated, not knowing how much she should share about her mom. "I'm not at liberty to discuss it right now, but I basically let him know we had no future together."

Becky gasped. "But why would you—oh, I'm sorry. You said you couldn't discuss it. I suppose you have your reasons for telling him that. Let me know when you're ready to talk about it, Julia. I'm here for you."

"Thanks." Julia rubbed her temples. "Would you mind taking me home? I have a headache." Seemed she'd been getting those a lot lately.

"No problem." Becky shoved her key into the ignition and started her car.

"I'm sorry to be such a downer. I couldn't be happier for you and George," Julia said.

"I know that. We'll get you through this, whatever it is," Becky said, perky spirit back in place.

"Yeah," Julia said. *If only that were possible.*

* * * * *

With the room addition completed, Julia had hoped to move back home this weekend, but with all that had happened between her parents, she didn't think she should leave her mom just yet.

"Mom, will you be all right if I go home tonight? I need to mow my lawn and check on my flowers."

"Doesn't your father mow your lawn?"

"Yes, but he's on vacation, so no one is there right now," Julia said.

The look on her mother's face made Julia wish she hadn't brought it up.

"It'll turn out all right, Mom." Julia placed her hand on her mom's shoulder.

Her mom cupped her palm over Julia's hand. "I hope you're right. I couldn't bear to lose him." A tear escaped her, but she blotted it with her hand and lifted her chin, cutting off further conversation.

"I'll check on you later, all right?"

"I'll be fine, Julia. I'm not a child."

Mom's fight was back. This time, Julia was glad to see it. She knew her mom would be all right.

Now, how in the world was she going to get her mom and dad back together?

* * * * *

A whole week had passed with still no word from Dad. Julia and her mom had stumbled through their week, one breath after another, each lost in her own grief. Much to Julia's relief, her mom agreed it was time for Julia to go home. With school starting soon, Julia needed to get things organized at home so she could deal with her classroom duties.

The perfumed sachet tucked in the corner of her dresser drawer in the guest room at her mom's house released a sweet, light scent that tickled her nose when Julia lifted clothes from the drawer and placed them in a large cardboard moving box. So many summer outfits she hadn't touched all season. She sighed. Grabbing another box, she reluctantly placed a forgotten pair of cotton pedal pushers in them. No sense in keeping them if she didn't wear them, as Becky so often pointed out.

Picking up a silky red blouse, she looked it over and leaned into it for a sniff. The sachet scent, sweet and flowery, lingered on it. She hadn't worn it recently, but she liked it as much as she did the day she saw it in the store. Still, she'd had it over a year and had only worn it a couple of times. Then there was that blue-and-white-checkered top. It looked so cute with the white pedal pushers—which were now a little snug. She simply had to stop eating Becky's cookies. Another sigh. She tossed it in the smaller box.

Over the next hour, she put clothes in a "giveaway" box and more clothes in a "to-be-taken-home" box. After the job was done, she went through both boxes one more time to make sure she wanted to give this away or keep that.

"Julia, would you like to take a lemonade break?" her mom called out.

"That would be great." Julia closed the boxes. Feeling rather pleased with herself, she stretched long and hard before going into the kitchen.

"Here you are, dear," her mom said, handing her the chilled glass of lemonade with a sprig of mint. "Let's go into the living room."

Though it was nearly lunchtime on a Saturday, her mom was still dressed in a light cotton housecoat. Bobby pins held her hair in pin curls all over her head. Beneath her eyes were half-circled shadows. Her feet were bare and Julia was almost sure she spotted cracked heels. Her mom never let her heels crack. She said it was against the laws of nature. Looking at them, Julia now understood why.

"Are you all right?" Julia asked, thinking surely hot flashes couldn't produce what stood before her right now.

Mother sighed. "No. But don't get me started. I can't talk about him."

They both knew to whom she was referring.

"The least he could do is call," Mom said with a frown.

"Maybe he just needs time. That was quite a revelation, after all." Julia's mom shot her a look and Julia pressed her lips together.

Mom's hardened jaw slacked and her shoulders dipped. "You're right. He'll never come home again." She slumped into a chair.

"He'll be back. He just needs time to work through it."

Just then a thud sounded at the front door. It definitely was not a knock. It was a thud.

"What in the world," her mom said, walking toward the door, with Julia right behind her. When Mom opened the door, Dad stood on the other side with a large bag slung over his shoulder.

If her dad hadn't been such a thin, wiry sort of fellow, Julia might have mistaken him for, well, Santa Claus.

"Are you just going to stand there, or are you going to let me in?" he asked with a definite edge to his voice that clearly knocked him out of the Santa Claus arena.

Speechless, Mom stepped aside, while Dad hauled his cargo into the living room and dropped it on the coffee table.

"What is this?" Mom wanted to know.

Julia was quite curious herself. The drama in her family grew more interesting by the minute.

He looked point blank at Mom. "These are for Julia. They're what I was looking for when I stumbled on your letter to Joseph."

Mom paled the color of milk toast. Neither one of them turned to Julia, which she thought a tad strange. If the package were for her, wouldn't it be the normal thing to do for them to turn to her right about now?

"What is it?" Julia asked, feeling quite pleased with the thought of some mysterious package coming her way.

"You kept them?" Mother asked, clearly shocked with the news.

Dad turned to Julia. "These are your letters."

On the other hand, if he brought her a pile of letters filled with family history, this could be a very long day.

Julia's breath hovered at attention, knowing her day could go either way.

"It took me several trips to the attic to finally find them." Her dad dumped the bag, quite out of breath. "I hid them years ago and couldn't remember where I'd put them."

"So that's what you were doing sneaking around the house," Julia said. Excitement surged through her veins…until she spotted the return address on the envelopes.

Nothing could have prepared her for this.

* * * * *

When the alarm sounded on Monday morning, Lukas slapped it off, stretched and yawned, then reluctantly rolled out of bed. The window to his motel room was open, so he could hear the morning bird chatter—sounded like black crows, and they weren't happy—and smell someone's garbage just beyond his window. He wanted to close it, but the smell inside wasn't any better.

After he showered, shaved, and dressed, he decided to take the "L" to his interview so he could avoid the traffic.

Walking downtown, he looked at the many buildings and numerous out-of-his-price-range hotels and other powerful edifices, clearly a strong arm of the Windy City. He used to love this place. But today, instead of his heart galloping at the sights and feel of the wind on his face, his boots kicked against the cement, reminding him with every step just how hard life could be.

He'd had no intention of hurting Julia. All he wanted were answers. He needed closure, so he could move on. Was that so wrong? He watched as a policeman stood in the center of the intersection and with a whistle and wave of his white-gloved hand, motioned a black Studebaker to move forward.

Obviously, now with her mom and dad's problems, she didn't want to pursue a relationship with him. He thought it might have something to do with the picture of his uncle and her mom, but he couldn't imagine why. So they knew each other once, what was the big deal? He had to admit he thought it was strange that his uncle hadn't mentioned it when he had stayed with them over the summer and fallen in love with Julia. Then the words hit him like a flying brick from a nearby building.

I'm pregnant.

Was it possible—could it be?

He stopped walking and stood in the middle of the sidewalk, people walking around him, casting strange glances his way.

But why didn't they get married? What happened to the baby, was it adopted? His temples began to throb. What was he thinking? That baby could have belonged to anyone. Just because his uncle had the paper didn't mean the baby was his. But why was the note in his Bible? If he and his aunt had children, it would explain the note, but they never had any. Otherwise, their house wouldn't have been left to Lukas.

None of it made sense.

Now, with Julia's reaction to him, he wondered if she knew something. So many questions without answers. But he wouldn't give up. He couldn't. He was tired of all the secrets, things left open-ended. What was the matter with people? Couldn't anyone tell the truth, be honest and open these days?

That thought made him laugh. He hadn't exactly been Honest Abe himself.

By the time he made it to the factory, he had calmed down. But once he finished the interview, job or no job, he was going back to Beach Village and find out the truth.

About everything.

CHAPTER TWENTY-NINE

Julia sat cross-legged on her bed, letters piled around her in two stacks. One was the "read" stack and the other was the "to-be-read" stack. She picked up the letter from the top of the "to-be-read" one. Looking at the return address, she still couldn't believe that Stefan had sent her all these letters and her mother had tried to dispose of them. If her dad hadn't retrieved them from the trash, she never would have believed Stefan really had tried to contact her. Over the years, her mind had given in fully to her mother's words that Stefan had never truly loved her. Though her heart never gave up hoping.

Line after line declared his love for her and swore that he would come back for her once he got out of the military. He gave little press to the ravages of war. He focused instead on his love for her. As the letters continued, however, his fervor decreased. The fact she never wrote to him—what? He said she'd never written to him? But what of all those letters she wrote? Had her mother confiscated those too?

Fueled by her anger, Julia got up and dialed her mother's number. They hadn't spoken since her dad dropped the bomb and the letters.

"Hello?"

"Just answer me this. Did you destroy the letters I wrote to Stefan as well?" Julia's voice sounded cold and unforgiving even to her own ears.

Silence.

"Mother?"

"Yes, I did, but Julia, you have to believe me, I thought I was doing what was best for you."

"Best for me, Mother, or best for you? You had no right," she whispered, just before she hung up the phone. Julia didn't want to hurt her mother, but she just couldn't talk about it now. Her mother's actions had changed Julia's future...forever.

Brushing away the hot tears that coursed down her cheeks, she grabbed the next letter and began to read....

* * * * *

After the interview and dinner, Lukas had planned to go home, but the idea to visit the cemetery where his parents were laid to rest would not leave him. Twilight had fallen over the city. The air smelled of earth and rain. Menacing clouds threatened overhead. The wind whipped through oaks and maples, sending birds flapping for refuge. Eerie-shaped clouds twisted and contorted, stretching long dark fingers one minute then blowing into bulky heads with imaginary eyes the next. He almost laughed as his boyhood imagination took over.

Almost.

He'd better make it quick if he wanted to find his parents' graves before the downpour that was sure to come.

By the time he spotted their headstones, the wind had died down a bit, giving him a moment of silence with his parents. He stared at his mom's grave, thinking over her laughter in earlier days, her gentle ways. Something he hadn't thought of in a while also came to him. The way she prayed. About everything.

How many people at her funeral had told him if there was a matter that needed prayer, they always called her? She was a—what did they call her?—a prayer warrior. That was it.

People sure wouldn't say that about him.

No. He was more like his dad. He turned a hardened heart toward his father's gravestone. Stone was a good way to describe him. The man had a heart of stone. Lukas couldn't remember ever being hugged or encouraged by his dad. Only his gruff admonitions of how to do something better. It was as though his dad watched and waited for him to fail so he could point it out.

No, son. You're remembering things wrong. Your father only wanted what was best for you. He wanted you to enjoy all the things he never could.

His mother's familiar words played in his mind. She had told him that over and over. But he had never believed her. Just once, he wanted to know that his dad was proud of him, that he loved him. But it never came.

"But what about how he treated you?"

I forgave him. You must forgive him too, my son.

Yes, his mother had told him that too. But he couldn't, wouldn't forgive him. The man didn't deserve forgiveness!

"Do you?"

Two words, but they hit his soul like a bolt of lightning. He knew it wasn't his mother's voice he was hearing anymore.

"No, I don't deserve forgiveness, but I never did the things that he did."

"Sin is sin."

He couldn't argue that. And he'd be the first to admit he had sinned, over and over. He didn't want to let go of his anger toward his dad. He didn't know how to let go.

"I'll help you."

A couple of big drops of rain plopped on his arm while his soul wrestled with letting go. He didn't want to hold onto his anger toward his father, yet when he had the opportunity to truly release it, he resisted. As though a light turned on, the verses in the New Testament where Jesus asked the sick man if he wanted to be made well suddenly made sense to him. In the past when he had read that passage, he always thought it strange that Jesus would ask that. Why wouldn't the man want to be made well?

Yet, here he stood, after years of agonizing over his father and wanting to be rid of the pain in his heart toward him, he had the chance to release it, and something stopped him. Why?

I will give you the strength. Trust me. You don't have to answer for your father. You only have to answer for you.

For reasons he couldn't explain Lukas had brought his uncle's Bible with him. Knowing his uncle to be a godly man, it somehow made him feel closer to his family. He flipped open to the pages marked by a ribbon. He'd probably placed it there the other day.

Ezekiel. He doubted he could find anything to help him in that book. It was one of those prophecy books, hard to understand.

Just as he started to turn the page, his eyes fell on underlined words in Ezekiel 36:26.

I will give you a new heart and put a new spirit in you; I will remove from you your heart of stone and give you a heart of flesh.

More drops of rain. Lukas quickly tucked the Bible into his shirt. His heavenly Father, who had walked with him over the years, had never left him. Only Lukas had moved. He had allowed his rage toward his father to get the upper hand and keep him away from the relationship he so desperately needed and wanted with his Lord.

The heavens opened and the floodgates deluged the earth below while Lukas poured out his years of pain and suffering, from a little boy to a man, until his last tear was spent and he could look at his earthly father's grave with great regret for the relationship he would never know. But miraculously, he could now do it without a trace of anger.

He knew only God could accomplish that miracle.

With a smile, and a shiver from the cold rain, he ran toward his car. He had no idea what God had in store for him, but he knew in his heart it was time to go home where he belonged—to Beach Village.

* * * * *

Julia sat on her bed and pored through Stefan's letters, one by one. His words of love and his confusion over her lack of response cut her to the core. She leaned back against the headboard of her bed. Her heart hurt. Oh, how she had loved him. And how she had hurt over the years absent from him. How many times had she envisioned him by the lakeshore? And his cologne, hadn't she dreamed of his scent? How she had ached to feel his arms around her—and when she found herself falling for Lukas, she struggled with betraying the love she had harbored so long for Stefan.

Now she found they were one and the same.

Nothing was what it had seemed. Lukas was Stefan. Her mother's prejudice was traced back to a love lost with Stefan's uncle. Stefan was a coward who had let her brother—no, wait—half brother—die. Her parents' relationship now hung by a thread.

Deep down Julia wanted to feel sorry for her mother, but the years of her mother's control hardened her. How had she not seen it? Little wonder Julia had trouble making decisions. Her mother had always made them for her. She should have known Stefan wouldn't leave her that way.

Her head pounded. Nausea rumbled in her stomach. Where would she go from here? A glance at her Bible on the nightstand provided the answer she knew she needed, but it was so hard to trust anything or anyone. Especially now. Hadn't she trusted her mother? Stefan?

Julia didn't know what to believe about anything anymore. Another glance at the Bible. She reached over and picked it up. God was truly her only hope.

* * * * *

Lukas took another glance through the curtain and noticed the red Bel Air convertible was still parked outside his house. It had been sitting there for about fifteen minutes, but the woman inside hadn't emerged yet. She could be a thief watching over the place. But why would she be out in the open? Maybe she was with a magazine and wanted to do an article on the place. He took in a sweeping view of the disarray. No, that couldn't be it. He decided to approach the stranger and find out.

Stepping through the front door, he waved to let her know he had seen her. "Good morning," he said with a loud, good-natured voice as he made his way toward the car. "I noticed you'd been here for a few minutes and thought I'd see if you needed help."

The woman appeared to be middle-aged, bright red lipstick, brown hair, pleasant smile. "Oh, no. I'm sorry. Not trying to infringe on your privacy." Her eyes watered. "My best friends used to live here. I moved away and came home for a visit. Just wanted to stop by and relive the memories, I guess."

"You're talking about the Zimmers?"

She brightened. "Yes."

"I'm their nephew, Stefan. I go by the name Lukas now."

"Stefan?" She looked at him with disbelief. "You're not at all what I remember. Guess I'm getting old." She chuckled.

"It's a long story," he said. "Why don't you come in and have some coffee so we can talk a bit?"

"I'd like that," she said.

He opened her car door and she stepped out. Once they were seated at the kitchen table with coffee mugs in hand, Lukas explained about the war and his injuries, the plastic surgery, and why he found himself back in Beach Village.

The woman, Mary Washington, listened intently. "I remember you as a youngster," she said with a smile.

He wondered if she would know anything about the note, but wasn't at all sure how he could approach the subject without marring his uncle's good reputation.

"So you were best friends with my aunt, you said?"

"That's right. I probably knew her better than I did your uncle." She adjusted the white gloves on her hands.

"They were great people. Too bad they didn't have children of their own to pass their place to," he said, looking into his cup.

"They almost did."

His head shot up. "They did?"

She nodded. "Catherine got pregnant once." She laughed. "I'll never forget it. She was so excited; she couldn't wait to tell Clay. We were in an afternoon emergency board meeting at church. Instead of waiting for him to come home, Catherine wrote a note to him and gave it to the church secretary, who took it to him. I watched him, because I always worry when unexpected notes interrupt a meeting. His eyes grew wide and he immediately excused himself. Then I was really worried. Suddenly, we heard crying then laughing. We all looked at one another and then jumped out of our seats and hurried into the hallway. We watched as Clay swirled Catherine around, both of them laughing. When he put her on her feet, they turned and saw us. The gleam in their eyes and the joy on their faces were palpable. Clay told us they were expecting."

Tears filled Mary's eyes and she wiped them away.

"Needless to say, when they lost the baby three months later, the whole church felt their pain."

"What happened?"

Mary shrugged. "Doctor said it was a miracle that she got pregnant in the first place. It never happened again."

"Excuse me a moment. I want to show you something." Lukas got up, plucked the note from his uncle's Bible, and brought it over to Mary. "I found this in Uncle Clay's Bible."

Mary looked at it and smiled. "Yes, that's the note. She carried that blue pad of paper with her everywhere." She chuckled. Carefully folding the paper, Mary gave it back to Lukas. Tears filled her eyes once again. "They were so precious. I still can't believe they're gone."

"I know."

They talked through two cups of coffee, then Mary had to go. Within a few yards of the front door, she turned to face Lukas. "They loved you dearly, you know."

He smiled, not knowing what to say.

Mary hugged him then walked to her car. He waved, satisfied that the pieces of the puzzle were coming together. Well, at least where his aunt and uncle were concerned.

Now, if he could only figure out things with Julia…

CHAPTER THIRTY

Julia stopped at her mother's to pick up the last of her things. Getting out of her car, as she looked around the property, sadness filled her. Her parents now had their home the way they wanted it, everything on the property looked picture-perfect, but her dad was living in an apartment and her mother was alone.

When Julia reached the door, she knocked. Given the current relationship—or lack of one—between her mother and her, she didn't feel right just walking into the house.

"Julia, so nice to see you." Her mother's face looked swollen, her eyes pleading.

Julia couldn't help feeling sorry for her. In her mother's attempt to keep control of her life and the lives of those around her, she had spoiled everything.

"I just came to pick up the rest of my things."

"Would you please have some tea with me?" The yearning in her mother's eyes broke Julia's heart. Though she hated how her mother had interfered in her life, she couldn't shut her out forever.

"All right, but I can't stay long."

Her mother brightened and immediately headed for the kitchen. "I'll hurry and get everything ready while you gather your things," she called over her shoulder.

By the time Julia had the rest of her belongings in the car, the tea kettle steamed on the stove and her mother had the cups and fixings in place on the table.

"So how have you been?" her mother asked as she slid into her chair at the table.

"All right." Julia scooped a teaspoonful of sugar into her tea and stirred.

"Getting your classroom ready for school, I suppose?"

"Yes."

Julia hated that their conversation was so stilted but had no idea how to fix it. With God's help, she had forgiven her mother, but there remained a chasm between them that she didn't know how to bridge.

"Have you heard from Dad?" The minute Julia asked, she wished she hadn't. The shadow on her mother's face said more than she wanted to hear.

"No. He's keeping his distance." Her mother absently stirred her tea. "I've made a mess of everything."

Before Julia could respond, their doorbell rang.

Her mother frowned. "Wonder who that could be?" She got up and answered the door, Julia watching from her chair.

"Are you Mrs. Hilton, Joseph Hilton's mother?"

Julia's heart paused.

"Yes, I am."

"Ma'am, my name is Greg Burrow. I was wounded in the war alongside your son. I wrote to you about that a long time ago. I wondered if I might talk to you for a moment?"

"Yes, yes, come in, Mr. Burrow." Mother opened the door to allow the man entrance. "My daughter is here, but you're welcome to join us for tea."

"Please, call me Greg." He looked at Julia. "Julia?" he said.

"Yes," she answered with a smile.

"I heard a lot about you. Joe was proud of his sister."

Just hearing that made Julia instantly sense a fresh connection with her brother.

"Thank you."

They settled at the table with their cups of tea, discussing families, life, the war.

Finally, Greg said, "I need to set the record straight. Let me start by saying how much I appreciated your son. He was a true hero in every sense of the word. The day he was killed"—he glanced at Julia's mother with a look of apology—"I was so angry. He was a great friend and helped me in so many ways. There was another soldier in our group, one I didn't like. His name was Stefan Zimmer."

Julia gasped.

"Something wrong?" he asked.

"No," Julia said.

"Stefan was a young man from around here too," Mother offered.

Julia braced herself. She didn't like where this was headed at all.

"I went into the war with some prejudice toward the Germans. The war only heightened my prejudice. It bugged me to no end that Stefan served alongside us. He was German." Greg's jaw tensed. "I was wrong."

Julia's mother had been staring into her cup of tea and his words made her look up at him.

"I spread the rumor that a German saw us wounded and turned away. I implied that he could have helped us, but he didn't." Greg fingered his mug. "The truth was" he stopped and took a deep breath "Stefan tried to save three of us. I managed to scoot to safety. Doug, another war buddy, and Joe were hurt badly. Stefan went to Joe first. Doug called to him and handed him a picture or something. Stefan stuffed it in his pocket then went back to Joe. Stefan grabbed Joe's arms just as the enemy planes returned. He tried to drag Joe to safety, and Joe cried out something to him. Stefan looked at Joe, dropped his grip, and closed Joe's eyes. He was dead. Then Stefan turned to help Doug, but he was too late. Several of the guys yelled at him to get out of the way. The enemy planes were getting dangerously close. Stefan ran for a nearby ditch and jumped in, head first. I heard his face was real messed up. I don't know what ever happened to him. But I had to come back and let you know that he was not a coward. Stefan Zimmer was a hero."

Tears ran down Mother's cheeks. "What made you tell us this now?" she whispered.

"You may not understand this, but I recently gave my heart to the Lord. I'm setting some things straight. Righting some wrongs, so to speak. I was wrong to spread my poison. Stefan didn't deserve that. If I knew how to tell him how sorry I am, I would do it." He stared at his fingers. "As I said, I've lost track of him. I don't even know if he made it through his injuries."

"He made it," Julia said.

Greg looked at her. "How do you know?"

She explained that Stefan had been in town, living at the home his aunt and uncle had bequeathed to him. Though she wasn't sure if he had come back from his recent trip to Chicago. She wrote down the address so Greg could go see him.

Greg's countenance glowed. "I can't tell you how much I appreciate that news. It shames me to know how I treated him, and I want to make it right. I have kids of my own now. I wouldn't want anyone to treat my son the way I treated Stefan."

"I'm so thankful you stopped by, Greg. I've had my own prejudices against the very same young man. It appears we both were wrong," Julia's mother said.

"Well, I won't keep you any longer. I just had to make things right. I think I'll stop by Stefan's and see if he's there. Thank you for the tea."

"One more thing," Julia said. "He goes by the name Lukas Gable now."

A puzzled expression shadowed his face.

"Long story. Maybe he'll tell you about it."

"Thanks." Greg went to the front door and gave a salute before he walked away.

"Looks like I have some work to do," Julia's mother said.

* * * * *

Becky popped her head into Julia's classroom where Julia worked preparing for the first day of classes that was scheduled to start soon.

"Want to take a break for lunch?"

Using her forearm, Julia wiped her brow. "I could sure use a break right about now. But I brought my own lunch."

"That works," Becky said. "I brought mine too. I'll grab it and join you."

"Sounds good."

Just as Becky started to leave she turned back and said, "They've hired the new teacher. Don't know who it is yet, but I know we have one." The fear in Becky's eyes said it all.

"Becky, even if it is Vicki, you don't need to worry. George loves you and nothing will change that."

"That's what I thought the first time around too," Becky said.

"George is different. You'll see."

Becky sighed. "I just pray I don't have to deal with her day in and day out. But whatever happens, I know the Lord will get me through."

Julia smiled. "Yes, He will."

"I'll be right back."

Once Becky returned, she and Julia settled into conversation about the start of school and what they hoped to accomplish during the year.

"How is your dad?" Julia asked.

"He's doing great. Oh, I forgot to tell you! He's working for George now."

"Really? That's wonderful."

"Yeah, he's so good with a hammer. I don't know why I didn't think of it. George came over when Dad was doing a little bit of remodeling in Mom's kitchen. He saw the quality of Dad's work and asked him to work with him. With Lukas gone, George was desperate for help."

Julia tried not to show her pain at the sound of Lukas's name.

"That's so cool. Sounds like George will fit in nicely with your family."

Becky's eyes sparkled. "I think so too." She took a bite of her sandwich. "Have you talked to Lukas lately?"

"No."

"I'm so sorry, Julia. I know how much you cared about him."

"Twice." Julia sighed. "I should have told him I know his true identity. I wanted to, but all this stuff with my parents, well, there was never a good time. And I can't deny it bothered me that he didn't tell me himself. I felt like part of a joke that he was in on and I wasn't."

"Well, you may still get the opportunity to talk to him."

"Why is that?"

"Lukas is back in town."

"He is?" A flood of excitement rushed through her. Lukas. Back home. To stay? Did they have another chance?

Becky nodded and smiled. "George told me. Seems Lukas has decided to stay here."

"Are you sure?" The hope that surged through Julia made her want to jump up and celebrate.

"That's what George told me."

"I wonder what he's going to do. Oh, Becky, I have to talk to him."

"Wait a minute. You can't go right now. We have work to do." Becky laughed. "But maybe after school?" she teased.

Just then the principal came into the room. "Hello, ladies. Nice to see you're getting a head start on your classrooms. I wanted to introduce you to our newest staff member."

Julia and Becky exchanged a glance. Julia cast a prayer heavenward for her friend, hoping Vicki would not be the new teacher.

The principal turned behind him. "Well, where did—" He glanced out the door into the hallway. "Ah, there you are. Come on in. I want you to meet a couple of our teachers," he said.

The new teacher walked into the room, taking every bit of breath from Julia's lungs.

"Lukas Gable, I'd like you to meet Becky Foster and Julia Hilton." Lukas smiled. "Hello, Becky, Julia. Good to see you again."

"Oh, I see you've met," the principal said.

"Yes, we have."

"Well, since you've met everyone else, I'll leave you here and I'll get back to my office. Let me know if you need anything."

"Thank you, sir," Lukas said. He turned and walked over to Julia.

"I need to get back to work too," Becky said, gathering her lunch sack and paper debris. "Good to see you again, Lukas," she said with a smile. "Welcome aboard."

"Thanks." He watched Becky leave the room, then he turned to Julia again. "I hope my being here won't be uncomfortable for you."

Julia's heart quickened. "Why would it be?" She walked to her desk, trying to keep her distance. "I'm happy for you."

He followed her. "You are?"

"Yes, I am."

"Did you know before the principal announced it? That I was a new teacher, I mean?" He stepped closer to her.

She shook her head. Then before he could say anything else, she explained how she knew he was Stefan, about the private investigator, the letters, everything.

He stood mere inches away. "Wow." He took a minute to digest all of it then looked at her. "Well, first of all, will you ever forgive me for not telling you who I was?"

Julia swallowed hard. She couldn't lose it here and now. She was at school. She needed to act like a professional. "You must have had your reasons."

He moved closer. "The name change came about to punish my dad. Stupid reason. And then I didn't tell you who I was because I wanted to know why you dropped me and figured you wouldn't tell the 'real me' the truth. I should have handled things differently."

She looked up at him. "I'm so sorry. Mother never should have interfered. She sees that now. We lost a lot of time together because of her. Can you ever forgive her?"

The smell of his cologne reached her. She told herself to stay calm, ignore the fact he stood so close that it caused her hands to tremble.

He put his hands on her shoulders. "Though I hate that we've lost all these years, I'm so thankful I've found you again. Of course I forgive her."

She looked in his eyes. His deep blue eyes. Her knees threatened to buckle.

"Please say you'll go to dinner with me tonight so we can talk more. Please?"

No matter how hard she tried, she couldn't pull her gaze away from those soft, pleading eyes. "Okay."

"I'll pick you up at seven." He stooped and gave her a kiss on the cheek and turned to leave.

"Is this technically our third date?" She grinned.

"You know, if you count the past, I think we've had a lot more than that."

"I think you're right."

Did she dare hope they could work through the pain of the past and look forward to a future together? And if they did have a future together, she'd gladly pay Becky the twenty-five dollars she would owe Eleanor.

* * * * *

Julia took a bite of her hamburger and noticed for the third time Lukas's glance at his watch.

"Do you have to be somewhere tonight?" she asked.

He took a sip from his glass of water. "No, why?"

"You keep looking at your watch."

"Bad habit," he said with a grin.

They ate for a while in silence. Julia wondered why he'd asked her out if he was going to be quiet all during their meal. Maybe he'd changed his mind about giving their love a second chance. Probably decided he couldn't be around her mother.

"So you wanted to talk," Julia said, hoping to get him started.

He glanced at his watch again. "Are you finished?"

Her heart sank. Obviously he needed some time to think over what she had told him earlier. She couldn't blame him. Her mother had taken years from them. "Yeah, I'm finished."

They got in the car, and when he took a turn away from the road that led to her home, he looked at her.

"Is it all right if we go to the beach and walk a little?"

"Sure."

Maybe they could talk it out, work through this. She shoved away the doubts that clamored to argue that point.

Stars twinkled in the evening sky by the time they arrived at the beach. They walked along the shoreline, just the way they had done so many times before in their youth.

"Did you talk to Greg Burrows?" Julia asked.

"Yes. It was good of him to come. I knew he had a problem with me from the beginning, and I knew it had to do with my heritage, but I didn't realize the resentment went so deep."

"That's how it is with some people," she said. "I'm glad he set the record straight."

"Me too. I guess we have Vicki to thank for that."

"Vicki? Why is that?"

"Vicki is his cousin. She was visiting his family recently and somehow your family name came up. He'd given his heart to the Lord and wanted to contact Joe's family and see if he could get any leads on my whereabouts, if possible. He saw her visit as a gift from God."

"That's amazing," Julia said.

They walked a little farther, each lost in thought.

"Your mother came over too."

The comment startled Julia. "She did?"

He nodded. "She apologized to me. Said she had thought she was doing the right thing to come between us but now she could see she was wrong."

"It took a lot for my mom to do that." Her mother's efforts blessed Julia clear through. Julia wanted to hug her. It couldn't have been easy for her.

"I know."

The night air had lost its intense heat of the day and now cloaked them in a warm, pleasant breeze. A sliver of moon cast them in a soft glow.

"So do you forgive her?"

He shrugged. "We all make mistakes. I've certainly made mine."

He shared more about his relationship with his dad and how he had gone to the cemetery where God spoke to his heart. "Anyway, I've made peace with God...and Dad."

"That's wonderful, Lukas," Julia said, meaning it. Her heart warmed toward this man in a way she wouldn't have thought possible. Just when she thought she couldn't have loved him more...

"Want to stop over there?" he said, pointing to "their" rock.

"Sure. Do you remember—"

"Of course I remember. This was our rock. I'll never forget. It's where we pledged our love and commitment to one another all those years ago."

Heat radiated on Julia's cheeks. She leaned against the uneven boulder. Lukas turned to face her, moonlight glinting in his eyes, a warm glow on his face.

Just then, the strains of "Love Letters in the Sand" lifted somewhere in the distance and floated over to them on the breeze.

He smiled. "Right on time."

"What?"

"I asked George to bring my portable phonograph to the parking lot and play Pat Boone's latest record at exactly nine o'clock. That's why I kept looking at my watch. Look." He pointed to the parking lot. George waved and they waved back.

"You did that for me?"

"All for you, baby." He nuzzled next to her ear and whispered, "All for you." He pulled her into his embrace and led her around the sand to the rhythm of the music.

Julia loved the song. Their song. Her heart felt it would burst with love all over again for this man.

His lips brushed against her ear. "Do we still have a chance, Julia?" he whispered. "Tell me we can start over, give our love a second chance?"

She pulled away slightly and looked up at him. "I can't start over."

The expression on his face broke her heart. "Oh, I see."

"That would take too long. I'm not getting any younger, you know." She lifted a smile.

He looked at her as though he didn't hear right. A moment's hesitation. Then a grin. He held her tight once more, their feet moving ever so gently over the sand. "So where do we pick up, my love?"

"How about we say this is the original night you came back for me?" Love soared through her so that she could hardly contain it.

Lukas pulled her into his strong arms and held her tight. "Oh, Julia, I have dreamed of this moment over and over again." He kissed her temples, her hair, her ears, her cheeks, her lips, softly at first, then with more commitment and longing than she could have imagined.

His touch made her dizzy. She didn't want to breathe for fear she would wake up from this wonderful dream.

Breathless from their kisses, he held her close for a long while then finally pulled away.

"So, where do we go from here?" he asked.

"I'm not sure," she said.

"I know where I want it to go."

She looked at him.

He bent down and with his finger drew a heart in the sand. Inside the heart he wrote the words, "Will you marry me?"

Tears welled in her eyes as she read the words.

He looked at her and smiled. "Is that a yes?"

"Yes! Oh, yes!" Julia threw her arms around him and held him with all her might. He laughed and scooped her into his strong arms, twirling her around, their laughter ringing through the night air.

"Let's go tell my mom," she said.

"But we still need to pick out the ring together," he said.

"We can do that later." She grabbed his hand and ran toward the car.

Just as they drove up to her parents' house, Julia was thrilled to see her mom and dad walking out of the house together, holding hands.

"Well, well, well," her dad said, smiling. "What are you two doing?"

"We've come to share our good news."

"Oh?" her mother said, eyes twinkling.

"We're getting married," they both blurted out.

"Does this mean I'll get a discount on my boat?" Dad asked.

Julia looked at her dad then at her mother.

"Lukas is building me a boat." He grinned.

So that explained the mysterious phone call. Now it made sense.

Lukas rubbed his jaw. "How about we work on it together."

"Get to know my son-in-law a little better, huh? I think I can do that," Dad said.

After the hugs and congratulations were over, Mom said, "I would invite you inside, but we were just leaving."

"Where are you going?" Julia asked.

"Who knows?" Mom grinned, a youthful glow on her face.

Dad got on his Harley. Mom eased on a shiny new helmet and climbed behind him while Julia and Lukas watched in disbelief.

"Does this mean you two are—" Julia didn't know how to say it.

"We're starting counseling tomorrow. We'll go from there," Dad said. "Talk to you later, Jules. We couldn't be happier for you both." Dad pulled on his helmet, revved the motor, and winked at her.

Mother blew a kiss and they went roaring off into the night.

"Do you suppose that will be you and me years from now?" Lukas asked.

"I hope not."

"How come?" he asked.

"I could never wear a helmet like the one Mom is wearing," she said.

Lukas let out a bellowing laugh, pulled her into his arms once more, and kissed her soundly.

"I'm going to run home and write our engagement on a stone of remembrance," she said.

"Oh, and what will it say?"

"It will say, 'On this night we pledged our love to one another.'"

"Uh-oh. We've been this close before, you know," he said.

"I know. But once it's on the stone, it has to come true. So don't get any ideas. There's no backing out."

He grinned and held her close.

She pulled away and looked up at him. "Wait. Will I be Mrs. Lukas Gable or Mrs. Stefan Zimmer?" She searched his eyes.

"Well, technically, my legal name is now Lukas Gable. Are you all right with becoming Mrs. Lukas Gable instead of Mrs. Stefan Zimmer?"

Julia snuggled into him. "The name doesn't matter. Sharing my life with you is all I've ever wanted, my darling. All I've ever wanted."

ABOUT THE AUTHOR

Best-selling author Diann Hunt writes romantic comedy and heartwarming women's fiction. Since 2001, she has published three novellas, eighteen novels, and co-authored a devotional for the CBA market.

Her novels have placed in the Holt Medallion Contest, won the prestigious ACFW Carol Award, and served as a Women of Faith pick.

Diann has five granddaughters and one grandson whom she loves to spoil (hoping one day they will throw her a fiftieth-anniversary bash in Hawaii) and she lives in Indiana with her real-life-hero husband of 36 years.

American Tapestries™
HISTORICAL ROMANCE IN NEW FRONTIERS

New to release in 2011, American Tapestries™ is a line of historical romances that celebrates America's history with heart-stirring love stories set across the expanse of her plains and prairies, coastlines and cities. Whether they helped build the industrial centers of the East Coast or forged new paths into the Western frontier, a diverse tapestry of immigrants and settlers flooded this Land of Opportunity in past centuries in pursuit of freedom and a brighter future. Behind each of these brave souls are the threads of a story begging to be told. Then, as now, the search for romance was a big part of the American dream. Summerside Press invites lovers of historical romance stories to fall in love with this line, and with America, all over again.

Don't miss these American Tapestries™ *inaugural titles!*

The Wedding Kiss BY HANNAH ALEXANDER

A kiss can be life changing. When Keara and Elam Jensen share their first kiss on their wedding day, a marriage of convenience becomes much less convenient! It also becomes more than they expected when God shows them what He really has in store for their lives. Will their mysteriously injured visitor ruin their future, or will her influence—and her personal battle—draw them into deadly danger? Visit Eureka Springs, Arkansas, in 1901, and discover for yourself what excitement and romance await along the White River Hollow.

From This Day Forward BY MARGARET DALEY

Penniless, pregnant, and newly widowed immigrant Rachel Gordon doesn't believe her situation could get any worse...until she meets her new neighbors.

Shortly after the War of 1812, Rachel and her husband set out from England for a plantation in South Carolina, which he had purchased sight unseen. However, while en route, Tom Gordon fell overboard and drowned, leaving Rachel, frightened and alone, to make a home for her and her newborn. Can a battle-scarred American physician who comes to her rescue also heal her wounded heart?

Watch for future Summerside Press historical romance titles by these great authors—
DiAnn Mills, Vickie McDonough, Janice Hanna, Susan May Warren...and more!

When I Fall in Love
Romance with a Nostalgic Beat

Do you remember the song that was playing during your first kiss? Can you still sing the lyrics to the tune you and your first love called "our song"? If so, you are going to love Summerside's When I Fall in Love™ fiction line. Each book in the When I Fall in Love™ nostalgic romance line, set in the 1920s through the 1970s, will carry the title of a familiar love song and will feature new, original romance stories set in the era of its title song's release.

{ Watch for the new WHEN I FALL IN LOVE ™
titles to release in 2011: }

Baby, It's Cold Outside BY SUSAN MAY WARREN

Five strangers with broken hearts, one raging blizzard. Will a warm fire and a string of Christmas lights provide the perfect remedy?

It's been years since Edith Miller hosted the annual Snowflake, Minnesota, Christmas Extravaganza. After her son was killed in the war some five years ago, her Christmas spirit died along with him. So she is more than happy to loan all her Christmas decorations to Stella Hanson, the new teacher in town. After all, what does she have to celebrate? But when the blizzard of the decade traps Stella—and four other wanderers—in Edith's home, Edith finds that by opening her door, she just might open her heart to a new reason celebrate Christmas.

Strangers in the Night BY PATRICIA RUSHFORD

All Abbie Campbell wants is to protect her daughter…and stay out of jail. But the handsome stranger with Frank Sinatra eyes seems determined to change everything.

Abbie Campbell has been running from the law for two years when Jake Connors, a friend of her parents, convinces her that it's time to return home. Back in the beautiful northwest, Abbie works to turn the old lumber town of Cold Creek into an artist retreat. But falling in love isn't the only challenge Abbie faces—the worst of which is a killer who seems determined to stop her at all costs.

Be on the lookout for future When I Fall in Love™ nostalgic romance titles by authors Deborah Raney, Anita Higman, and more.